Martin Scattergood
Drowning in a Sea of Air

2

Martin Scattergood

Drowning in a Sea of Air

4

December 2010	Initial print run of 250pcs
January 2018	Kindle edition completed. Appendix 3 added.
January 2019	German paperback edition published on Amazon. Appendix 3 updated
February 2020	English paperback edition published on Amazon. Appendix 3 updated

Prologue

As I woke on the 11th of February 2005, after a troubled, almost sleepless night, I instantly knew something was seriously wrong. I was concerned, but had no idea that I would be fighting for my life forty hours later. Paralysis crept up my body, engulfing all of my extremities and finally strangling my throat and lungs, leaving me unable to move, breathe, talk, eat, smell, taste, or communicate. I became a prisoner in my own useless body.

During the weeks of excruciating pain, anxiety, and the ballast of total physical paralysis, I struggled and suffered, but survived. I lived as a quadriplegic on life support for eight weeks with terrifying thoughts of death and long-term disability. I experienced fantastic medical care and received huge amounts of selfless kindness from family and friends. Finally, it was the magical healing powers reflected as the love of my family — my wife Fiona and my two kids, Alexander and Francesca - that saw me through the deepest darkest moments of a horrible ordeal.

This is the story of a dreadful illness called Guillain-Barré Syndrome (GBS).

6

Acknowledgements

I started this work as a handwritten diary around nine weeks into my hospital stay, when holding a pen was a major task. All in all, it has taken five and a half years to complete and all the words are mine.

I would like to thank Rob for taking time to read my first few raw chapters and then encouraging me to complete it. Without his interest in my story and me, I doubt I would have finished it. Rob dedicated a lot of his precious free time to editing the first drafts. For the final edits, I am extremely grateful to Rachel who took on this difficult job with such enthusiasm and Maureen from First Editing.

I would like to pass on my thanks to the GBS organisation in Germany, Albert Handelman and Josef Berger, for their support and understanding for me and my family while I was hospitalised and in rehabilitation.

There was a massive army of people in Germany, the UK, and Taiwan that supported Fiona and me. They visited, offered practical help, called on the phone, cooked meals, drove the kids to their activities and looked after them when we were both in the hospital. I will be eternally grateful to you all. Special thanks go to Fiona's sister Gillian, who has since passed away, Pia and Jörg, Bernie and Dennis, Andrea and Christian, Andrea and Stefan, Hans and Friederike, Fiona and Iwan, Máire and Mick, Susanne, Angelika, Gertrude, Nick, Rachel, Noah, Mark,

Ros, Angela, Caroline and the British Women's Club friends.

Several medical staff treated me with unbelievable dedication and professionalism. I would like to mention two specifically. The Registrar in a local hospital who recognised I had GBS and Thomas a superstar nurse who was simply the best of the best.

To all of my family: thank you for your love and support. In Manchester: Mum and Mike, Jean and Gordon, Lesley and Brian, Julie and Deborah. In Edinburgh: Margaret, Jan, Liz, Melanie and James. In New Zealand: David, Zoë and Charlotte.

Finally, hugs, kisses and lots of love to Fiona, Alexander and Francesca. Without you, I would not have made it.

Authors note; for reasons of confidentiality, I have changed the names of the medical staff.

December 2010

Nine years after completing my book and fifteen years after contracting GBS, I am fit, extremely positive and totally immersed once again in my favourite sport of triathlon. I have updated the book with Appendix 3 which details my sporting exploits since 2011.

February 2020

Index

Part 3 – Starting Life Again

Appendix 1

Appendix 2

Appendix 3

Introduction

This story is not a chronological account of my illness, but rather an insight into my thoughts, treatment and life both in and after hospital. I have split it into three parts. Part 1 deals with the rapid onset of the illness; part 2 with my treatment and recovery in hospital; while part 3 is about my new post-GBS life.

I spent a total of sixteen weeks in hospital, with the first eight on life support, literally being kept alive by a machine. Of this, the first two weeks were in Düsseldorf and the next fourteen, near Bonn. I was then back at home in Düsseldorf for three weeks, followed by five weeks as an outpatient attending a clinic for seven hours a day. It was a total of twenty-four long weeks of illness, recovery, and rehabilitation. For more details on my condition over the weeks, please refer to Appendix 2.

In writing my story, I hope to try and help others who have GBS, or who are suffering in some other way. I would also like to convey three things: Firstly, how our health is the most precious thing we have; Secondly, how to communicate with sick and disabled people; and thirdly how the power of the mind can drive the body to survive almost anything. If with my words I have achieved even one of these goals, the effort expended in writing this will have been so very much worthwhile.

12

Part 1 — Unexpected Illness

14

Chapter 1 — Running Scared

Guillain-Barré Syndrome (GBS) can strike anyone, young or old, male or female, fit or unhealthy. It attacks the peripheral nervous system, destroying the coating on the nerve linings along which the electrical signals from the brain travel to our muscles. The brain remains unaffected by GBS and is not to be confused with other diseases, such as motor neurone disease, that irreparably attack the central nervous system. GBS results in a rapid onset of muscle paralysis, as brain signals fail to arrive at their chosen destination. It affects around fifteen to twenty people per million each year. The disease was first identified in 1916 by the two French doctors who gave their name to it, Georges Guillain and Jean Alexandre Barré however the actual cause remains unclear. What is known is that around half of the cases occur after patients contract the flu, or worryingly, after a flu vaccination. GBS also occurs after operations, gastric problems, and when the body's immune systems are low. Usually the body starts a slow improvement after a period of weeks with the majority of patients able to achieve a near or in some cases full recovery.

Nine days before I entered hospital, my wife, Fiona, was suffering with the latest flu scurrying around Germany. Running my own business, I was very keen to avoid any debilitating illness, so I started taking preventative herbal medicines. Fiona really suffered over the next two days, but I remained symptom free. After a boozy party that I attended alone on Friday night, I spent Saturday in bed with a headache and flu-like aches and pains. I convinced myself it was a hangover, but when the symptoms persisted on Sunday, I gave in and took Ibuprofen to numb the flu. Each tablet brought four hours of relief and allowed me to get back to work on Monday. Fiona continued to suffer until the following Thursday, which was when I started on my downhill slide.

Work can be a great distraction. I was busy and under a lot of pressure from customers and my supplier. I did not have time to think about having the flu. While the aching joints, fever, and general listlessness continued, Wednesday brought about a further deterioration. My hands and feet started tingling. Not a mild pins and needles type of tingle, more like the painful variety experienced when, for example, ice cold feet start to warm up too quickly. Bizarrely, when I washed my hands in cold water I noticed that the water felt hot and when I touched a hot radiator it felt cold!

As Fiona was just emerging from a painful and sick week in bed, understanding and sympathy for my complaints were in short supply. I brushed off her suggestion to see the doctor, insisting instead on taking our son, Alexander, to watch the German national team play Argentina at the Düsseldorf Arena. The game was okay, resulting in a 2-2 draw, but I spent most of the time trying to fight off what had become quite uncomfortable pain in my legs, pelvis, and back. Business commitments on Thursday meant I had to be in the office. Ibuprofen was still bringing relief for the standard four hours, but failed to make any impression on the tingling. The opposite hot and cold feelings were persisting in my hands and feet. What I remained oblivious to was that the virus was now starting to take hold, and I just wrote off the pain and discomfort as flu symptoms.

I went to bed early, but awoke at midnight with more intense pain in my legs. I got up and was aware that my legs felt unsteady. I thought it was the after-effects of flu or perhaps I'd simply stood up too quickly. I decided to sleep in the guest room and wished for the calming distraction of sleep, but it only came in staccato steps. By morning the unsteadiness had not improved. I tried to stand but had to grasp the nearest piece of furniture for support.

It was Friday 11th of February. A visit to the doctor was now imperative. I asked Fiona to drive because I knew I couldn't get behind the wheel. We had an appointment at 10:30, which gave me time to think. I started to feel anxious and scribbled down my symptoms, ready to recount them to the doctor. I wrote:

1) Saturday: Flu symptoms, joint ache;
2) Wednesday: Lower back pain and into legs. Pain all over. Severe joint ache in left thumb. Muscle pain;
3) Thursday: Tingling. All muscles hurting. Feel hot when I touch cold. Feet and hand tingling. Tingling feels numb like after injection at the dentist. Tongue and lips affected as well as face muscles. Intake of breath is sensitive, feels like after injection;
4) Friday: Legs weaker. Feel as though I might collapse. Feet feeling numb. Shoulder pain.

Fiona drove and conversation was kept to a minimum. The pain and tingling were increasing and I felt nauseous. *What is happening?* I asked myself. I searched my head for a point of reference. I wanted to know if I would be all right and kept looking for that past experience, that recovery path, the road back to health that would allay my fears. I found nothing. The fear was gripping me tighter. I knew I was fit. Marathons and triathlons were not a problem; they had become my way of life, with intense training six days a week over the previous two years. I'd always, always battled through and had never given in. But this was different and I was scared.

We were called into the surgery. As we were both in need of a doctor, we took the opportunity to share our appointment, Fiona started and recounted the very difficult week she'd been through. Dr. Thoms prescribed some tablets. I listened patiently, but was in a lot of discomfort and tried to shift my weight to relieve the pain. Dr. Thoms turned to me with his usual calming smile and asked, "And how are you Mr. Scattergood?" I took out the crumpled paper and read my scribbled notes. My reflexes were tested, several questions were asked, and he concluded that I was also suffering from the flu. I was told to "continue with the Ibuprofen and all will be right soon." Little did I know that this was the last day I would walk under my own steam for an exhausting sixteen weeks!

Somewhat relieved, although uncertain, I stood up, steadying myself on the chair. As we left Dr. Thoms's room, I held onto the door and walls for support. He was immediately very concerned and told me that the unsteadiness was not due to the flu. I was told to lie down, was given an intravenous drip, and he quickly arranged to get me admitted to our local hospital. I was glad something was happening despite the prospect of hospitalisation clicking up my anxiety levels even further.

We arrived at the hospital around 1:00 p.m. Fiona dropped me off at the entrance and I walked, rather unsteadily, to the reception desk, using the supporting backs of several chairs on the way. I presented my referral note from Dr. Thoms and could not help being amused by his description of my condition — "tendency to collapse". I was called in to see a junior doctor. Fiona helped me in and I hauled myself onto a bed. The doctor was pleasant, but after examining me appeared sceptical. She ordered a blood test and advised, "It will take some time to get the results."

Content I was in safe hands, Fiona returned home and I was on my own, in this most sterile of examination rooms. It would be the first of very many days in hospitals for me. My eyes were drawn to the clock on the wall. I could not have imagined how this simple instrument would soon come to dominate every waking second of my life over the next weeks, eventually becoming my main focus of attention. On this day, I watched the clock drag through one hour, two hours, and three hours. I moved from the bed to the chair and back again. My legs got weaker. The pain began to intensify in my legs, my back, and now my arms. I tried to move the pillow on the bed — it was too heavy. I was tired, hungry, and felt extremely sick. As I waited I tried to find answers ... self-diagnose the cause ... recall my travel, meals ... *Was it something I'd caught on my last trip to China three weeks before, or was it the after-effects of a nasty stomach bug contracted in Turkey?* Hell, I had no idea.

As I moved back once again from the bed to the chair, the doctor finally returned. The blood tests had proved negative. I had a slight infection, but nothing to explain my present condition. *Oh no, don't send me home,* I thought. I nervously explained the worsening of my condition over the lonely three hours since we'd last met. Her scepticism did not waiver, yet she had no facts at hand to work on. I knew I was deteriorating by the minute and becoming increasingly desperate. She had no answers and it annoyed me that she didn't recognise how scared I was. Possessing extra insurance that allowed me to be seen by a senior doctor or consultant when in the hospital, and although I'm never comfortable with this type of exclusivity, I set my principles aside and pushed to be seen by more senior staff. She told me, rather unconvincingly, "I am not sure if the Registrar is available, it is Friday afternoon you know. I will check and come back to you." *Who cares what bloody day it is; just get me better*, I thought.

Less than two minutes after leaving, she arrived back with the Registrar — so much for Friday afternoon and not being available. I told the story once again; I recounted my trip to China in mid-January, previous illnesses and every bloody thing I could think of. "Nothing conclusive" was the best reply I got. Finally, the Registrar advised I would be admitted, but "just for observation." The junior doctor was visibly relieved that she would not have to make any diagnosis. She busied herself with the administrative paperwork that is annoyingly necessary to arrange admittance into German hospitals. I was rather generously told that a porter would come with a chair to take me to my room "so you don't need to walk." I considered spitting back "well, I can't naffin´ well walk anyway," but decided politeness was probably the better course of action. It was 5:00 p.m. and the last time I would see a doctor until 9:00 a.m. the next morning. What lay ahead of me was the most wakeful, painful, and terrifying sixteen hours of my life. I would have to endure it without any medication, observation or tender (loving) nursing care — in fact just the opposite!

Expecting a chair to take me from A+E to the ward, I was surprised to see a bed being wheeled into the examination room. It seemed a trifle over the top, but it did the job. More immediately my thoughts turned to where to put my feet on a bed that I would soon be sleeping in. I never resolved that problem and heaved them up in front of me — I was past caring about dirty shoes on a clean bed. My home for that night was a double room on the fifth floor, shared with a very flatulent man and occasionally his very obnoxious wife.

As with all hospital rooms, it was sparse, impersonal, and worrisome; it provided no relief for my pain or answers to my questions. I hated the sterility and the atmosphere of that room, I hated the man next to me as he farted his way through the next few hours and I hated his wife, who had the cheek to ring for a nurse to bring her a cup of coffee. I was angry and in a great deal of pain, I knew I was very ill — and I couldn't care less about this self-important couple bemoaning the state of the German health system and the lack of service on a private ward. My insurance had bumped me up to this ward, but I still had no medical care. Just as my neighbours' complaints reached a crescendo, I threw up in my kidney bowl and shut them up.

Sometime later Fiona arrived. I tried to walk around the bed to see her, but my legs gave way. We were both worried, but had no explanations. She helped me to feel more comfortable, changed me into my pyjamas, and tried to reassure me. It was a relief to have her there. She stayed as long as she could, but had to leave to be home with the kids.

I ate a sandwich but immediately threw up again. I didn't have enough strength to reach over and press the nurse call button, so asked Windy Miller next to me to do it. A nurse came, I was cleaned up and I suffered my way through to the night shift changeover. Later on in the evening, I asked the night nurse for a sleeping tablet. He was a slight man with thin grey hair. Not very tall and probably in his early fifties, his less than imposing presence hid a streak of nastiness that one really only hears about in medical disaster stories. He left; I took the tablet and promptly threw it up. My neighbour knew the routine by now and pressed the call button. Nurse Nasty, as I christened him, arrived at my bed oozing slimy disgust: "Well, what did you expect? No more tablets for you." He left and I was glad to see the back of him.

Thankfully, I've had very few totally sleepless nights, but this was one of them. I had pain in muscles all over my body; I was uncomfortable lying in any position, but nevertheless kept trying to move, constantly searching for relief. Breathing, as well as talking, was becoming more of an effort. My body control was slowly being taken away from me — it didn't slip away quietly, but fought with massive cramp-like pain, a horrible sweat, and slow strangulation of my throat. Those were the physical problems, but the indescribable pain was in my head — I had no idea what was wrong. I was in hospital, but nobody was looking after me. Then, for the first time, I realised I was almost totally paralysed from the neck down.

I was desperate for some attention and relief from this slow waking nightmare. I managed to get a hand to the call button and summoned Nurse Nasty. He slithered into the dark room and hissed his way to my bed. He produced a small torch from somewhere deep in his scaly white coat and shone it at me. With considerable effort, I told him that I was paralysed. His mood immediately changed from downright horrible to positively demonic. He moved to the end of the bed, lifted the cover from my legs, yanked one leg up and scored the sharp end of some medical implement along the sole of my foot. "Did you feel that?" he spat. "Yes," I groaned. He repeated the same painful process on the other foot. "Did you feel that?" I nodded once again. He then shouted, "Don't tell me you are paralysed when you are not — I was just about to take you to the quadriplegic unit. You would have made me look a right fool and there are other patients on this ward that need my help!" He then bent down and lifted the foot of my bed violently up and down several times. I was tossed about on the bed like a cork bobbing in a pond. He continued to shout, "What is wrong with you? I am in here all the time, you don't know if you want your bed up or down and you tell me you are paralysed. I've got work to do!" He then strode out, leaving me gawking.

With all these histrionics from this most despicable man, he had woken my sleeping neighbour. In almost complete and utter exasperation, I asked Windy, "What was all that about?" I didn't get a reply, but didn't need one. I was left with my fears. I kept asking myself, *what did I do to provoke such a reaction? Why is nobody helping me?*

I struggled through the remaining hours — sleep being an unreachable goal. Breathing was getting harder as every intake of air dragged through my constricted and increasingly paralysed throat. The night shift changed and Nurse Nasty's terrorising was over. I clearly remember filing his horrible actions away in my mind, vowing to come back and terrorise him. Revenge occupied my thoughts, but it was soon drowned and forgotten in the pain and torment swirling around me. A new nurse came into the room. I begged her for something, anything, to bring relief from this unknown world. She wasn't unfriendly, but her tone, like the junior doctor the day before, was one of indifference to my plight. I couldn't help thinking that when confronted with the unknown, medical staff are extremely sceptical and categorise you as a potential time waster. I was told to wait for the doctor.

It was now after 9:00 a.m. I hadn't eaten for over twenty-four hours, had not slept or received any medical attention or pain relief. The last time I'd seen a doctor was at 5:00 p.m. the previous evening — so much for observation in my local hospital! My junior doctor appeared. I studied her expression to see if she had any answers, but knew instantly from her attitude of indifference that my struggle would continue. I was examined once again. I recounted the dreadful night, the total paralysis, the pain and the increasing struggle for each breath. There was no reaction from her, absolutely bloody nothing. I was reaching a point of total and utter exasperation and let the doctor know it. "Look, I want to see the boss."

I am a great admirer of professionalism in whatever form it is demonstrated to me. If a tradesman or a nuclear scientist does a good professional job, they'll get my complete respect, regardless of their profession. Unfortunately, too many doctors that I have come across seem to demand and not earn my respect. Frankly it annoys me when people feel they cannot challenge a doctor lest it be seen as disrespectful, because I have experienced unbelievable levels of incompetence far too often. This was one of those times. The young doctor was way too far out of her depth and seemingly unprepared to acknowledge it. If I hadn't reacted with my demands, I could have died on that ward.

It was after 10:00 a.m. when the Registrar who had seen me the day before arrived. I was desperate, telling him "You need to do something — I am paralysed." He was a slim, fit-looking man, with short grey and slightly receding hair. I guessed he was my age or slightly younger. In contrast to my emotional state, he was very calm and asked his junior colleague some questions. He then crossed his arms in front of me and placed his hands close to mine. He asked me to hold his hands and squeeze them. I couldn't. In fact I couldn't even lift my hands to get close to his. He then enquired, "You told me yesterday that it had started with tingling in your feet and hands, right?" "Yes," I confirmed. He continued, "Okay, we need to transfer you to the neurological department at another hospital; this is something for real specialists. We are not equipped to look after you further here. I will make immediate arrangements to get you transferred there by ambulance." I suddenly noticed I had an audience, Windy, my flatulent neighbour and his irritating wife, were listening intently, two nurses had joined the two doctors and as the Registrar delivered his diagnosis, the mood in the room changed. Finally, they realised I was not a time waster. The scepticism dissolved almost instantly into a caring, almost obsequious attitude. The two doctors conferred. I heard the letters GBS for the first time as the Registrar told his junior colleague "I think he has GBS. I've seen it only twice in more than twenty years of medical practice." Boy, was I pleased he had come up with something. I didn't know what GBS meant, but something was finally happening. It is funny how relief can mask physical pain. But it was only temporary — I knew something would happen now, but I was still extremely ill.

The nurses busied themselves clearing up my belongings and packing them in the case that Fiona had brought the night before. They were now concerned about my comfort but I couldn't help feeling angry about the previous hours of torture. When the Registrar came back over I asked what exactly was wrong with me. "I think you have Guillain-Barré Syndrome," he explained, "It is a disease that attacks the nerves. The prognosis these days is quite good, with a near full or even full recovery possible, but it will take some time. I will call the hospital and arrange for a bed there. We will get an ambulance and transfer you as soon as possible." I thanked him and asked for oxygen, as breathing was now really, really hard.

Able to breathe again, the registrar's words started to slowly sink in. Nerve disease, ambulance, neurological department, specialists, prognosis quite good, long time. *Help! This is really serious.* I was alone and immediately thought about Fiona. I realised that she was none the wiser about my condition. There had been no communication between her and the hospital since the previous evening. I knew she would be worried and I wanted to talk to her, but family life had to carry on. Saturday morning was dedicated to golf lessons for the kids and she would be ferrying them from home and killing time over a coffee until they finished. I needed them now more than ever, but, in no position to make a quick phone call, I was going to have to face the next bit on my own.

I was told the ambulance would be arriving very soon. My case was packed. I was ready; desperately hoping the move would bring some miracle cure and relief from the pain. In this situation nothing can happen quickly enough. Impatient to get into that ambulance and start moving, I asked the nurse how much longer the wait would be. She looked at me reassuringly, touching my hand in recognition of my plight and said, "They will be here soon." This was of little comfort when I could feel the slow onset of strangulation.

Eventually, two heavily dressed paramedics arrived in their fluorescent orange jackets, thick black boots, and ridiculously white trousers. With them came a stretcher on spindly legs - the type that seems to miraculously collapse when thrust into an ambulance - and they positioned themselves at the side of my bed. A 'heave-ho' transfer delivered me onto the stretcher and I was strapped in. The oxygen tube from my nose was connected to a small canister, papers were thrust into the paramedic's hands and my case was placed beside my legs on the stretcher. The doctors, nurses, plus Windy and his wife, formed something of a departing committee. The Registrar reassured me that everything was arranged and I would be taken straight to a specialist. As I left, everyone looked very concerned and wished me all the best - I was simply glad to be on my way, but I had no idea of what lay ahead. I was wheeled out and the first chapter on my journey came to an end. The Registrar had just saved my life.

Chapter 2 — Drowning in a Sea of Air

As the ambulance was about to depart the paramedics agreed amongst themselves that I should only be accorded flashing lights, with no siren. They told me they would make haste, but not drive at top speed. The stretcher - in which I was rather too tightly cocooned - had been set just high enough so I could look out over the frosted parts of the windows in the rear of the ambulance. I recognised the trees and tops of the buildings as we turned out of the local hospital and set off for the neurological department of a clinic 15km away.

I was very uncomfortable. A paramedic was sitting with me, making sure I was okay, but conversation was not on the agenda. I was glad I was on my way to the "specialists", but sheer terror continued to dominate my thoughts. We sped on our way to the clinic. The complete paralysis made any movement impossible, although my brain was acutely aware of everything around me — the sounds, the speed of the ambulance, the pain, the nausea, and the smells. I smelt illness! I was ill.

We arrived at the emergency room of the neurological department of the clinic. I was unloaded and my belongings were placed on the stretcher again. I had stupidly and naively expected a reception committee, all gowned and scrubbed up *ER*-style ready to whisk me off to administer some immediate cure. Reality was different. I was soon to learn that things do not happen quickly in hospitals — exception being a life-threatening emergency. I accept that doctors and nursing staff are human, they have their routines and systems, meaning that they will get round to you when they are ready, but only if it fits their system. I was ill, really ill, in pain, and shitting myself with fear. I had arrived under the emergency flashing lights of the ambulance, yet my case did not constitute an emergency in the eyes of the doctors. So my first frustrating hour at the clinic began in much the same way the previous day had started, just waiting around.

My papers were handed over to a sandwich-eating nurse at the reception desk. No bed was available! *Damn.* The Registrar in my local hospital had told me everything was arranged and they were waiting for me. The bored-looking paramedics who'd accompanied me in the ambulance apologised. Until a bed could be found, I had to lie there on my very uncomfortable stretcher, strapped in, with no place to go. My thoughts turned to treatment. I was finally in a specialist department at the clinic and I was convinced I would soon be getting medical help to free me from my predicament. It was all so slow, with people looking ever so busy doing things other than looking after me. I wanted help and with hindsight should have made a song and dance about it. Eventually, a bed was wheeled in and I was transferred. Finally, I was on a bed, albeit in a hallway. *All set, bring in the doctors — I am sick, give me some drugs and send me home in a day or two, then we'll all be happy.*

I waited and waited. Nothing happened. Eventually, I was pushed into a twin bed consulting room where I occupied the bed next to a very fat man. While he continued to receive treatment, again I waited. A nurse came in and filled in some more forms. A doctor finally arrived, shaking my paralysed hand, yet I couldn't return this most basic of greetings. He introduced himself as an internist. *What! Where are the specialist neurologists?* He turned to the nurse and asked, "Have we taken an ECG? Have we taken blood?" "No," was my frustrated answer spoken through gritted teeth. And so began another long wait; pain, suffering, and blind panic do not constitute an emergency. A spidery ECG system was wheeled in. A nurse hooked me up, a printout was made, and she seemed happy. Blood was taken and an extremely painful IV tube was inserted into my wrist. The internist completed his examination and departed, while the fat man's treatment was over and he too left. I was on my own again. Breathing was becoming more and more difficult. Swallowing was now a problem and adding further insult, as my ability to talk was deteriorating, evil tasting saliva was collecting in my mouth. My bodily systems were shutting down. It was 1:00 p.m., Saturday 12th of February. Within the last twenty-four hours I had deteriorated from being able to walk, albeit unsteadily, to having difficulty breathing and swallowing and the onset of full paralysis from the neck down. The disease was now moving up my neck and entwining itself around the muscles in my throat — my lungs would be next.

A young neurologist arrived with a nurse and introduced himself. He explained that I had suspected GBS; *tell me something I don't know.* To complete his diagnosis and confirm the disease, he would have to take a lumbar puncture. *A what?* I was told in detail how he would remove some fluid from my spine and then send it for analysis. GBS could be confirmed if the protein levels in the spinal fluid were at an elevated level. He calmly and kindly told me that it would be unpleasant and painful, but very necessary. I was racked with pain and so bloody uncomfortable that one more wallop wouldn't make any big difference. "Go ahead," I told him.

He returned with what looked like a horse syringe with a javelin on the end of it. I was asked if I could sit up and bend over. *Funny one doc, I can't move*, I thought sarcastically. Visibly embarrassed to have asked such a question, the doctor and the nurse manoeuvred me to the edge of the bed, my feet hanging down above the floor. My very elegant hospital gown, courtesy of the first hospital, was opened at the back. I then had to lean forward onto the shoulders of the nurse, rounding my back as far as I could in the process. The doctor moved around behind me and proceeded to feel down at the bottom of my spine. He kneaded the area for a long time until finding the right spot. Eventually, he was ready and forewarned me of the impending insertion. It is strange how when you cannot move at all, you still try to tense up. I tried, but my muscles would not respond. The needle crunched into my spine and the pain was extreme. He told me to bend over further. I tried to coax my muscles but was only able to lean forward when the nurse sank further down. We made a very interesting sight. I was in great danger of falling off the bed and as the pain bit, I felt like ripping the head off the doctor as I went down. *Come on,* I told myself, *you can do it*.

"Nothing is happening," sighed the doctor. *What! All of this for nothing*, I thought. The needle was removed and I was told to bend even further forward. "Don't worry, the nurse will hold you." The three of us tried again, I tensed up imaginary muscles, the nurse held my 75 kg floppy, unresponsive body with the doctor testing and prodding until finally inserting the needle in my back.

He struck fluid! *Hooray!* There were imaginary high fives all round. I was pulled even further over as he extracted the liquid that would determine my treatment over the next sixteen weeks. The needle was in my back for around two minutes, but I never saw how much he withdrew. The team was satisfied and made their preparations to leave with their liquid pain. It was now around 2:30 p.m.

The doctor and nurse returned and Fiona, Alexander, and Francesca were shown into the room. They looked at me, not knowing what to say or what to do. I was so happy to see them but saw only absolute and sheer terror on all of their faces — especially Francesca. Her big eyes are normally so full of expression, radiating her warmth and love. On that day her eyes reflected her fears. Fiona was fighting back tears and she kept saying, "Sorry, sorry, sorry." She then added, "We have only just found out. We were at golf and the hospital called to say you had been transferred." It was around twenty hours since Fiona had seen me. She didn't know about the terrible night, the pain, the nausea, and worst of all, the paralysis. I looked and listened and then managed to say, "I am extremely ill and I am totally paralysed."

I don't know what they were thinking at this time, but it wasn't time to talk. I could see and feel their concern. We were together. It gave me great comfort to know that I was no longer alone with this terrifying illness. I was so afraid that this might be the last day of my life and I might not see my family again. We had so much left to do together;

Alexander and Francesca were only fourteen and twelve, far too early for me to leave them fatherless. Fiona and I had a lot of living to do. I couldn't leave her. I couldn't go. This focus would give me so much strength over the next few immobile weeks and I never gave up or let myself get down; well only once or twice, but more of that later. Here we were, in the cold atmosphere of a hospital room and I have never loved them more or been happier to see them. I suddenly didn't feel quite as bad. As Fiona held my hand, Alexander busied himself and tended to the ever-increasing amounts of saliva that I could no longer swallow. He placed paper kidney bowls under my mouth and wiped my face as Francesca remained terrified and immobile.

The doctor returned and confirmed I had GBS. A severe form, he explained that it would necessitate a transfer to an intensive care ward, as there was the potential for some breathing complications, and that the next twenty-four to forty-eight hours would be critical. As he was telling me this, I was slightly relieved that the terror had finally taken definite shape. It was known. I was in a hospital; they knew what to do, or so I thought. *Just give me a few pills, doc, and I will get on home*. My faith in modern medicine to administer instant relief was so wide of the mark; with hindsight, it was both laughable and naive. I continued to believe that something could be done until the doctor said, "We will give you some immunoglobin intravenously to assist in the treatment and speed recovery, but I'm afraid you will be in the hospital for some time." The obvious reply was "how long?" I was not prepared for the hammer blow that came, "Several weeks or even months. However, the prognosis of this disease is good and you have a high chance of making a full recovery." *Wooooh! Slow down here, doc, I am fit and healthy; I run marathons and eat triathlons for breakfast. This is not happening to me. Me, the nutter, who at forty-seven still refused to recognise that whilst the mind was able to achieve those sporting goals, the body was no longer that of a twenty-year-old. Me, the ever so health conscious goody-goody that cut out as many food evils as possible and dropped down a clothes size, so that I was now slimmer than I was at university. Me, Martin, the ever so optimistic and downright annoying sporting evangelist does not get ill.* In those few moments I was shattered, devastated. However much I did not want to hear it, I knew it was true. I was very, very seriously ill.

Sport was my stress release valve, my health insurance, and my life insurance. I honestly believed that by continuing my commitment to sport into later life I would be able to dodge lifestyle illnesses and plough into old age without serious health problems. But sport had not saved me. This angered me later when I was left alone with my thoughts as I tried to resolve why I had contracted this horrible disease. Looking back now, I can say quite frankly that I was just simply unlucky. Despite my anger and realisation then, sport was, however, to play an immensely significant role in my recovery. Physically, going into this illness, I was fit, which meant I was able to recover my muscle strength reasonably quickly as the recovery process got under way. Mentally, though, was where sport helped me the most. My, sometimes monastic, slavery to physical exercise over the last thirty years has given me incredible reserves of mental strength to fight on, when giving up would be the easier option. Giving up to me represents defeat, weakness, and cowardice. It is the antithesis of what I admire in great sports people who put themselves on the line and give absolutely everything. I had not envisaged that I would need to fight like my sporting heroes, but I would soon have a life or death struggle on my hands. *No sir-reeh, this one is not for giving up and is ready to take on this challenge head on.* It proved to be the hardest challenge I've ever set myself and those reserves were tested right to the very limit.

As the nurse busied herself with preparing for the arrival of the immunoglobin, the mood amongst my family was sombre. Drip lines were set up and a stand was wheeled into place. The doctor prepared his notes and told us there were no spare intensive care beds in the neurological department, but one was available on the surgery ward. He reassured me that everything would be okay and he would come with us to the surgery ICU. An ambulance had been ordered and I would shortly be transferred. I was in bed, propped up at an acute angle watching and listening to all of the action. I had gone from the relative inactivity of a local hospital to a slow start at the clinic and now to a rather rapid transfer from outpatient to intensive care. I knew I was ill, yet remained blissfully unaware of what was going to happen. I did not for one second think that I would need the attention of the intensive care staff. In fact it was to the contrary, I was already cheerily considering my next move from intensive care to a normal ward once the obligatory twenty-four to forty-eight hours of observation were over.

The immunoglobin arrived and it was hooked up to my drip. I heard a nurse say each bottle costs the same as a small car, although I was well past caring. I watched the slow rhythmic dripping into the tube and continued to secretly hope it would course through my veins and impart immediate relief. What fantasies, your mind can imagine, but the cold reality was paralysis, pain, and ever-increasing breathing problems. I took great comfort in the closeness of my family. We tried talking, but there were no words for this situation. Instead we all seemed much happier being involved in trying to relieve me of my discomfort, hence a routine had developed: My mouth was cleaned up, tissues and kidney bowls were collected and then thrown away. This went on while we waited for the liquid to dispense into my veins and for the ambulance to arrive.

When the first bottle was finished I noticed that my left shoulder and left leg had regained some, albeit slight, motion. Encouraged, I told the doctor. I was happy at this progress and wanted more of the liquid to speed the recovery process even further. He advised me that the second one would be hooked up in the intensive care unit, so I had to wait. This was the very first piece of slightly encouraging news that we'd had. The paramedics arrived and I was transferred yet again to the collapsible stretcher. We left in higher spirits, out of the examination room and into the ambulance. For the second time that day, I was loaded up and driven the short journey to the surgery intensive care unit. The doctor travelled with me in the ambulance while Fiona and the children had to find the car and drive it within the labyrinth of buildings that made up the clinic.

It was now around 5:30 in the evening of Saturday 12th of February. I was wheeled into a gleaming, new, lavishly appointed and spotlessly clean cubicle in the ICU. The facilities were exceptional — all flat screen monitors, tubes, bottles, and expensive looking equipment. The lighting was bright and harsh. Beeps and alarms cut through any periods of silence with irritating regularity. Doctors and nurses were constantly on the move giving the place a sense of heightened tension.

Now physically useless and almost unable to speak, I was transferred to a bed and the staff busied themselves with hooking me up and plugging me in. The array of signals on my monitor included pulse, blood pressure, ECG, oxygen saturation levels, and countless other things. I was impressed with my pulse at sixty-five or lower and played games by holding my breath to force it below sixty. Anything under fifty was probably alarm time, so I spared the nurses that worry. I remember being pleased with myself that I was so fit, despite a marked reduction in training, that I was still able to have a relatively low heartbeat, even in the stressful situation of intensive care. Once again, I had not grasped the severity of the situation. I was still allowing myself to be carried off into my own little fantasy world. Little did I know that in a few hours, those games of holding my breath would turn into an ever desperate struggle to get any air; a battle that I would eventually lose.

My doctor wrote endless notes and seemed oblivious to my situation. A very pleasant nurse looked after me. She was slightly younger than me, small with a plump, friendly face. I was struck by her professionalism with the techno-array of equipment around me and also her gentle caring attention to making sure I was as comfortable as possible. I was connected to at least three drips and had countless electrodes and sensors around my body. She adjusted the positioning of my bed, so my head was up and my feet were down. She skilfully negotiated the electronics of the bed to place me in a sort of sitting position, while still lying down. I was just about comfortable, but the drip did not contain any painkillers so I was in serious pain searing from what seemed like every muscle in my body. The nausea had eased, but was still present. Intensive care units are many things; one thing they are not is cold. I was also hot, very hot.

The dreaded word catheter was mentioned. I wanted to shout, kick, and scream *NO!* But I couldn't move and verbal communication had become a barely audible whisper. I knew, or thought I knew, that I was in control of my bladder, *thank you very much*, and nobody, but nobody was going to stick anything down my willy! As I got my message across, I realised that I had not had anything to eat or drink since breakfast the day before.

My nurse left and brought Fiona and the kids in to see me. Fiona explained that getting into the intensive care unit was a major exercise involving filling out countless forms, washing of hands and moving through an air lock consisting of two sets of separate doors. I was just glad to see her and the kids again. We all looked around and marvelled at the modernity of the unit I was in. It's times like these when it is easy to realise how incredible the

German health system really is, which makes the moaning of Windy Miller and his wife the day before seem even more pathetic. However well it is appointed, an ICU is not designed for comfort; the various alarms and noises were incessant. The blinking of the monitor transmitting my life functions dragged my weary eyes to it constantly. I was seduced into watching the figures and counted them against the damn clock that was strategically positioned directly in my line of vision. I was exhausted, but knew sleep with all these sensory distractions was going to be impossible. I was going to have a very bad relationship with that clock. It was going to be a long night!

The duty doctor, a surgeon, came in and the young neurologist explained my situation to him. I had GBS, I was on my second bottle of immunoglobin and I needed to be monitored because of possible breathing complications. If all went well, I should be all right and out of the ICU in twenty-four to fourty-eight hours. My family and I all looked and listened, but only the two doctors spoke. I am naturally positive and optimistic. I have my moments, like anyone else, but I am generally a happy or very happy person. I castigate myself when I get down or things are going wrong. I tell myself to stop being a wimp and just get on with the task at hand. This is my mechanism to stop seeing things as too black or to avoid self-destruction spiralling into a depressive state. Now, lying in my very expensive ICU room, I was in the absolute worst possible physical condition I could have ever imagined, unfortunately it was to get worse, yet I was STILL positive. I thought that breathing difficulties were not for me; they were for other, less fortunate people. I expected the observation would be over soon and I would be moved to another ward very quickly. Analysing it now, I can only comment that I was unable mentally to comprehend the severity of my problems. I was naively stupid in my belief that I would get out of this one, like I had done all the others. The surgeon told me in quiet, but practised tones that I was in the right and best place. He talked me through the monitors and alarms and reassured me that nothing could go wrong. He was trying to calm my nerves. I was in pain, uncomfortable, very ill, and still very scared. As for something going wrong, I hadn't even considered it!

I couldn't really talk and the family didn't feel like talking; there were really no words to say. We glanced at the clock and it was after 7:00 in the evening. It had been a long and tiring day for them. I was in bed, wired up and as the doc said, "In the best place." There was nothing they could do for me right now. I could just about whisper that I was okay and they should go home. I knew Fiona didn't want to leave, but the kids needed something to eat and hospital is not a place for them to be. We said our goodbyes. They kissed me and told me it would be okay. I wouldn't see the children again for another three weeks.

Time was moving slowly. My condition was not improving. My nurse came in and I tried to talk. A very dry whisper came out. I tried to force it out harder. "I need the urine bottle." Although I hadn't drunk anything in more than twenty-four hours, I was now on numerous drips and I needed to go. A bottle was produced and I was left wondering what I was to do. In fact, there was nothing I could do. The nurse took charge, pulled the bed sheets back and popped my willy into the bottle. *Well here we go lad,* I thought *Let's hope the waterworks are still working.* I was so desperate to avoid a catheter. I willed the fluid out. It worked. It was at least something positive and helped to motivate me to try the same routine three or four times over the next couple of hours.

I felt comfortable with this nurse. She had the calm reassured air of a professional in full control of her job, such a contrast to the junior doctor who checked me in at the local hospital. I got to know many medical staff over the next few weeks. There were those that did their jobs and those that cared and went the extra mile. They knew when to help me and when to gently push or coach me to do it myself. Their touch was sometimes not gentle, but always reassured, and I developed an unbelievable trust in them. Those staff tended to be nurses rather than doctors. The trust I put in one male nurse later in my recovery helped save my life. He gave me the strength I needed to meet and overcome the challenges of pain and uncertainty each and every day. This ICU nurse, who I never got to know by name, was the first carer to add her own touch to the medical necessities of my situation. She made me feel warm in the few hours that I spent in her care. In fact her care seemed to distract me from my plight and I failed to notice that my condition was continuing to deteriorate as she neared the end of her shift.

It was approaching 10:00 p.m. when she told me she would be going home. I was so disappointed. She left to get changed and then spent several minutes talking to colleagues by the nurses' desk. I watched them through the glass walls of my cubicle. She left, giving a small wave. I whispered "bye" and resumed the observation of my life functions on the monitor. I was alone again, alone with seemingly no relief from this horror. I thought about sleep, but the noises, the stifling heat, and the extremely bright lights meant that natural sleep would be impossible.

My thoughts turned to my chest and upper body. I looked at the clock. It was now 11:00 p.m. and I realised that the limited movement I had regained in my left shoulder and leg had gone and they were once again paralysed. The GBS had met the immunoglobin head on and after brief resistance had brushed it aside, allowing the continued march towards the life-sustaining muscles in my throat, lungs, and heart. GBS had me in a vice-like grip. I could move my head, but nothing else. As I checked my breathing, which was laboured, I realised it was getting worse. I tried to attract somebody's attention. Nobody was there. I began to panic and tried to shout. Nothing came out. I tried my forced whisper, but nobody heard me. My heart rate started rising, I was sweating. I tried again and again to attract somebody's attention, but could not make myself heard. I started thrashing my head about, trying to shout, but could only manage a barely audible whisper that I repeated over and over again. "Doctor, doctor, nurse, nurse." Panic was setting in. I wanted to kick, scream, and thrash out. I was drowning in a sea of air.

My chest was tightening. Breathing was more and more difficult. The pain in my upper body was increasing. I was frightened, frightened like I have never been frightened before. Eventually, the surgeon arrived. I had panicked my way through until 11:40pm. In a terrible and stressed state, I wanted to shout to him, but only had the muscle strength to manage a pathetic whisper. I gulped and gulped

precious air between words spewing them out as quickly
as possible and just about completed the sentence "I need
more oxygen." I trembled with fear as he checked the
monitors. He was calmness personified and I was a wreck.
He told me reassuringly, "It doesn't matter to me if you
breathe on your own or we start artificial breathing. I am
looking at your stats. Your oxygen saturation is good. I
think you can do it on your own." He tapped me on my
arm and left!

I wanted to shout and scream *Doc! Help, help!* The
gulps of air did not contain enough oxygen and I was
slipping away. I used all my will power to draw in as much
air as possible and thought *come on Martin, fight. Fight
for it. Fight like you have never fought before. You can do
it.* My heart was racing as I was now struggling to stay
alive. I tried to calm down, but it was as if a huge weight
was pushing down on my chest. I tried to gulp in more air
but the invisible hands of death were tightening around my
throat. GBS was circling and moving in to take me. My
chest was rising and falling in a desperate attempt to keep
breathing. It wasn't working. I flashed a glance at the
clock. It was 11:50 p.m. on 12th of February. The surgeon
came back again. I was desperate. I looked at him through
frightened, terrified eyes.

And that was the last I remembered.

Part 2: Coma, Intensive Care, and Rehabilitation

46

Chapter 3 — Waking Up

I slowly came to, aware that I was emerging from a long and very deep sleep. It had taken me away from the pain, discomfort and panic of a debilitating illness. Sleep had been a haven of comfort, but now as I awoke, the stark reality of my situation started to come into focus. I could recall every second leading up to my struggle for breath in the intensive care unit, but then all was blank. I knew that I had been out for a long time, that I was in a different bed in a different room, but I had no idea whether it was day or night, or if I had been out for days or weeks. I was fully aware that I was ill and that I was paralysed. My brain was working and did not seem to be affected. I remained blissfully unaware of how serious my predicament was. Perhaps this is a protection mechanism, allowing the brain to remain optimistic, filling the body with positive energy which no doubt assists recovery.

My mouth was propped painfully open by a large and fat tube. I guessed it was some sort of breathing tube, but in fact had no idea. My jaw ached. As I tried to look down at the tube I realised that I was lying on my side, making any movement of my head very difficult. The tube was opaque with a red tinge, dotted with rivulets of condensation that rattled about as I breathed. My body was motionless, yet the pain was very intense. I felt hot, very hot, and was in a great deal of discomfort. My eyes turned to my surroundings. Everything was fuzzy, courtesy of my poor eyesight, but I could just make out that I was in a single room. The bed was in the middle and there was a sliding door. The electric lights were very bright and the radio was on. It was Antenne Düsseldorf, the local radio station. The music stopped and was replaced by the news. I listened intently for clues of the time or the day. It was 9:00am in the morning, but I had no idea what the date was. The news finished without any reference to the day of the week — and I calculated that I would need another fourteen hours until 11:00pm in the evening, when my useless body might eventually fall back to sleep. That haven away from the world of paralysis was so far away as the 9:00 a.m. news finished. I would have to listen to another thirteen more news bulletins, twenty-seven more traffic updates and countless numbers of songs. My helplessness was overwhelming and I knew I would have a difficult struggle ahead.

Unbeknown to me, I'd woken up at 9:00 a.m. on Thursday 17th of February. The last recollection I had was at 11:50 p.m. on Saturday 12th of February. I don't know exactly what happened in the next few minutes; only the surgeon on duty in the intensive care unit can fill in those gaps. What I do know is that sometime after my last thoughts, GBS had finally strangled all the life out of my throat and lung muscles. I stopped breathing. Reacting to the situation, the doctor intubated me and put me on a breathing machine. To conserve my energy and promote recovery, I was put in a medically induced coma with the aid of heavy sedation. I was given a cocktail of drugs, including opiates, to relieve the pain. With these actions, my life had been saved. Twenty years ago, GBS and its treatment were little known. In my condition I would have died as a simple addition to the statistics of unexplained deaths. Fortunately, at the age of forty-seven, my time was not up.

I later learnt that the surgeon called Fiona at 1:50am in the morning of Sunday 13th of February. The call woke her up and the doctor told her the cheery news that I had stopped breathing. She was, naturally, devastated and had no idea what to do. She rang the hospital back and asked if she should come in to see me, but they told her to get some sleep. Your husband has just stopped breathing...the perfect way to induce a comfortable night's sleep!

I was transferred from the surgical ICU on Sunday and placed in the neurological ICU. Fiona came to see me every day, talking to me and willing me back to a waking state. It was a very difficult time for her. I was gravely ill. I had a very serious form of GBS and nobody was prepared to give her any guarantees. Most of the medical staff talked to her about a minimum of six months in hospital, which was if I survived. The coma was necessary to give my body strength to recover. I had drugs to keep me in the coma and drugs to numb the pain. My body swelled and I was unrecognisable. Visitors came to see me and were shocked at the poor physical state I was in. Several cried and left feeling helpless.

When I first woke up, I had the intubation tube in my mouth. Sometime later, I cannot recall when, I was anaesthetised in my room and given a tracheotomy. A J-shaped tube was inserted in my neck and connected to a ventilator. The tube, a cannula, was my lifeline, but it cut off the power of speech, taste, and smell. It would be more than seven weeks before I could talk, eat, or drink again.

I keep on writing that I had no idea how seriously ill I was. Looking back, I find it difficult to believe I was neither aware nor mentally able to process the information. I knew I could not move, but have no recollection of realising that I could not talk — perhaps I tried and nothing happened. I don't remember seeing or noticing the nasal feeding tube or the catheter. Similarly, I cannot remember the ventilator and the life it was gifting me. In fact, those first hours and days of my recovery are very cloudy and I can only recall certain items.

I woke again, after the tracheotomy, with no idea that I had just had an operation. To my great surprise and joy, Fiona walked in just as I woke up. She later told me that she was there before and when the surgeons had arrived, they asked her to leave. It was magical to see her and I longed to be able to say hello and give her a kiss. "Oh Scattie, you are awake!" she gushed. I could not communicate, but I desperately wanted to ask some questions. I tried to talk with my eyes, fluttering them. It didn't work. I became frustrated and opened my eyes wider to signal that I wanted to say something. Again communication was impossible, Fiona couldn't understand me. I decided that sleep would provide relief from this world. I wanted to talk, but couldn't make Fiona understand. I rolled my eyes left and right and then simultaneously closed them and dropped my head to the side. In my very confused state, it was totally obvious to me that this pantomime was a very clear demonstration of my request to go to sleep. I wanted to escape, to slip into a calming and comfortable sleep, leaving the nastiness of my new world behind. There was no reaction from Fiona and my frustration level increased even further. It was my first hard lesson in the loneliness of paralysis.

Just then, a grey-haired man with glasses and a white coat walked in. He looked at me, then acknowledged Fiona and shook her hand. He introduced himself as Professor Drews. He then asked me if I could hear him and if I could understand German. I nodded slightly in painful agreement to both questions. Something then happened that shook me to the core — he asked Fiona if she could step outside with him. *What?* I was waiting for him to give me some information or diagnosis, possibly even some words of encouragement. Instead, he took Fiona outside, which signalled to me that it was not only a serious illness; but I was also going to die!

Boy was I scared. It seemed like forever before Fiona finally came back in. I have no idea if it was twenty seconds, two minutes, or twenty minutes. It seemed like an awfully long time and I was alone with my dark and troublesome thoughts. I searched her face and her eyes especially for clues. *Had she been crying? What had he said to her? Was I going to die?* I strained every single immobile muscle in my body to signal to her and say, "Well? What did he say?"

Fiona composed herself and said, "He said you have a very serious case of GBS. It is going to take a long time. But recovery is possible."

I could not make my mind up if she had been crying, but I know her well enough to know at that time she was not telling me everything the professor had told her. I was furious that this man had come to my bed, introduced himself, asked if I could understand him and then walked out to speak with my wife. *He could not do the decent thing and talk to me*; instead his actions worried me greatly. I thought it could only mean bad news and I was to spend a long time questioning if I had a finite time left in this world. Later on in my recovery, I read a great deal about GBS and its effects on the body and mind. One clear guideline offered by the truly exceptional GBS self-help group (www.gbsinfo.de) is to avoid worrying the patient unnecessarily, as this can easily lead to depression, resulting in the loss of the will to live. Whilst there was no doubt that he was an extremely experienced medical man, Professor Drews had zero understanding of the human effect of the cowardly act of avoiding talking to me. Sadly, it was a trait that I was to encounter on more occasions.

Professor Drews had actually told Fiona he was not sure if I could make it. He was not able to give any guarantees because mine was such a bad case. Showing remarkable strength, Fiona managed to keep this from me. Only slight redness around her eyes and our intimate knowledge of each other betrayed the fact that she was hiding some comments from me. She picked up my hand and said, "Oh Scattie, we'll get through this together. Just, as we have got through everything else together." And we did.

Chapter 4 — Foundations of Recovery

I was now just at the start of my recovery and I very quickly realised that the key to survival would be mental. Two fundamental thought processes underpinned my loose strategy to make sure I would succeed. The first involved just being positive, the second was bizarrely related to a clock.

I am a keen runner and when I push myself to the limit, whether in training or in a race, two opposing sides battle each other. The bad side is always telling me to slow down or stop; it tempts me with immediate relief from the exercise-induced pain. The good side is always pushing me harder; counting down the kilometres and telling me to never, ever give up. It is a battle neither seen nor heard by outsiders, an internal struggle that brings out extraordinary depths of inner strength when I am faced with the most extreme and adverse of situations. The good side nearly always wins. In 2004 I was running in the Hamburg Marathon. It was my second marathon and I'd set myself a four-hour time goal. I was moving well until I hit the "wall" at 36 km and I was no longer able to run without severe cramp or pain. With a determined inner strength and the 'good side' pushing me along, I shuffled, jogged, and walked the next 5 km to the 41 km mark, battling against cramp and dehydration. I looked at my time and calculated I had an easy ten minutes to complete the last kilometre and still come in under four hours. Unfortunately, in my exhaustion I'd miscalculated the time. It wasn't ten but a very difficult five! I immediately shot down the thoughts of giving up and just focused on getting to the finish line. The good side of my brain now had a new target and I found myself accelerating, running really hard through the pain. I passed countless weakening runners and pushed on ever faster and faster. The 42km mark and the final straight came into sight. I had only seconds to go to achieve my four hour goal. A marathon though is not just 42 km, it is 42.196 km and because of those extra meters, I missed my target by 45 seconds. I had run the final kilometre in five minutes, eight seconds, my fastest kilometre in the whole race. I had not succumbed to the bad side. Instead, the positive side had won. I'd fought on and despite the pain and exhaustion I'd nearly, oh so nearly, got to my target on time.

As I lay in my horrible bed, in that damn intensive care ward, surrounded by those bloody beeping machines keeping me alive, I knew that I had to switch the positive side into action again. The target this time was a lot more important than a magical four-hour marathon. It was the will to live. I wanted to live and I wanted to kick this bloody illness in the teeth. I fixed the target and very clearly remember saying to myself, "Don't let this get you down. This is the way life is now; we have to go with it, not against it."

I can report with pride, that although I had some dark moments, they were only that. I never got depressed and never really lost the will to live. I remained extremely positive and was ready to take on new and painful challenges every day. I am convinced the mental strength that I drew upon had developed through my addiction to sport. Sport had not protected me from GBS, but it would save my life when it came to the mental struggles that I wrestled with on many occasions in those early days.

A clock was responsible for the second foundation on which to build my recovery. Every room in the hospital had a clock. I could see one every second of every hour of every day of every week during the nearly eight that I lay paralysed and immobile in my bed. I started that first day, on waking from the coma, calculating how many hours I needed to endure before I could go back to sleep for temporary relief. I knew it was a mistake to count the time like that, but it was hard to drag my eyes away from the bloody thing. Showing a mental awareness that still surprises me today, I shifted my thinking into a positive mind-set and told myself that the clock should never, ever be my enemy. Instead it was to be my friend and every second counted down was a second closer to surviving and recovery.

I have considered these two pivotal thoughts many times, especially during the writing of this story. I was very fortunate to have realised the mental dangers early enough and switched the positive side on as I started to take stock of my situation. If the negative side had won, I would not have made it. This and my attitude toward the clock were the two foundations of my recovery. I would be lying if I said I was happy and content all the way through my treatment. My thoughts though were laser-focused on refusing to give in. At the time I did not see it as mental strength, just plainly very sensible actions to keep me on an even keel. Later in my rehabilitation, comments were often passed to me about my "iron will". I found them embarrassing. Now, with the benefit of time and the possibility to reflect on my hopelessness, I would say it was simply a survival instinct.

Chapter 5 — Mind Games

My initial memory of those first few days at the clinic in Düsseldorf and indeed the first weeks after I was transferred to Bonn are very sketchy as I passed in and out of consciousness, no doubt helped by the drugs I was on. The drugs included morphine for pain relief, anti-depressants (apparently good for promoting nerve reconstruction), blood pressure tablets, heart rate regulating tablets, and countless other pharmaceutical delights. They were all necessary. They helped me overcome some of the pain and brought blessed relief as I drifted into sleep. At other times they seemed to sharpen my senses and I became acutely aware of pain. As the level increased, I desperately sought help but could only attract attention by violently moving my head from left to right on my pillow (later, I was to get an alarm I could press with my head, but during the first two weeks in Düsseldorf I had nothing like this). I then increased the frequency of the movements, only stopping when I was exhausted. After one long particularly violent head shaking incident, I remember the back of my head hurting and I was concerned I would rub away the very little hair that I have, very much like that of a new baby when lying in its cot.

As well as a form of communication, the head shaking was a sign of my frustration. I was not happy, I was uncomfortable, and I wanted out. Eventually, if or when somebody came to me, I might be asked what I wanted. *Well heh*, I couldn't tell them. If the nursing staff were on good form, they would ask me questions and I would nod that I wanted pain relief after the appropriate question. I do not remember any of the staff in Düsseldorf trying to establish any method of contact with me, they only reacted to me. The absolute opposite was later true in Bonn. There the staff would communicate with all patients as soon as possible — they would calmly and reassuringly move closer to the patient, usually with some form of touch such as a hand on the shoulder and ask the patient to open or close his or her eyes if they understood. Every action was explained in detail and the patient was kept informed. The patient felt engaged and to be honest, wanted. This was alien to the people in the clinic and because of it I came to resent the nursing staff there.

After one particularly violent head shaking session, Bernd, the nurse who looked after me a lot of the time, demanded to know why I was always shaking my head. If truth be known, I was seeking attention and wanted to go back to sleep, or get some pain relief, but could not articulate this. He shouted at me and asked if I was doing it on purpose, or if it was an epileptic reaction. He waited for me to answer, but the only way I could answer was to shake my head more! He went ballistic. He was not as horrible as Nurse Nasty during my first night, but he would have made a very good understudy as he threatened me with some drugs to stop my head shaking. When his female companion joined him in their nursing duties, I hoped for a more tender loving approach. But she only seemed to support him. I was shouted at and they both man-handled me in a very rough way as I was moved from one side to another. My worst memory was of them turning me over and then dropping me off the bed. They half caught me, saving me from serious injury, but my upper body and arms did hit the floor.

I am totally convinced that the verbal abuse happened on many occasions. However, I need to concede that the incident of being dropped on the floor may have been a result of my imagination. Having said that, at the time I was 100 percent sure that it had happened. It also sent me into a very stressed and agitated state some days later when Fiona and our great friend Dennis, who was on one of his many trips from Belgium, told me that I would soon be transferred to another hospital in Bonn. They presented me with a paper, explaining that it was a consent form for my transfer. Normally, I would have had to sign it, but was unable to do so. Therefore, Fiona told me she would need to sign it on my behalf. This was the reality of the conversation, but my understanding in my possibly confused mental state was somewhat different. I thought the nurses had given Fiona and Dennis a form to say how good they had been to me and on signing the form we agreed not to take any action against them, should they have hurt me or treated me badly. Naturally, as Fiona was about to sign the paper I became extremely agitated and wanted to scream to her that Bernd and his sidekick had abused me and dropped me on the floor. Unable to do anything else, I went into a very violent head shaking session and was determined to stop them signing the form and letting those bastards off the hook.

Fiona and Dennis tried for a very long time to understand the source of my violent concern. They asked question after question where I could only indicate a yes or no with my head, eventually determining that the form was the problem. However, no amount of questioning could have determined the reason for my unhappiness. The situation was resolved by all of us agreeing not to sign the form without consulting me once again. My stress levels were extremely high and I was very glad to get away from those bloody nurses. Frankly, only Bernd and his female sidekick can say what really happened. Fiona told me they were very kind and looked after me very well. Unfortunately, my memory, however wrong it may be, only tells me that I was a victim of abuse rather than a receiver of care.

Being dropped or not was a confusing state and I can safely say that I was not in full control of my mind. It was playing tricks on me. It was not the first one though. My first recollection was when I struggled to move my head to assess where I was in the clinic as I awoke from the coma. I had established that I was in a single room and after the usual four hourly positional changes to avoid the onset of bed sores, I found myself staring at a bright blue wall. I could see that the wall was only blue in the middle and I reasoned in my less than lucid state that its intense colour was provided by bright backlights. Occasionally, white areas appeared on the blue and I was quite impressed with its calming effect. My mind then took me off to Frankfurt airport. I was on the moving pavement in the subterranean tunnel transferring between terminals. There, you can find strange fluorescent lights that change seamlessly from red to green to blue, presumably to effuse calmness so avoiding any claustrophobic passengers panicking during the long underground passage. Back in my room I was impressed by how thoughtful the hospital planners had been to provide this wall to calm me down and soothe me through the day. Actually, I was looking at two large windows. It was a stunningly sunny day after a snowstorm, with a brilliantly blue sky. The white areas on the blue wall were occasional clouds. It was my first psychedelic trip.

Dennis no doubt inspired my next hallucination. A warm Yorkshire lad, we have a lot in common, except that he is from the wrong side of the Pennines. We first met in Düsseldorf when Fiona and Bernie, Dennis's wife, got to know each other at the British Women's Club in 1992. We have been firm friends ever since and spend holidays and weekends in Germany and Belgium together. As I fell ill, Fiona turned to Bernie and Dennis and our other close friends Pia and Jörg for support. Dennis came to visit me in the ICU two or three times and was upset to see me drugged up, with a very swollen body, and so close to death. After one visit, my tortured mind must have picked up on Dennis living in Belgium and sent me into a virtual world. This time, I was moved from Düsseldorf and my bed was changed from a hospital bed to an aluminium slab in a fish shop, close to Brussels. I was surrounded on both sides by fish and lay on a bed of ice. Customers were happily coming into the shop and buying their fish around my lifeless body. I was there for three days and seemed quite happy being surrounded by shoppers. The only strange thing that occurred to me was that I was in Belgium but all the people spoke German and not Flemish!

When I was conscious and floating between sleep and the real and imaginary worlds, I had a lot of time to think. I was frustrated but my mind did wander in some wonderful directions. Apart from the fish shop, I thought about the artistic creation of menus, especially extremely colourful and tasteful starter and main courses. I remember thinking for hours and hours about specific starters, putting together the ingredients, cooking them and then arranging them onto plates. Photographs were taken of my creations and the crowning glories were the huge posters that hung on the wall in my room and the hours I spent admiring them. The colours and the ingredients seemed to match my mood exactly; they issued a very calming effect on me. I longed for a pen to write down the ingredients and tried in vain to recall the last menu as I awoke after yet another dose of sleep. Once again, this was complete fabrication in my mind, but it succeeded in reducing my stress levels.

The opposite happened once I had transferred to Bonn. Thankfully, I was no longer so heavily sedated or so totally reliant on drugs, but I was still taking some medication and possibly in a very fragile mental state. Lack of muscle power combined with the life support machine connected to the tube in my neck, prevented me from eating via the conventional route. Instead, I was kept alive with liquid food and cold tea that dripped into a feeding tube up my left nostril, down my throat, and into my stomach. I was advised that after a certain amount of time, usually four weeks, the tube needed to be renewed. Sara, my nurse for the day in Bonn, talked me through the procedure. She would take the tube out and then insert the new one. With increasing astonishment, I watched as she slowly pulled the incumbent tube out through my nose. The colour changed from clear to light brown and then to yucky brown. And still the tube came out. It crawled up the back of my throat, took the bend up, came round the top of my nose and emerged out of my nostril leaving me with the opposite feeling of sucking a string of spaghetti off your fork. The grunge on the tube resembled the bottom of a muddy pond and fortunately for me, taken away before I could think too much about the contents of my stomach. Sara then collected the new tube and removed it from its sterile packaging. She told me to keep swallowing as hard as I could and inserted the new tube up my nose.

The experience was not pleasant, but it surprised me how easily she could feed a long tube up my nose and into my stomach. Sara tested if the tube was in the right place by placing a stethoscope on my stomach and squirting water into the tube. Her verdict — bull's eye! However; I could feel that something was wrong and as I swallowed hard the discomfort was very noticeable. I was convinced the tube was thicker than the previous one and as I fought hard to get used to it, the pain and irritation in my throat caused me to vomit. Unable to communicate, I tried hard to indicate to her that the new tube was the problem — but I was not successful. Concerned about my sudden vomiting, I was prescribed drugs for nausea and another painful drip was inserted into my arm. I threw up again and again but I was not feeling nauseous, just gagging on the tube.

Despite many attempts, I could not make any of the staff understand that the tube was the problem. Consequently, I had to try and learn to live with this hideous lump at the back of my throat. Once again my mind started wandering away from reality and I convinced myself that the lump in my throat was in fact caused by two tubes. The second one had a knot in it and, more bizarrely, was also connected to a fellow female patient who was also receiving liquid food. Over the next few hours I had imaginary explorations into my throat and tried unsuccessfully to retrieve the second tube and remove the knot. I knew that if I removed the knot I would survive, but my fellow patient would be condemned to die. As I fought in my mind to free myself of the knot in this horrible hallucinogenic trip, I became enormously agitated and seriously unhappy. In my virtual world, I finally removed the knot and although I survived I felt real compunction and shame at having condemned my fellow (imaginary) patient to die.

Another hallucinogenic experience occurred when my bed developed a massage function that moved and rumbled under my body. It started with wave-like motions and I was sure I was being gently carried further and further down the bed. I panicked and thought that in time I would fall out of the bed. Unable to move, the thought of being thrown onto the floor well away from the safety of my bed was absolutely frightening. As I lay on my right side, the bed continued to rumble and gyrate beneath me. Paradoxically, I was sufficiently mentally aware to realise that my bed had never done this before. I recall asking myself if I was imagining it, but it all seemed so physically real with the massage functions switching between rippling waves, then circular movements and vibrations, all as if controlled by an electronic box of tricks. I decided I needed to really know if I was moving, so I fixed my eyesight on the edge of the bedside cabinet and lined it up with a spot on the wall. I reasoned that if I were moving down the bed, the two spots would no longer be in line. The bed continued to rumble and vibrate, but the spots remained in line. *I was not moving at all, there was no massage function!*

On a less sinister note, I would spend hours and hours lying in bed willing my legs and arms to move. I focused on my feet, because the nursing staff had warned me that I would get "drop foot syndrome", where through lack of movement, my ankle joints would cease to function, stiffen up and I would no longer be able to hold my feet at 90 degrees to my legs. Whilst immobile in my bed, drop foot was in itself not a problem, however when my leg muscles started to regain some strength and walking became a possibility, I would need to lift my feet up before planting them down. With "dropped feet", walking would be, at best, extremely difficult. In an attempt to prevent this, the nurses put my shoes on during my waking hours, wedging a pillow between them and the end of the bed. This meant I was lying on my back with my shoes on and my feet covered by a blanket. With very little to do, I would spend time concentrating hard in an attempt to exercise my feet. In my mind, I allowed my feet to drop down towards the end of the bed, so pushing against the pillow and then, with monumental effort, lift them back up at right angles to my legs. Each foot was very stiff at first but they loosened up after I'd performed the exercise several times. My left leg was far worse than my right and it was a real challenge to get it to move at all. My feet were in fact immobile. The mental effort to move them and the very real physical feelings were complete fabrications in my head.

I was very glad of the drugs for the pain relief and assistance they gave me in my recovery. However, the resulting hallucinations caused severe anxiety at a time when it was least needed. The moving bed, the problems associated with my feeding tube and phantom limb movements were made altogether more sinister simply because I was conscious. It was my first insight into the dangerous power of my brain to make imaginary situations feel, quite literally, extraordinarily real. Put bluntly, I could not control my body or my brain, and it was frightening.

Chapter 6 — Paralysis and Inspiration

Paralysis means the total and complete removal of choice. It means dependence, dependence on others and on drugs and on equipment. When lying or sitting, it stops you from shifting your weight and searching for a more comfortable position. It means enduring pain until the nursing staff decides to move you to prevent the onset of bedsores or administer a further shot of medication. It prevents you from walking, reading, eating, or talking to relieve boredom. I could see and hear, but had no taste or smell. The GBS had attacked my throat and lungs, meaning I was not able to breathe alone or swallow. Life-giving air was forced into my lungs by a ventilator that hissed, clicked, and buzzed away for more than seven helpless weeks. I was unable to eat or drink so I was kept alive by a nasal feeding tube.

The muscles controlling my eyes had also succumbed to GBS, leaving me with severe double vision. Reading was impossible. When sleep came, the muscles in my eyelids could not close them properly. My eyes were in danger of drying up, so eye cream was regularly applied, which stung and caused even more double vision. Communication with visitors was only possible by closing my eyes or moving my head from side to side. Every single muscle in my face except my jaw muscles was also paralysed. I could open and close my mouth, but all facial movement: eyebrows, mouth, nose, and cheeks were frozen into useless inactivity. Not only was I motionless, I was also expressionless. Two drips delivered a constant concoction of drugs and, just as a tube was used to feed me, a catheter was used to remove fluids from my body. The ultimate indignity was the adult-sized Pampers I had to wear. It was a cruel blow, but there was nothing I could do about it.

In the first waking hours after the coma my first mental struggle started. I fought hard as my drug-induced haze wore off. I tried to close the new situation I was in out of my mind. I tried to go back to sleep. I tried to get away. But whatever I did, I could not get away. I was a prisoner and this was torture. This went on for a couple of days and eventually I decided I'd had enough. I was ready to give up. I wanted to throw in the towel. The pain was horrible. I was hot, uncomfortable, and not sure if I was going to die. I told myself, "Martin, you are forty-seven now. You've had good innings. It's time to go." I wanted to die. I wanted to escape. I discussed it in my head twice and who knows — if a switch had been there I just might have turned off the ventilator.

Fortunately, I recognised this mental turmoil very quickly and set about severely chastising myself for thinking such negative claptrap. I took stock of my situation and tried to think of examples of how others had fought on and not given up. I immediately arrived at the name of the first Superman actor Christopher Reeve. I recalled details and pictures I had seen of him on a television programme and in various articles. I thought about how he required constant twenty-four hour attention, how he had learned to speak whilst on a ventilator, and how he lived his life in a wheelchair, with only limited movement of his head. I admired his will to live — in fact, I thought to myself when I'd seen him on

TV; *What is there to live for? He needs constant attention, cannot move, can only speak with difficulty, cannot eat and is a prisoner in his own body.* It seemed to be the worst possible nightmare. Well here I was, in exactly the same situation. I was at life's T-junction. Turning left I could have succumbed to my negative thoughts and given up. Right was life, in its most basic form. Faced with a decision, I asked myself, "You are a quadriplegic now — do you really want to live like this, totally paralysed?" I thought for a very short time and wanted to shout a resounding YES! Inspiration coursed through me as I thought of Fiona and the kids, not myself. I thought, *I am in a crappy situation, but I can't leave the family. I want to live for them.* And in that moment I shut out all negative thoughts and built an impenetrable wall of optimism and will to live that not even the most deadly of thoughts could penetrate — although as you will see later, the Pope and Terri Schiavo came very close.

I drew further inspiration from a second person — that of Markus Babbel, a German international footballer who starred at Liverpool and was then at Blackburn Rovers. He contracted GBS in 2002. Fiona told me his name after talking to Professor Drews in the ICU. Coincidentally, I'd read a long article in the Sunday Times about him in 2002. I could recall seeing pictures of him in a wheelchair in a German hospital and some details of his paralysis. He was out for ten months, during which time Liverpool and their manager Gerard Houllier had stuck by him. He recovered sufficiently well enough to play again for Liverpool, Blackburn, Stuttgart, and even got as far as the national team squad once again, in 2004.

Remembering all this about Babbel gave me tremendous motivation. Here I was, a leisure sportsman, fit and healthy, yet nevertheless struck down by this horrible illness, and the same thing had happened to him. GBS had taken a professional footballer, an international, playing for one of the top clubs in Europe! He had made it back; he was playing again and not just playing, playing at the very highest level. I could do it. I would do it! I will always be thankful to Markus Babbel for the inspiration he gave me at that time. Most probably unbeknown to him, he is a shining example to many GBS sufferers. Later on when I had time to analyse my predicament and study the illness, I realised that the majority of people with GBS (seventy percent), have some mild to severe form in their extremities and in their skeletal muscles. In the most extreme cases (up to thirty percent), facial muscles, throat and lungs are also affected, requiring a tracheotomy and a ventilator. In around five percent of all cases, the patients die. My case was one of those extreme ones and I was saved only from death by quick reactions in the intensive care unit. Fortunately for Babbel, his was less severe. His face and throat muscles were not affected and his physical skills returned after his period of rehabilitation.

So now I had two people to inspire me: Christopher Reeve and Markus Babbel. I kicked out the negative thoughts and started to think that I had been given an opportunity. I was alive, not dead. I never looked back, because I knew I was going to do it for the family. I am not a religious person and am unable to understand the true meaning of religious faith and belief. When I was at my lowest point, thoughts of dying or giving up were occupying my mind and threatening to hijack it. My weapon against it was family. I believed in them, I had faith in them, and I wanted to live for them. They were my focus. I can imagine that a religious person could similarly use his or her faith to set a focus and move away from negative thoughts. But if neither of these is available, recovery must be truly monumentally difficult.

The dark thoughts threatening to empower the negative side of my brain only really visited me during the first two weeks in Düsseldorf. It was at this time that the frustration with my situation was at its greatest and the discomfort was at its worst. Once I was moved away from Düsseldorf, I was able to focus on recovery and rehabilitation. The struggle to survive was replaced by a struggle to get better. It was not without equal amounts of pain, discomfort and frustration, but I was surrounded by positivity in Bonn that undoubtedly contributed to my recovery.

Chapter 7 —Transfer to Bonn

I was prepared for my move from Düsseldorf and was very glad to be transferred. I knew something was happening; I was told I was going to a very good place and that I now needed rehabilitation. Frankly, I was not able to understand what rehabilitation was, but I knew it was the next stage in my journey and I was happy to get away from the nurses that had, at least in my mind, abused me verbally (this was real) and physically.

It was Friday 25th of February. I'd spent thirteen days in the clinic ICU. I have no recollection of any departure committee, but Fiona was there and a doctor asked me if I would like to be sedated for the journey. I nodded and the next memory I have is of being wheeled into a much brighter and friendlier ward in my new home in a clinic in Bonn. The journey was critical — I was transferred to a portable ventilator and hooked up to further life support systems. Fiona followed in the car, desperately hoping that the systems employed to keep me alive in the ambulance were doing their job.

In contrast to Düsseldorf, there was a major reception committee when I arrived — in fact in every aspect, from the staff to the rooms to the whole atmosphere, the Bonn clinic was so much warmer, friendlier, and all together a much nicer place to be. The nursing staff and doctors greeted me, all wearing full surgical masks and gowns! It was a shock, leaving me unsure if I had suddenly become contagious! I subsequently learned it was normal procedure for staff to take precautions for all new admissions and after four days they approached me in their normal clothing.

One of those to receive me was Thomas, an extremely special and dedicated nurse who I came to trust with my life. True to form, he immediately tried to engage in communication with me. He introduced himself, explained where I was, and told me this would be my new home from now on. I tried to talk and for the first time, at least to my memory, I suddenly realised I was not able to speak. I moved my lips and was aware I was not making any sound, but was sure my exaggerated lip movements would make what I wanted to say obvious. Thomas, to my dismay, dismissed me by saying, "I am sorry, but I cannot lip read." At the time it was a real put down and another challenge I would have to overcome.

My bed was wheeled into a room with one other patient. I was on an intensive care ward and on the third floor, where they could treat a maximum of ten patients. At all times there were three nurses between the ten patients and at least one, sometimes two doctors on duty. The senior doctor in charge, Dr. Mertz, approached me to say, "You are in good hands, but if you want to walk out of here, you have to do what we tell you to do. It will not be easy and you'll need to be patient." He repeated, "You just need to be patient." I was unhappy about his comment. *How could he tell me to be patient? Did he know what it was like to be immobile and a quadriplegic?* I had been patient for the last two weeks and I was in need of some TLC. However, his words forced me say to myself that I was going to walk out of that hospital and I was going to do it unaided and as quickly as possible. He did not know it, but he had given me the target — much like the magical four-hour time goal in the Hamburg marathon —and I used it throughout my struggles with the pain and the negative side in my head.

My only sense that was not affected by GBS was my hearing. My sight is not too good without glasses so everything is normally blurred and with the lack of muscle control in my eyes I had double vision. When I was turned onto my side every four hours, I only had limited movement in my head, so my field of vision was very narrow. Consequently, I had very little sensory input and my head and thoughts became my life, my communication, my amusement and my salvation. Up until arriving in Bonn, I had lived my life almost exclusively in my head. I craved contact both verbal and physical, but because the emphasis in Düsseldorf was on stabilising my condition only essential (and cold) nursing prevailed; rehabilitation was definitely not on the agenda. I was now in an altogether more welcoming place. The staff communicated with me, a nurse would spend up to an hour with me each day cleaning me and straightening my bed. Even the cleaner was cheery and always said good morning and passed the time of day with me. The change of surroundings also helped my visitors, who felt less intimidated and I could enjoy my time with them without thinking that we were a nuisance to the nursing staff.

I was now receiving more attention on a day to day basis. It had started with the nursing, then rehabilitation in the form of daily physiotherapy and speech therapy but also more visits from family and friends. Alexander and Francesca had not been allowed into the ICU in

Düsseldorf. I hadn't seen them since 12th February, the day I stopped breathing. It was great when they visited and Fiona did a remarkable job in preparing them for the horror of seeing their dad on life support. They must have been shocked and sick with worry to see me in such a bad way. To their amazing credit, they never showed it. I was also able now to see so many dear friends who made the almost 200 km round trip journey. Not one single day passed in seven weeks without a visitor coming to see me. It was their attention that dragged me away from the world in my head. I solemnly maintain that physical and verbal contact is equally as important as medical care.

After a visitor or nurse left my bedside, I drifted back into my own world. I had conversations with myself, I played some games, and I thought a lot. At the beginning of my time in hospital my thoughts were mostly negative, based around frustrations, boredom and anger. These drove me to the struggles in my head centring on the positive and negative. However, as time progressed, the level of negativity subsided, possibly due to the extra stimulation that I was getting, but more likely because I was getting used to my situation and predicament. The further I progressed in my rehabilitation, the more relaxed I became with my lot in life. One day in about my sixth week in Bonn, I had finished my physiotherapy session at around 3:00 p.m. The physio had left the room and I knew there would be no more visitors that day, no more exercises to do, no more stimulations until 11:00 p.m. when I would get my next dose of medication to send me to sleep. The radio was on and I looked at the clock on the wall. Unable to move, I just lay there and watched the clock for the next eight hours. I watched the second hand and counted it as it stepped through its sixty clicks per minute. There was always a slight pause at fifty-seven, the next move delayed and then a quick rush to sixty to complete the minute on time. Normally, clock watching would have driven me mad, but I was immobile and very content.

Basically, my brain had slowed as my body had dramatically stopped functioning. During recovery I was not able, nor did I need, to make any decisions at all. Everything was decided for me. I was fed, washed, and turned. I was woken up and sent to sleep. I was physically useless without the need for any brain gymnastics, so my brain slowed down. In short, I was getting used to my situation and becoming content. One afternoon as I lay in my bed and I thought about how I did not have to plan or decide anything, I realised I did not need to get up to go to the toilet in the middle of the night because of my catheter, which I knew would really please Fiona. And when I realised I could pooh in my Pampers and somebody would come and clean me up, I could not help but smile (only inside, because my face was paralysed) and feel happy. I realise this is bizarre, these thoughts were all played out in my head, but it was a dramatic change compared to a few weeks previously. The change may have occurred because I was confident I was now getting better and that it was only a matter of time before discernable improvements in my condition would materialise. But, it was more likely to have been because of my institutionalisation.

The contentment became a further worrying development and threatened to derail my determination to reach my target of walking out of that hospital. In my seventh week, Thomas came to my bed with a huge smile on his face. "I have something for you," he told me as he hid something behind his back. He produced a urine bottle and told me, "I'm going to take your catheter out — you will be really pleased about that." *Hell no,* I was upset! I was no longer incapable. I would have to start making decisions and this caused me a great deal of consternation. For weeks I had been unable to make any decision. Now, I would have to take responsibility and call for a nurse when I needed to relieve myself. It was a very strange feeling and one that again caused me to search for further depths of motivation. I needn't have worried though because I was snapped out of the contentment by the excellent cajolement of the staff pushing me further with my recovery.

Chapter 8 — My Daily Routine with GBS in Bonn

Around the fifth week of my recovery I was coming off the drugs and had more of a clear head. It was a relief to feel that I was getting back to rational thoughts. Yet, it was also a problem, as I had to face up to the daily challenges of getting my body and life back with a mind that was now exposed to the rawness of my limited capabilities. For five of the seven weeks in Bonn, I was in a single room. The door was always closed and it only opened when either my nurse came to see me for my regular four-hour visit, the liquid food and drips ran out, which set off an ear-piercing alarm, the delightfully cheerful cleaner came in, I was having my physio, speech therapy or medical visit, or lastly, a visitor came to see me. I was bored and devoid of contact most of the time.

My twenty-four hour day began when I was woken up around 3:00 a.m. by the night staff bursting into the room, switching lights on, and talking to me as though I'd been awake for hours. Fuzzy with sleep in my useless body, I was turned onto my opposite side as they tidied up and straightened my bed. Despite the rude awakening, it was always a relief, as the muscles on the current side had seized up after the immobility of the previous four hours. My Pampers were removed and changed. If necessary, I was also cleaned up (delightful). Then, the part I hated, a thermometer was stuck up my bum and my temperature recorded. It was bad enough being woken up, but the thought of a cold blunt instrument thrust into my backside dominated my thoughts constantly as I was prepared for the next four hours of sleep. My tubes to the food and drips were checked, and if necessary, the food was refilled. The pillows and blankets were rearranged behind my back, between my legs, and under my arms to prevent me from rolling onto my back. Some staff members were extremely skilled at this making it a treat to have nicely fluffed up pillows. Others were definitely not so adept and I was left feeling uncomfortable. The next action was dedicated to my throat and life support machine.

To the left of my head was a suction pump attached to a long hose with a removable flexible tube on the end. When a patient is on life support, air is forced into the lungs under higher pressure. This is different from natural breathing where we create a lower pressure in our lungs, allowing air to flow in. When using positive pressure, one of the side effects is a build-up of fluid that cannot be expelled by the patient. If this is left, infection can easily develop, which rapidly leads to pneumonia; a very common cause of death in ICU patients. After an hour on the ventilator, it was possible to hear the fluid rattling around in my lungs like an eighty-cigarette-a-day man. I could cough, but could not clear it, so it had to be removed, especially after a few hours of sleep. To do this, a new semi-flexible tube was removed from its packaging and attached to the suction pump. When switched on, it hissed as it sucked air. The nurse then fed it into an opening in the J shaped cannula in my neck. With skilled movement it was pushed down into my throat, immediately inducing pain and violent coughing. When it was pushed further down, it suddenly cut off all the air into my lungs. It was instant strangulation that caused me to convulse as I tried to cough out the liquid and expel the tube. The fluid rattled away as it was sucked up, but the discomfort and near panic were both quite terrifying. As soon as the tube was removed, my air supply would resume and I was able to start breathing again. I suffered this eight to ten times a day!

The life support machine was about the size of a portable twelve-inch tube TV. Two 30 mm diameter tubes, supported on spidery metal arms, came out of the front and joined to become one via a valve close to my neck. A single thinner tube then connected to the cannula in my neck. The air was forced out of the machine and it wooshed and bellowed as my lungs inflated. Whilst flexible, the tubes had some inertia that prevented complete freedom of movement, so when they were aligned to my new position in the bed, there was an inevitable force tugging painfully on the cannula. I also had a bandage, rather like a dog collar around my neck to keep the cannula in place that was very often adjusted to be just too tight, leaving me one again with a feeling of mild strangulation.

The whole visit and clean up lasted around twenty minutes. The final action was a shot of medication into my feeding tube and I drifted off to sleep. I cannot recall having any problems getting back to sleep, even with a bum that was still smarting after its nightly violation.

I would wake up naturally around 6:30 or 7:00 in the morning. In the beginning I assumed I would sleep at various times during the day, as I had done on previous stays in hospital. Unfortunately, either GBS or my medication robbed me of this relief and I only slept again late in the evening when I was given my drugs. Once awake in the morning, I would long for somebody to come into my room just to say hello. It was the worst time as I waited for the nurse of the day to come in to see me. There were ten patients on the ward and usually three nurses. This gave them enough time to get round to each of the patients they were assigned to in order to administer attention and the care needed. All too often, one of the nurses was ill or there was an emergency and the staff numbers were reduced, leaving very little time for each patient. Depending where I was on the rota, the first visit from the nurse may have been at 6:30–7:00, or it could have been three hours later. I found these hours the most taxing, as I was always desperately waiting to have contact with somebody.

I would always try to shift my position from lying on my side to lying on my back. I would try to move muscles in my neck, back, and pelvic area, and in doing so move the pillow or rolled up duvet from behind me. I would work on this for hours before the nurse came in. Occasionally I was successful and would enjoy the relief of being flat on my back. Whilst I was doing this, an ear-piercing alarm signalling that I no longer had any food or medication might go off. Strangely the boredom and the alarms never really angered me. Yes, both were incredibly frustrating and annoying, but in fact having GBS was a zillion times worse.

One major improvement in Bonn was the availability of an alarm button. It was the size of a jam jar lid with a large button in the middle, and was placed beside my head on my pillow. I was able to lift or turn my head onto the button and set off an alarm to attract the nursing staff.

Great — I had my first form of communication. Actually, there was very little that I needed the staff for, except the dreaded tube down my throat to extract the rattling fluid. I have to admit though, I sometimes pushed the button in the mornings just to attract attention and have some actual human contact. A nurse would eventually come in and ask me what was wrong. I usually coughed, rattling the fluid around in my lungs indicating it had to be removed. When that was completed I clicked my tongue and moved my head, nodding towards the radio. These were my first really successful attempts at communication and filled me with a lot of hope. I also got what I wanted when the radio was switched on. Always on SWR3, it became my escape from the monotony of the day. The nurse would then tell me he or she would be back in half an hour or so. It was inevitably longer, sometimes three hours later, before they returned to prepare me for the day ahead.

If it was a weekday, I would receive treatment from a physiotherapist and a speech therapist. An occupational therapist would also visit twice a week. This broke up the day, with each session lasting thirty minutes. If it was a weekend, there were no such visits and the days were inevitably longer and broken only by the visits of friends and family. As the early shift prepared to hand over around 1:30 p.m., my nurse for the day might pop in and say goodbye. The next shift would then be in sometime in the afternoon to turn me and then again around 7:00 p.m. ready for my evening of either listening to the radio or trying to concentrate on the television news.

The night shift started their rounds at 10:00 p.m. and I always willed them to come to me first because I knew they would pump me full of drugs and I would be off and away to sleep for the next few hours. Sometimes, I was lucky and they did come to me first, but other times it was midnight, which made it a long day doing nothing. When the night shift came to my room, I was moved, cleaned, and turned quickly. The crud in my lungs was extracted to the sound of strangulation and my life support tubes were arranged for the night's sleep. The absolute best part though was the final act when the nurses took a massive syringe and squeezed its contents into my feeding tube. The syringe contained my medication, which had been mixed with a milky liquid that must have been in the fridge because I immediately felt a cold sensation as it entered my stomach. Only a short time later I was off and I had some blessed relief for the next few hours. My day then started again early in the morning.

Chapter 9 — Realisation of My Predicament

It was the week before the Easter holiday period. I was still not able to move, but had the luxury of a single room, courtesy of the fact that my roommate had developed some contagious infection. The room was big enough for two beds and had light-coloured walls. I had a large picture window to my left and a door to a balcony. My bed was in the middle and I had a table, decorated with cards and a religious cross. I was surrounded by medical equipment and although on an intensive care ward, it was reasonably pleasant and not the sterile, bright, high tech of the Düsseldorf clinic. There was the usual ever-present clock on the wall and a toilet and shower in a separate room. Outside, I could see trees and over to the next building, which was an old folks' home. I had cards, get well messages, and photos on the wall. I had a collage of photographs from Christian, my next-door neighbour, which had a photograph of me in Carnival fancy dress the week before I entered hospital. I was smiling profusely and it was an ever constant reminder of how paralysed my face had become since the onset of GBS. I also had another photograph of Fiona and me in Sienna in 2003. These two images were a constant source of interest for my various visitors. To my frustration, most of them assumed I was a huge Carnival fan (I am not). On the other hand, so many people recognised the main square in Sienna that their conversation transported me back there to the warmth of the sun and the joy of physical movement.

The Carnival photograph was taken one week before I entered hospital and the night before I started with the flu. I have not been able to smile like this since.

Spring was well on the way and as the sun was getting higher, it streamed in through the balcony door; practically blinding me if I was turned onto my side late in the afternoon. Alexander taped a temporary sun block made of card to the upper half of the window. My initial days in the Düsseldorf clinic had coincided with a snowy and cold snap, but I was so ill that I was not aware of the winter outside. Now, several weeks later in the comfort of my single room, spring had arrived. I could see the sun and the new season gave me renewed energy. There was talk of pushing my bed onto the balcony and getting me a sun umbrella, all nice words and whilst I wanted this, it was a frightening prospect because outside had become the unknown. It was a world that I had inhabited before, a world made up of movement, eating, smiling, and independence. It was a foreign world to me now and although I wanted to re-enter it, I was safe and secure in my bed, attached to my noisy ventilator and looked after by the nursing staff. I had lost confidence, was becoming institutionalised, and I was still not fully aware of how seriously ill I was. I know this sounds unbelievable, but I can only assume nature gives us inherent optimism or our minds balk at processing information to conclude how bad things really are.

Mentally, I was able to process information, albeit not always true reality, and I was able to think. Unfortunately, I had hours and hours of time doing absolutely nothing because I only had a very limited ability to concentrate on anything. For example, I was able to read, but could not concentrate long enough to read. I had a radio, but it melted into background noise as I retreated into the world in my head. Much to the great credit of Fiona, my family and all our friends, I had at least one visitor every day on that ward, which was indeed my only stimulus. During one visit, our friends Stefan and Andrea brought a television for me to watch. The get well cards on the table to my left were moved and it was turned towards me. I could receive up to fifteen channels via the hospital cable network. To watch it though, I had to be positioned on my left side; this was usually the last of the turns I had late in the day and well before the night shift arrived. My afternoon shift nurse would finish sorting me out, make my bed and then ask if I wanted to watch the TV. There were fourteen German channels and BBC World in English. My German is pretty good, some would say fluent, but I was simply unable to watch anything in German — it was impossible for me to concentrate on it. Therefore, by default I became an avid evening watcher of BBC World. The nurses would put my glasses on my face and always very thoughtfully place the remote control on my bed close to my useless hands. I was then left in peace to watch and also wonder how on earth I could use the bloody remote control to either turn up the volume or switch the TV off. Neither was possible, but as I now had limited but uncontrolled movement in my right arm, I spent a lot of time willing my arm to move towards the remote and with an outstretched finger try to target the correct button. It was a pathetic attempt every time and not only did I fail to hit the right buttons, which incidentally were small and would normally require a significant amount of dexterity, I missed the remote completely, my finger stabbing the bed instead. I persisted with my attempts, but would end up laughing to myself as I missed the damn thing time and time again. In those early weeks, simple controlled movement was impossible.

The week before Easter 2005, two very tragic stories, the failing health and death of Pope John Paul and the slow starvation and death of Terri Schiavo, dominated the news on BBC World. Pope John Paul was at the end of a very complete and full life. Terri Schiavo was once a vibrant young woman, but was now a rather pathetic figure that had been in a coma since 1990. She was confirmed to be brain dead and her husband had campaigned for seven years to allow her to die with dignity. Her parents were against the decision, so tragically a court case was conducted that had to rule between the two sides. The court sided with her husband and the feeding tube, the life source through which she received food and liquid, was removed, resulting in a slow, probably excruciatingly painful death by starvation and dehydration.

Each bulletin on the news showed a picture of Terri Schiavo in her wheelchair. The chair was very heavy with neck and head supports. Her head drooped to the side and was supported only by the chair. Her mouth was open and her face was gaunt and expressionless. She looked extremely ill and obviously very disabled. I watched bulletin after bulletin and tried but failed to understand the anguish that her family must have been going through and every time they showed the same picture of this poor woman who was dying a horrible death. I don't know why, but her predicament and tragic image remained with me even after the television was switched off.

It was during this time that Peter, one of my favourite nurses, was looking after me in the afternoon. He was very competent, in his late twenties and admirably working as a nurse to fund his way through medical school, which he completed the following year. Peter asked how I was feeling and I proudly showed him that I was able to move both arms, albeit with very limited control. As he was due to give me a bed wash, as well as a shave and clean my teeth, he asked if I would like to clean my own teeth. I knew this would be a challenge, but I was up for it. Unfortunately, it wasn't quite as simple as giving me the electric toothbrush, it necessitated a move for me from the bed into my wheelchair and then into the bathroom, so that

I could clean my teeth in front of the sink and begin the first step towards social integration and independence.

He placed the wheelchair by the end of my bed, on the right hand side. It was a huge contraption; nothing like the chairs that you see people use to propel themselves along in, this one was far too heavy. It had leg, arm, back, side, and head supports. I was readied for the transfer into the chair and moved from a prone to a sitting position — always an excruciating and horrific exercise — the various pipes and tubes were disconnected and a portable oxygen bottle attached to provide me with supplementary breathing support. Peter lifted me into the chair. I was wheeled into the bathroom and placed in front of a mirror for the first time since 11th of February. It was now 23rd of March. It was a devastating moment for me. My newfound motivation was crushed as I took the first look at myself in the mirror. I looked dreadful. I was thin, gaunt, with a drooping mouth and dark, deep-set eyes. I saw the feeding tube in my nose and the ventilator tube in my neck and was shocked rigid by the sight. My eyes moved to the chair and I saw the neck support for my head. I was crushed. I immediately saw Terri Schiavo — the same expression, the same position of the head tilted to the side and the same disabled pathetic look. *Boy, you look ill and so disabled,* I said to myself. My brain had actually shielded me from the worst of this horrible debilitating illness by refusing to contemplate how bad things were. But now, reflected by the mirror I could finally see how bad I was. The world in my head, to which I so often retreated, had not prepared me for this. In that world, my face was unchanged; I was able to smile and communicate and the life-giving tubes were nowhere to be seen. I stared and stared at the reflection and knew the pathetic person in the mirror was me, but it was a stranger, who was seriously ill and drastically disabled.

My gaze never moved from the mirror as Peter placed the electric toothbrush, with the appropriately chunky handle in my right hand and bent my fingers around it. He then brought my left hand on top of it. He applied the toothpaste and I tried to move my arms towards my face and open mouth. It felt as though I was trying to move my arms through porridge and everything seemed to happen in slow motion. I opened my mouth and Peter switched the brush on. My pathetic features did not register the sense of achievement I had at this simple act and although my lack of dexterity prevented me from actually touching too many teeth, it was one of the first major steps in my recovery. Satisfied, I was happy to leave that mirror and retreat back into my world where I looked fine and well. If I couldn't see it, it wasn't there.

After my visual shock, Terri Schiavo and her dreadful suffering dominated even more of my thoughts. With each television bulletin I longed to hear the news that her ordeal was finally over as her body was now starved of food and water. Naturally, as hers had been removed, I found myself focusing on my feeding tube, dripping liquid food and then tea into my stomach. I was on four bottles of what my nurses called astronaut food every day, each containing five hundred calories. The liquid food was a disgusting brown colour and when it finished the same bottle was filled with cold tea. I was not aware of the liquid entering my stomach and could not taste it. I was never hungry and only occasionally thirsty.

I experienced at first hand the horrible effects that the lack of both food and liquid has on your body. My weight dropped by over 16 kg in the first seven weeks and I often looked down at my ever-thinning legs and arms wondering whether I was going to fade away. Worse than the weight loss was the pain in my hands and feet resulting from the lack of fluid and nutrients in my body. The skin on my hands and feet started to crack, leading to open sores that had to be treated regularly with cream. My lips cracked and bled. The skin around my toes receded, pulling strongly against the nail on each digit and resulting in horrible pain. Relief was only temporary with the use of cream. These were the problems that I was having whilst getting two thousand calories of food. Terri Schiavo's body was not receiving anything and it was almost impossible to imagine a worse lingering death. I felt so connected to this poor woman and she made me realise for the first time how precarious my situation with my feeding tube was.

I also followed the ever-worsening condition of Pope John Paul on the news. As he became weaker, a report from the Vatican updated the waiting world that the Pope had been "intubated and placed on a ventilator to aid breathing. A feeding tube was also placed into his stomach." Then the hammer blow that I was not expecting. "The Pope is now being kept alive artificially." These words slammed into me and shook me to the core. I repeated them — ventilator to aid breathing, feeding tube in his stomach, being kept alive artificially. I looked at my ventilator and my feeding tube; *I was being kept alive artificially! Take away the feeding tube like Terri Schiavo and it would be a slow, dreadfully painful death. Take away the ventilator and it would be curtains in no time at all.* I was once again devastated and started to assess my own mortality through the real life drama of these two suffering people. During my first few days in the ICU I was in fear of my life and did not know if I would survive. Now, I was able to process information and could see an improvement in my condition but the realisation of the seriousness of my situation caused me enormous amounts of anxiety and a different type of fear.

On the Thursday before Good Friday, Thomas was on the early shift, starting at 6:00 a.m. He told me that he would finish his shift and then have five days off, returning on Wednesday afternoon the following week. I will dedicate a lot more words in a later chapter to Thomas' skill, but at this time of mental torture where the onset of my recovery was matched against the realisation of my condition, he was the one medical person that I needed the most. I was not going to see him for nearly six days. I also knew that over the Easter weekend there would be no physio or speech therapy sessions during the day to break up the boredom and the TV bulletins would continue to deliver bad news. It was a very dark period and I really struggled as I explored the deepest recesses of my mind. I had an enormous amount of time to think, worry and question why this had happened and why to me. I turned on my fitness and became angry about my sport and its lack of protection. Fortunately, I never let my anger or anguish really get me down, but I wanted to talk or share my plight with somebody. I felt alone. Relief did come when I received visits from family and friends over the next few days. They never knew how I was feeling over Easter and I never showed it —well, who wants to visit a miserable bugger anyway?

Sometime over the next few days, both the Pope and Terri Schiavo passed away and the news bulletins returned to items that contained less personally emotional issues for me. It was naturally a huge relief that afforded me some peace of mind. Moving forward a week, our friends Fiona and Iwan Williams came to visit Fiona in Düsseldorf for the weekend. Our friend Fiona (referred to as Fiona W. to avoid confusion with my wife Fiona) stayed a week and helped enormously, driving Fiona the 200 kilometre round trip to see me on several occasions in the hospital, since my wife was unable to drive herself because of a debilitating back condition. The Saturday following Easter, all three of them came and it was brilliant to meet up. It was always a lot easier for my visitors when there were multiple people in my room, as I couldn't really participate in any communication. I was told about the recent rugby and football results and we caught up on other issues that had been happening in the outside world. I'd had my very first outing in my wheelchair the weekend before, so Fiona asked if I'd like to go to the hospital café in the other building. I readily agreed and she asked the duty nurse, Claudia, to ready me for a transfer into my wheelchair.

Claudia was young and I got the impression she was not the sharpest knife in the block. Her attitude toward patients was more that of work than a genuine interest in going the extra mile to help and really care. I'd had a run-in with her on a night shift when she was unhappy that I had spent the previous two hours minutely shifting my weight in an attempt to move myself from lying on my side to lying on my back. The pain when you lie on your side for prolonged periods of time becomes intolerable, but once on your back, it is very easy to develop a lung infection as the fluid caused by the air forced into your lungs is not removed. Hence the constant attention of the nurses in making sure those patients are on their side. When she saw that I had moved on to my back, she shouted at me and with her fellow nurse Toby, moved me onto my side and wedged the bedding further and harder into my back. If you are a good patient and not prone to infection, it was possible for the nursing staff to place you at an angle of sixty to eighty degrees on one side. If there was a higher risk, it was a ninety-degree angle, which was a lot more uncomfortable and painful. If you were a naughty boy, as I was, the nurse would put you at one hundred five degrees, meaning that my face was also turned in towards the bed, making looking around almost impossible. She shouted at me, put me in this position and told me that one hundred five degrees was necessary to prevent me getting a lung infection and I should not mess her about. I normally had a touch alarm that I could press with my head in case I needed something. Whether by accident or design, I later found out the alarm had been disconnected. I was totally helpless in this position and had to endure excruciating pain and discomfort before the drugs that were injected into my feeding tube worked their magic and I was released off into the land of nod. The problem with this type of abuse was that I was totally and utterly helpless to either say anything or to react in any way. But, it also ran counter to everything that I had come to expect from the excellent staff in Bonn, namely that they really looked after the patients and abuse was very far from their agenda. I was upset about this development and complained bitterly to Thomas the next day, via a pen and alphabet board setup I had started to use. He had words with Claudia and it didn't happen again.

For the trip to the cafe, Claudia came in and readied me for my transfer to the wheelchair. I was disconnected from the ventilator and she positioned me on the side of the bed. The next stage is extremely critical as the patient is moved from bed to chair. There are techniques and every nurse, whether large or small, had his or her own method. Claudia seemed to have learned her way in the farmyard tossing bags of potatoes. She moved into position to lift me and then proceeded to very nearly drop me on the floor. I could see Iwan moving towards her to help, but she managed to recover, tossed me upwards, realigned her grip and then rolled me into the chair. By far the worst transfer, but I was safely installed. My feet were put onto the footrests, the oxygen bottle was connected up to the tube in my neck, and I was prepared for a couple of hours in the chair.

I was wheeled to the café and the four of us sat in a corner. Several patients were sitting around and the atmosphere was more relaxed and less sterile than on the wards. Iwan brought coffee and some cakes. Fiona asked me if I minded them eating in front of me and I shook my head to say no. I was only being polite though, and would really have liked to try the cake. Alas, my tubes wouldn't allow this and I had to endure the others enjoying food that I'd not tasted for seven weeks. It was hard watching them.

I had a table on my wheelchair where I could rest my hands and place the alphabet sheet that I used to communicate. During the previous week I had recovered sufficient dexterity in my fingers, which allowed me to point to a letter and thus spell out a word and then a sentence. With the aid of the alphabet board I managed to ask some questions and just enjoyed the banter with old friends. Fiona asked me to pull the face I used to show displeasure. I opened my mouth and pushed my lower jaw forward — together with the lack of expression on my face it was classic gurning and caused us all to laugh. Oh it felt good to laugh — there had been precious little to laugh about over the previous weeks.

We started talking about my illness and how I was feeling. I typed out my answers by slowly moving my finger around the alphabet board. Sometimes my finger moved involuntarily to another letter or my finger was shaking so badly that I would seem to circle the target letter and then suddenly stab down and come to rest on the appropriate character. I decided to ask a question that had been bothering me since I had woken from the coma — I wanted to know what had happened to me in the ICU in Düsseldorf. I could remember everything up until the doctor had come to see me for the second time. I knew that I was really struggling with my breathing and that it was just before midnight, then my mind went blank. I typed out my message "What happened to me in Düsseldorf?" I was leaning forward, hunched over the table, fingers poised ready to respond and carry on the conversation. I looked at Fiona and showed her with my eyes that I was expecting an answer.

She enquired, "In the ICU?"

I nodded yes.

She looked at Fiona W. and Iwan and then replied, "Don't you know?"

I found this to be a strange answer because I wouldn't have needed to ask if I knew, so I tried to show her that I was still expecting an answer. She took a deep breath and said, "Well you stopped breathing. The surgeon intubated you and then called at 1:50 a.m. to tell me."

It was a catastrophic piece of news that hit me like a steam train. I threw myself backwards in my chair, rolling my eyes upwards, my mouth open wide in a silent scream. I was gutted and my shock was obvious for everyone to see. Iwan immediately jumped into the conversation and tried to reassure me by saying, "Hey, it is okay now. That was a long time ago. You are getting better now." Fiona grabbed hold of my hand and squeezed it hard. But I was really in shock.

This was the final piece of mental torture for me over the Easter break. I had never contemplated my own vulnerability. I suddenly realised that I'd been only seconds away from death. It was true what Iwan had said, I knew that I was now living and breathing, but I kept on staring at this black abyss that was my death, the end. I tried to shake myself away from this negativity and make my way back to Fiona and my friends, but it was very hard. They left me that evening and I was alone with my thoughts. I had thoughts of total paralysis, looking so disabled, of being on life support, to have stopped breathing and finally to have been only seconds away from leaving this world. They were real bombshells and I now had hard facts about how ill I'd really been. Terri Schiavo and the Pope were current affair issues that caused me real concern, but being close to death was a trauma that refused to leave me. It became a poison that infected my mind with a negativity that threatened to take over my life and drag me into a depressive state. In hospital I was okay because I was preoccupied with my physical rehabilitation, but later when I was back at work and attempting to function as a near normal person again, the poison seeped into my life, causing anger and resentment at home with my loved ones, only to be rescued by post-traumatic stress counselling. Meanwhile, I was thankful that I had got through the Easter week, and the next day's saw some remarkable improvements in my condition, not least because I was to attempt to start talking again, which changed all communication with visitors and staff alike.

Chapter 10 — Communication

Communication is a magical and truly wonderful gift that we possess and use in many forms. Our voices are used to promote contact and to ask for information. Hands are used to attract attention or to point. Nods, winks, eye movements, and facial expressions add subtlety or effect to verbal or non-verbal communication. Touch offers a greeting or intimacy. We write, draw and gesticulate with all available limbs when we want to understand or be understood in another language that we are not proficient in. Finally, our body language communicates, usually without us realising it. I took all these methods of communication for granted. GBS removed all of them and left me only with the ability to open and close (not completely) my eyelids, to move my head from side to side and to open and close my mouth. In those early weeks the only sound I could make was to click my tongue, which struck me as terribly rude, but it was sometimes the only way I could attract attention.

I was initially confronted with the need to communicate as I was slipping away in the ICU in Düsseldorf. It terrified me as I was struggling to breathe and I could not attract the doctor's attention. It continued as I came out of the coma and I was looking for answers, comfort, and relief from my condition. At first, I refused to understand or was not able to realise that people could not understand me. I craved attention and I wanted answers, so moved the only part of my body that I could, which was my head. I thrashed it from side to side in silent anger and with an almost epileptic type force whenever I could sense that somebody was in my room or simply walking past. Very rarely did it generate the contact that I was looking for, causing my frustration levels to rise even further, and prompting my nurses to threaten me with some horrible medication to quieten me down.

Despite my best efforts, all the exaggerated eye gymnastics and slow deliberate mouthing of words that I practised were spectacularly unsuccessful in producing any kind of response from the medical staff or visitors. I was therefore condemned to days and weeks of one-way communication. I could hear and see the people in my room, I was aware of them, but they had no idea if I was able to register them. One would assume that experienced medical staff would know this — I had a rare but well-documented condition. It was known that my hearing and brain functions would not be affected and similarly that a very real threat could be the onset of depression. This threat of depression is best countered by including the patient in their nursing, communicating, and explaining to him what was happening — in short treating him as a normal person. It was therefore always a shock when medical staff would shout at me because I did not respond to their words. I wanted to scream out that I was neither deaf nor stupid. One nurse complained to me with very genuine disgust that I always looked so miserable, never smiling, and never talking to her. She was right, I did look miserable, but I was simply unable to do anything about it because all the muscles in my face were paralysed. I was so upset about this form of abuse and I vowed to tell as many staff as I could when I was able to talk (I only got round to one of them about eight weeks later and she was really shocked when I told her).

The utter lack of communication got to me as I started to live within the confines of bodily imprisonment. Most of the staff in Bonn were superb at establishing and maintaining communication with patients, in total contrast to the ICU staff in Düsseldorf. I remember watching two of my favourite nursing staff, Rolf, an incredibly cheery twenty-eight year old (he later qualified as a doctor in 2007), and Nicole, a lovely warm young nurse, as they separately nursed an extremely poorly roommate of mine. His condition was very severe, the result of suspected brain damage after being knocked over as a pedestrian. He suffered terrible physical injuries, which required constant attention in the form of wounds being dressed, traction weights being adjusted, and plaster casts replaced. These two young nurses would always come into the room and address him by his name with a warm hello. They would then move round to the side of his bed, look him in the eyes, talk in a normal voice and ask him how he was today, usually with a comforting hand on his shoulder or arm. As far as I am aware, there was never any reaction from him, but they would continue to talk to him as they went about their job, nursing him. It was a great pleasure to watch dedicated professionals at work. But, it reminded me of how alone I'd been when I was not able to attract anybody's attention in the ICU in Düsseldorf.

During my daily routine, there were no highlights based around food, reading a book, taking a nap, or having a chat with my roommate. My highlight was seeing people. Even better was to try to engage these people, and the ultimate was to communicate with them with whatever means were at my disposal. At first it was clicking my tongue, shaking my head or bashing it on the pillow, in fact, I would have done anything to try and get my message across. I also saw the same desire to communicate from other patients later on in my treatment when I was transferred from the ICU to a normal ward. I'd become more mobile in my own wheelchair and was able to see and meet other patients. I frequently saw a young woman in her late twenties who was very severely disabled. I learned from the nurses that she'd had an accident and had been starved of oxygen, resulting in severe brain damage and great physical disability. She was married and her dedicated husband came to the hospital and read to her in the library every day. I often saw the two of them as I passed through in my wheelchair on my way to another treatment session. She was reclined in her wheelchair, her arms and legs locked by her disability in tortuous positions. He would always sit next to her, reading quietly from a book. Her open-eyed stare did not convey any indication that she was understanding or even aware of her husband, or so I thought. To be honest, I did not have the opportunity to try to establish any communication with her but I had learned from my own experience that when you are locked inside your own body you will use anything you can to try and get a message to the outside world. One day, I passed her in the corridor; she was in the same convulsed position in her chair. Her parents and husband were talking to the ward sister. Suddenly, she started to move her leg up and down, thumping it into the chair, lifting it up and sending it crashing down once again. Her parents seemed embarrassed and tried to stop her moving. They talked to her gently at first and then physically restrained her and held her leg down. I felt distressed for this young woman as her family carried on their conversation with the nurse. I am absolutely convinced that she was trying to communicate and tell her loved ones or the medical staff something. As with Terri Schiavo, I felt instantly connected to her and was able to feel her frustration and sense her will to communicate. I would have never reached this conclusion if I had not experienced being locked inside my own body. You have so much you want to bring out and life is so joyous when you can share it with others. When you are imprisoned in the deep chasm of a lifeless body, it is a long way to the outside and life is very lonely. This young woman had a profound effect on me, but I was lucky, I'd escaped from my prison and was moving every day closer back to a world of interaction.

The steps to verbal communication were a long way off and inextricably linked to the life support machine I was connected to. The tube in my throat prevented me from talking, so I explored other means. What I learned from the visit of the therapists, apart from the medical treatment, was that the sensation of touch was a brilliant and comforting way of communication. The treatment would start with a matey rub of my shoulder or a hand on my arm. They would always look me in the eye and ask how I was doing. Many of my visitors, especially men, found it difficult, even impossible, to touch me. I know this is a man thing, but experienced male visitors knew what to do.

Early on during my time in Bonn, the GBS Initiative sent along a fellow, but recovering, GBS sufferer to see me. Josef Berger was a lovely, calm and understanding man. He visited me on four occasions, always cheerful, bringing a thoughtful present and taking time to talk to me. He had contracted GBS fifteen months previously. At the age of fifty-nine he had decided to retrain as a doctor — a very admirable move. He had completed all his studies and his clinical year in the hospital and was four days away from his final aural examination at the age of 64 to become certified as a doctor when he contracted the flu, which subsequently developed into GBS. His condition deteriorated rapidly and he, too, was on life support for more than twelve weeks. He suffered terrible hallucinations and great hardship, but here he was standing in front of me walking, talking, and moving like any normal healthy person.

He was a superb inspiration to me and I was eager to ask him many questions, but I just couldn't do it. Yes, my condition was immensely frustrating, but he knew exactly what I was thinking and how I was feeling. He asked me if he could touch my hand. I nodded my head in agreement. He moved his finger in steps up my hand and into my arm, at each step asking if I could feel his finger. Just beyond my wrist and up into my arm all feeling had gone. He could have said, "Wow you are really in a bad way aren't you?" But instead, he turned it round and told me, "Well that is good that you have the feeling in your hands. You are in better shape than I was at this stage." He made me feel great and he kept hold of my hand. This would normally have been highly unusual to have a strange man holding my hand, but this was not a usual situation. He knew as a fellow sufferer how comforting it felt when people would touch or hold his hand. Consequently, I now know that I would always ask any immobile or severely disabled person if I could touch their hand, or stroke their arm. It is an intimate gesture; hence the reason I would ask for permission, but it is a very simple way of communicating that is infinitely more powerful than a thousand words. As a patient, it always left me feeling warm, content and a lot more in "contact" with my visitor. In short, I always thought they had some idea how I was feeling, as Josef had done, and it was truly delightful. Incidentally, Josef completed his final exam and qualified as a doctor.

My female visitors were much better with personal touch and I was nearly always greeted with a kiss, which was blissful and made me feel "normal". Of course Fiona would always hold my hand, but the first recollection I have of somebody holding my hand and then actually massaging it was Barbara, who visited me with her husband, Jochen, and son, Nick, on the Saturday before Easter weekend. I was not able to move at the time, but Barbara took my hand and as an experienced physiotherapist, she was able to gently massage it. My hands were paralysed and there was very little feeling in them, but I was able to sense the warmth and the movement of her hand on mine. It was sensational. I didn't want her to stop, but she was worried that I wouldn't like it, so she stopped. After that I tried to ask as many people as possible, that is when I could actually let them know what I wanted, to massage my hands or my feet, much to the amusement of the nursing staff!

A massive leap forward on my journey back to interactive dialogue came when Thomas presented me with my alphabet board. It was a plastic laminated A4 sheet of paper with all the letters of the alphabet printed on it. I cannot remember the actual day this was given to me and with hindsight, it must have been at the time when there was a visitor in the room, probably Fiona, and I guess Alexander and Francesca as well. Thomas put a pen in my mouth and told me that I could point to the letters on the sheet, so spelling out a word, and in effect talking to my visitor. It was a revolution! Here I was surrounded by enormously expensive pieces of medical equipment and living in a very sophisticated new digital age and the best way forward for me was to have a piece of paper held in front of me and a pen shoved in my mouth. Suddenly, I was able to see light coming into my prison and I was able to send information back to the outside world. It opened up an enormous amount of possibilities; Fiona could finally ask me questions. I could tell people what I wanted, that my feet were hurting, I wanted a massage, my pillow was too hard, or I was absolutely desperate to have a drink (which I couldn't have). I was on the way back!

There was always a routine for the use of the pen and paper. I would signal to my visitor, usually by clicking my tongue that I wanted to say something. They would pick up the paper and the pen, which by now had sticking plaster wrapped round the end to make it easier to grip between my teeth. I was usually lying down, with my head propped up on a pillow and the bed raised slightly upwards. With some contortions around the life support, feeding and medication tubes, a visitor would approach the head of the bed and place the sheet 20 cm in front of my face. They had to stand level with my head and place the pen gently in my mouth. This was always a tricky bit because a first-timer often put the pen in too far and I would gag. *If it wasn't the bloody vacuum tube strangling me, it was the flaming pen sending me into convulsions.* Once we established the right position for the pen, a conversation could start.

It was a laborious process. I first had to think what language I was going to answer in. If Fiona or other international visitors were there, I would answer in English. If I had German visitors, obviously I would answer in German. But when Pia, our German friend, brought Fiona to see me, it could be a dual language conversation. To inform my visitor, I would start by first tapping an E or a D. Once the language was established, I had to think what I was going to say or how I was going to answer. I would try to keep everything very short because it was very tiring on my neck. I had to move my head up, off the pillow, and forward. I then had to focus on the sheet, hitting the correct letter and then moving on to the next one. After a few days, my neck muscles were much stronger and I could really fly around that piece of paper tapping out my words at the rate of about one letter a second. The main problem for my visitors was that I would start with a question like "How are you?" and then stop. It is very easy to recognise the words when you see them written down, but I never thought about tapping a space between the words in my question, so it would come out as "howareyou". Again, when written down this is possible to decipher, but when the person behind me had to remember every letter and add it to the next one that I was merrily tapping out one a second they often encountered problems understanding what I was trying to say. Oblivious to any confusion and exhausted from my efforts, I would flop back down on to the pillow and wait for the answer to my elegantly tapped out question. More often than not, the answer came back "Er, sorry, I didn't get that. Can you please do it again?"

I wanted to type out, "Bollocks, do you know how hard this is?" But I resisted and went back to my original question by dragging myself off the pillow and starting again. I would tap slowly and when I got to the end of a word, try to turn my head to my visitor to register if it was understood. The method worked haphazardly, but it was generally hard work, especially with adults. With teenagers, it was absolutely no problem and I could tap away at top speed and they would call out the words even before I had finished them. I think it would be probably true to say this was because our kids have grown up with SMS and other types of shorthand that use predicted text — which I find baffling and unusable — so when I started with a word, they would immediately spring into this mode, guess the word, and our conversation would flow much faster. It is also true to say that if I had hit a space bar between words, my adult visitors would probably have got to my question a lot faster.

One amusing incident occurred when Bernie and Dennis visited me. It was March and I knew it was the climax of the 6 Nations rugby championship the weekend before. I wanted to ask who had won. I clicked my tongue, signalling to them that I wanted my alphabet board. Bernie positioned it in front of me and I tapped out " R U G B". Before, I could get to the Y, she launched off into a great long diatribe about her recent trip to England and what she had done there, who she had seen, and what she had brought back, on and on. I was thinking, *Bernie, this is very nice and I am interested in this, but why are you telling me? I only wanted to know who won the 6 Nations*. She had thought I wanted to say, "Are you going to Great Britain?, "r u gb", and was horrified when I eventually got the question out about the rugby (I think Wales won). We have laughed many times about this and it was one of the lighter moments that punctuated my recovery.

I used the board and pen for around four weeks. The major disadvantages of it were that I needed to have somebody prop it up in front of me and then place the pen in my mouth and it was quite tiring for me to be lifting my head off my pillow and bobbing around like a nodding dog in the back of a car. As I got stronger, the paralysis in my arms started to recede first and then I recovered limited movement in my hands. I had very little coordination, but could move my arm in a required direction and was just about able to control my index finger, so that I could point to something. This improvement lent itself to using the board when I was lifted for my daily two-hour torture into my wheelchair. Once safely in the chair, a tray was placed in front of me, rather like a baby's high chair, with the board on it. Mustering up all my concentration to direct a finger to the correct letter, I set off to spell out a word. Not very successfully in the beginning, because I was unable to control my movements with sufficient accuracy, so I often tapped on the wrong letter. The major advantage though, was that I was sitting up and could easily make eye contact with my visitor, to check if the words were understood. Consequently, conversations were much faster and less tiring for me. As I recovered more coordination in my hands, I was able to direct my finger to the correct letter without too much trouble and my board accompanied me wherever I went in my wheelchair. When I was pushed out into the corridor for some change of scenery, the nurses would stop by and ask me questions. I was able to tap out a reply and I could feel a much greater rapport building up with them.

The day after I discovered from Fiona that I had stopped breathing, Dennis visited me with Alexander and Francesca. It was a Sunday, a glorious day, so I was lifted into my wheelchair and we went outside into the sunshine. Dennis asked the kids to go and get some ice cream so that we could be alone together. He and Bernie had been a tremendous support for Fiona whilst I was in the hospital and they regularly came to see me. As we sat in the sun together he asked me, "How are you in your head?" It was the first and to the best of my knowledge the only time anybody asked me about the state of my mind. With a debilitating illness that renders you paralysed, it is all too easy to focus on the physical side of the problems. I suppose this is only natural and because we as humans are on the move all of the time, it is nothing short of a nightmare to be mobile one day and paralysed the next. In fact, the mental side of GBS is one of the most dangerous and taxing issues, and can directly lead to depression. The depression stems from the seemingly hopeless situation in which one finds oneself and can mean the patient has no desire to move on with their treatment or rehabilitation. In other words, they give up or perhaps worse, fail to come off the life support machine. Both can lead to complications that may result in death.

It was a good question from Dennis and one that I actually didn't need to think about too much before I tapped out my answer. I told him I was okay. I knew that I had not been and would never be depressed about my situation. I knew that I was in fact getting better, so life was looking up. I rapidly moved on to telling him that I had been counting the days and weeks to our planned family holiday together in Turkey in the summer. I wasn't at all worried about the state of my head, but really quite concerned about the fact I might still be in hospital at the end of July, which would mean missing my holiday. I am not sure if Dennis was surprised about my reaction and why he was the only person that asked me how my head was, but I was glad he asked it. Perhaps people avoided asking direct questions for fear of upsetting me, but actually the opposite was true. Maybe I was somehow able to show people that I was okay and not depressed — Fiona says she knew I was okay and doing well in my head. However, I was pleased to be able to answer Dennis's question and proud that I was on good form. If the question had upset me, I would not have answered, but the fact that it was posed made me feel more that Dennis was trying to understand, or maybe had understood, my predicament.

The alphabet board was really a godsend and I will always be eternally grateful to Thomas for suggesting it, as it opened up the world of interactive communication to me after four weeks of existing on a one-way street. In the end it was just a stepping-stone on the rehabilitation road to full verbal communication. I desperately wanted to talk, especially when Fiona called from home to check on me because she was unable to visit, or having a well-earned rest. I knew when she was on the phone because the duty nurse would come into my room, tell me she was calling and check for her that I was okay. I would execute a pathetic wave that was transmitted back to Fiona. I found that public expression of my love really emotional. Yet, it also highlighted the deficiencies of the board, because it was purely limited to one-on-one, face-to-face communication. So when Thomas told me on the Sunday evening after Dennis had left that I could try my second attempt at talking, I was bursting with excitement, albeit a little nervously since my first attempt, three weeks earlier with a speech therapist, had been quite traumatic.

But this brilliant spring evening with the dimming sunlight streaming in through the windows, I was ready to try again. Thomas placed a speech valve on my cannula. I was ready for yet another new challenge. He stood back from me, smiling, and said, "Well Martin I am really looking forward to hearing your voice."

The valve immediately stopped me expelling my breath and I took an exaggerated deep intake of air. I then summoned up the strength in my chest and pushed the air out, saying to Thomas, "Hi, how are you?" I gasped in another lungful of air and then expelled it, using the pressure to speak again. We talked for a few minutes more. It was truly magical, even though hearing my voice punctuated by deep intakes of breath reminded me of how Christopher Reeve spoke.

Thomas had the ward phone with him. He asked me if I wanted to call home. I readily agreed and immediately thought, *what a nice gesture and one that is not taught in any manual* — it was just a lovely thing to offer. He held the receiver to my ear. It rang and unfortunately Fiona was not at home, so I left a message on the answer machine. "Hi, it's me. I can talk again," sharp intake of breath. "Need to get off now," sharp intake of breath. "See you tomorrow. Love you." Thomas took the phone from my ear and he had a beaming smile on his face. I was exhausted but smiling inside. *Scat was on his way back.* Fiona told me she heard the message with her friend Fiona W. later that evening and they were so excited. She didn't delete it for weeks!

Thomas took the valve off and I was connected back to the life support machine. Talking for just a few minutes had really taken it out of me. The muscle effort to force the air out of my lungs was huge. The sound that came out was similar to my voice, but it sounded strange, as though I was talking through tissue paper. Several letters were really difficult to pronounce, such as P and B, and I had a strong lisp courtesy of the immobility of the muscles around my lips. Fiona and her friend Fiona W. came in to see me the next day and we had a wonderful time talking to each other. It was magic. Fiona W. left us alone and we had the first opportunity to chat to each other for eight weeks. We talked about talking and what the kids were doing. They were just mundane things, but it was a real joy to be back in two-way contact.

The next day, I was talking to my friend Jörg on one of his many visits, breathing in very deeply and then pushing the words out as I exhaled. After forty minutes, I was utterly exhausted. It was as if my battery was suddenly empty and to use a marathon analogy, I had hit the wall. I was dizzy, short of breath, and sweating profusely. A nurse was summoned and I was disconnected from my speech valve. A hasty transfer was executed back to my bed and the life support tube was docked into my neck. A huge feeling of relief came over me as I was back in the sanctuary of my bed and could rely on assisted breathing from the hissing machine by my right ear. Bathing in the joy of speech, I'd drifted into deeper waters and forgotten that I was not strong enough to handle this new world. My muscles had reached their absolute limit in a very short space of time, but my brain had ignored the warning signs because I was so happy!

I was now able to communicate regularly and it made life so much easier. It wasn't instant communication, because I was still on the life support, so when I wanted to talk, I had to signal to a nurse that I needed the speech valve. I was then disconnected from the machine and the valve was plopped into place. The change was enormous. One day a business colleague came to see me. We had spoken on the phone, but never met. He bravely came to the hospital and I was in the corridor in my wheelchair when he arrived. I had my alphabet board on my table and I tried very hard to have a conversation with him by tapping out the letters and looking at him to see if he had understood. Frankly, it was painfully embarrassing for both of us because he couldn't understand what I wanted to say. I then asked a nurse to wheel me back into my room and to put the speech valve in. Instantly, the conversation was a lot easier and a lot faster. We both relaxed and enjoyed a few laughs. Simply put, it was communication as he knew it and he was a lot more comfortable with it, so I was able to relax allowing the conversation to flow.

Being comfortable with verbal communication was a natural reaction, but it highlights how most of us, myself included, are uncomfortable when dealing with disabled people. I saw and experienced this time and time again with people shouting at me as though I were deaf, stupid, or both because I could not answer. Visitors were very reluctant to touch me, even to shake my lifeless hand, perhaps for fear of it being construed as too personal or possibly they were afraid of catching something. If there is one message I would like to try and convey here it is that a disabled person has the same emotions and desire to be in touch with other people as much as you and I. Treating them differently and avoiding contact or communication is extremely upsetting. Conversely, treating a disabled person with dignity and respect can bring untold amounts of joy and, as in my case, huge amounts of motivation, which I used to push myself even harder during my rehabilitation.

118

Chapter 11 — The Medical Staff

Thomas

Over a period of twenty-four weeks in medical care, I experienced a lot of different contact with doctors, nurses, therapists, and counsellors. For the most part, they are remarkable people who treat their job and the care of others with great professionalism. I am eternally grateful to the Registrar in the Düsseldorf who had seen GBS twice within twenty years of medical practice, acknowledged the inexperience within his own hospital, and therefore knew he had to send me to a neurological department for specialist treatment. In doing this he saved my life. I am thankful to the many other doctors who imparted instructions to nurses and therapists on the amount of medication and therapy that I needed. I had superb nursing care, especially on the intensive care ward in Bonn. It was there that I met the most professional, dedicated and my all round superb medical hero Thomas. He was head and shoulders above any of the other staff that I met throughout my treatment. The doctor in the Düsseldorf saved my life. Thomas brought me back to life.

He was two years younger than me at forty-five years old, of average height at around 1.75 m. He had a full head of hair, a slightly round face, and carried a kilo or two of extra weight. He had married the previous year and was a fan of fine food and wine, which we discussed endlessly when I was able to talk. He did his apprenticeship as a purchaser in a company, but decided to go into nursing, as he was bored in his job. His work took him into intensive care nursing, which is physically and mentally very demanding. I was fortunate to spend seven weeks of my life being nursed by him. My relationship developed from respect to trust and eventually to a deep platonic love. Each day in the hospital, I longed to see him at the start of his shift, I missed him terribly when he was on leave or vacation — the five-day break that he took over Easter was so lonely and dark for me. I trusted him so much that I did everything he asked of me, even when I knew it would hurt, be uncomfortable, or downright unpleasant. He rescued me from the clutches of eternal misery, cajoling, encouraging, and motivating me to push myself harder in my rehab, very often when I wanted to stop and do nothing. He was never gentle, sometimes even slightly rough and nowhere near as good as some of the female nurses in some areas of nursing. Despite this, he was always happy, with a huge smile on his face, treating me with dignity and respect. Thomas was one in a million and it was a privilege to observe a true master at work.

We first met on 23rd of February when I was delivered to Bonn from Düsseldorf. Fiona came into the room and Thomas, along with all the other staff, was clad in a gown and mask to protect him from any potential disease that I may have brought with me. After the complete medical team had departed, he handed Fiona an information folder that included details of the care I would receive and a questionnaire about me that she had to fill in. It asked for my name, those of my family and the usual details of whom to contact. It listed the names of any children and asked if I would like to be addressed by my first name and whether the staff could address me with "Sie" or "Du". I nodded to Fiona that I wanted to be called Martin and that using the familiar "Du" form was perfectly acceptable. Actually, I have no idea why they asked me this question as everybody addressed me as Herr Scattergood and used the "Sie" term until I was able to talk to them and I insisted on being called Martin. Finally, Fiona filled in my nationality as British or as the Germans insisted on saying, English. Later, when I was in a single room, Angelika, one of the nurses, put a sign on the door declaring that I was "The English Patient" after the popular film.

To my great fortune, Thomas was assigned as my nurse. This meant that except for a few occasions, he would look after me when he was on duty, either on the early or late shift — he had given up the night shift sometime earlier in his career. When he came into the room he religiously washed his hands with the disinfectant that was placed on the wall by my door. On the early shift, despite the ungodly hour, he was interminably cheery and asked me how I was as he put on up to six pairs of rubber gloves, one on top of the other. He was the only nurse to do this and it showed his level of experience and professionalism. Once he had completed one task on me, say removing the fluid rattling about in my lungs, the first pair of gloves would come off to be discarded in the bin, assuring that bacteria was not transmitted to others via inadvertent contact.

His absolute top speciality, apart from his mastery in intensive care nursing, was weaning patients off life support machines. This is not an easy task as the machine, by virtue of its function, is to keep you alive. Therefore, when you are told for the first time that it will be switched off, it quite literally scares patients to death. Some never make it and are discharged from the hospital still connected to their machine; a full recovery then becomes impossible. The very first time the machine was switched off next to me, it was Thomas who was in control. He reassured me that I could do it and that nothing could go wrong. He explained that he would disconnect the tubes and put another small connector on the end of the cannula in my neck. A small oxygen bottle was then placed close to this connector — it was not fed directly into my lungs, but was sufficiently close so that I could breathe in oxygen as well as air to keep my oxygen saturation levels up.

When we breathe we absorb oxygen into our blood stream. If there is not enough oxygen (i.e. the saturation levels are too low) our brains become starved and we begin to feel dizzy, eventually passing out. A painful test was carried out regularly to check my blood saturation levels with a needle pricked into my ear lobe and a drop of blood placed on a glass plate for analysis. A portable meter was used to measure the levels and they were recorded in my notes. To begin this process, a gel was first placed on my ear lobe which stung and made the area hot, so more blood would flow to the surface. This was applied about ten minutes before the sample was taken, so the nurse would carry on with other duties before the sample was collected. The prick in the lobe was usually quite painless and when done skilfully, the nurse could almost instantly scoop up the blood sample, ready for analysis. Not Thomas though! He was the absolute worst at getting the sample out. He would stab me, then squeeze and push my lobe until some minute specimen was collected — it was really quite painful and he was very poor at it. I forgave him, though.

For my first time off the ventilator, the tubes were disconnected from the cannula in my neck. I looked up into Thomas's eyes as he moved the tubes away and described in detail what he was doing. I guessed he could see in mine how scared I was as I started to breathe unaided for the first time in more than five weeks. He remained very calm and continually encouraged me to carry on, telling me that I was doing fine. Unfortunately, I began to hyperventilate, convinced I was not getting enough air into my lungs. My heartbeat rose and I started sweating profusely. I was on the verge of panic, but he kept reassuring me. "Try and calm down Martin. You are doing really well. Breathe more slowly. We will only do it for five minutes. Come on slow down. I am here. Nothing can go wrong." My rate of breathing slowed and I began to calm down. More encouragement from Thomas came and he carried on talking to me. Looking back, I am sure we were well over the five minutes at this time and I was clinging to his every word, but longing to get back on to the machine. To my consternation he suddenly said he had to nip out of the room and get something. He reassured me he would be back soon and nothing could go wrong — I was connected to monitors that were transmitted to the nurses' office outside and I could always press the alarm button. He left. *Yikes, I was breathing on my own, lying next to this machine that only five minutes before had been keeping me alive.* Again, I became very anxious and started to breathe heavily. No Thomas to help me. I looked around the room and felt so alone. I forced myself to calm down and breathe more slowly. I tried very hard and wanted to do it for Thomas, to show him that I could do it.

A minute went by and he did not return; then two, three and four. No sign of him. I was still breathing and still alive, but it was hard work and my lungs were hurting! Finally, he came back in and full of his usual smiles, hooked me up to the blessed machine and I could relax — *phew*.

I guessed later that Thomas had planned all along to scoot out of the room when I was off the machine, as long as I was okay in the first few minutes. He knew from years of experience that a patient needs a combination of encouragement and firm help to make this first step. Too much pussy-footing about worrying that panic will set in is counterproductive. So, his direction was to firmly encourage me to breathe alone and to extend it every day by five minutes or more. He would distract me by talking, or simply leave me on my own and force me to spend longer off the machine, so training the muscles in my lungs to gain strength. It was a classic example of being cruel to be kind and a method that he used with me because he had the experience to judge if I was okay and just how far he could push me.

The life support machine was my constant companion night and day. It made an annoying noise as air was forced down my throat. Eventually I no longer registered the usual whooshing and whirring — unless something went wrong! If my breathing pattern changed, for example with the onset of panic, and I began to try and draw breath faster, the machine would deliver the air at the increased frequency. As it was forced into my lungs the natural reaction was to breathe faster until I was getting closer to hyperventilation. A deafening alarm would then sound that was very close to my right ear and continued as long as I was breathing at this accelerated rate. The alarm would make me panic even more, leaving me feeling hopeless in the face of an incoming tsunami of air, and the noise drove me mad. As I neared exhaustion, a nurse might respond to the alarm and check to see if all was okay. Eventually, I realised that the best way to break this cycle was to calm down and try to slow my breathing. Easier said than done in a panic situation, but after a few weeks of experience I was able to control my reactions. It reminded me of a programme that I'd heard about drowning on Radio 4. The presenter was at the Naval Research establishment in Portsmouth and was investigating the claim that most people drown within three metres of safety. A microphone was strapped to him and it recorded his breathing and heart rate as he jumped into a pool of water with a temperature of 10°C. The effect of the cold water was to "take his breath away". His heart rate immediately rocketed and he began to hyperventilate as panic set in. In a real life situation, the person in the water is then gulping in huge amounts of air and likely to swallow water, especially if it is choppy. The advice given to the listener was to try to overcome your fear and to calm down, so reducing your heart rate. Whilst I was not about to drown, the effect of my panic was to increase my heart rate, setting the machine on its quest to keep up with me. Survival was controlled by chilling out — not the first thought one tends to have, though, about life support machines.

The converse was also true. As I was getting stronger, I was spending less and less time on the machine during the day, but always hooked up at night time. I was given my medication by the night shift and I really looked forward to drifting off into the comfort of sleep. The machine whooshed and wheezed and I slowly drifted off. Unbeknown to me, just as I was about to move from consciousness into sleep, I would momentarily either stop breathing, or significantly slow down my rhythm. The bloody machine would then sound an alarm, jumpstarting me awake and sending me into a mini panic. You know what comes next; yes, I started hyperventilating, feeling that my lungs were being inflated like a kid's balloon. To break this, I had to calm down and try to keep my breathing constant as I slipped into sleep. Not an easy task and it only compounded my love/hate relationship with the bloody machine.

Thomas continued to work his magic with me in my rehabilitation by treating me with dignity. He was always ready with the next action or words of encouragement to either push me to do more or to make my life more comfortable. He was the one to give me the alphabet board; he was the one to wrap sticking plaster around the pen because it was easier to grip between my teeth. He talked to and explained my condition to my visitors. He noticed my rancid tongue, asked Fiona to get a tongue cleaner (did you know there was such a thing?) and he used it whenever he cleaned me up. One day, he noticed how dry my lips were. They had cracked and the dead skin was looking unsightly. He grabbed two cotton buds and proceeded to use them like mini chop sticks to remove the skin. He really looked after me, so I was not surprised when he came into my room in my seventh week of hospitalisation and asked if I would like to have a shower. I was so happy and I readily nodded my agreement. My first weeks of illness were characterised by enormous amounts of sweating caused by the GBS and the layering of pillows and blankets on and around my body. The prospect then of having a shower was very exciting.

Thomas summoned Nicole to assist him. She wheeled a stretcher-type bed into the room. I looked to my right as she came in, on top of the stretcher was a blue waterproof, thinly padded mattress. It looked very similar to the self-inflating camping mattress we had bought from Aldi the year before, except it had semi-rigid sides that could fold up and, by means of Velcro in the corners, form a shallow waterproof tray. Thomas and Nicole removed my various tubes and disconnected me from the life support machine. Finally, they removed my gown and the delightful Pampers, leaving me naked in bed.

The stretcher height was adjusted to the same as my bed. I was turned on to my left side and the mattress from the stretcher was placed from my right underneath me. I was rolled back on to it and winced as my warm skin hit its cold surface. The next part was the tricky bit because they had to get a totally paralysed body from the bed onto the stretcher. I absolutely hated this bit as they positioned themselves for the lift. I could for the first time in weeks look down at this white, emaciated, and useless body. The bones around my wrists were very prominent. My knees sat like huge knotted humps on thin branches. My feet looked so large in comparison to my frighteningly thin legs. It was only seven weeks since I had stopped walking but the muscle and weight loss I suffered were extreme.

Yet again a very vivid reminder about how cruel GBS could be.

I snapped out of my dark thoughts as Thomas and Nicole positioned themselves at the top and bottom of the mattress to lift me onto the stretcher. One, two, three, and I was airborne from the bed and onto the stretcher. Safely on, the edges were folded upwards and I was lying in my waterproof tray. I was reasonably comfortable, but I was cold lying on this sterile surface. Thomas wheeled me into the bathroom and opened the window — it was late March and cold outside. I started to shiver lightly and longed for the warmth of the shower water. The stretcher was tipped up slightly so my head was above my feet. They donned waterproof aprons and clogs; it was a major effort for all concerned to get me showered! Thomas tested the water, which was blissful as it warmed me. I was on my back, and after I was wet all over he turned off the water. The combination of the open window, lying on a cold waterproof surface whilst stark naked and totally wet sent my body temperature plummeting and I started to shiver. Thomas ignored this and started to wash me all over. Fortunately, he removed the soap with more warm water from the shower head, bringing some temporary relief. I was then turned on my side, with Nicole holding me to prevent me falling, and he sprayed my back. The water was turned off and I was so cold it was impossible to stop my body shaking. The movements became so violent that Thomas was concerned that I was indeed having a fit and he asked me if I was okay. I wanted to scream at him — *Yes I'm okay, but extremely cold. Just get me dry! Please get me dry!*

I think he must have caught my brain pattern because he and Nicole jumped into action with a couple of towels and they started rubbing me dry, at the same time trying to warm me up. It was nice to be clean, but I was so relieved when I was transferred back into my bed and was able to warm up under the mountain of pillows, towels, and quilts.

Thomas wasn't always perfect, but he redeemed himself so many other times, the next of which was a week or two later when he came into my room hiding a urine bottle behind his back. He was going to remove the catheter. He knew, but crucially I didn't, that this was very unpleasant. The bed covers were pulled back and he snapped his several pairs of rubber gloves on. He looked at the tube and then looked at me, telling me to take a deep breath. He then totally distracted me by asking, "What was it that you do again?" I breathed in ready to try to talk (it was possible at this time) and he skilfully withdrew the tube. I winced. It was unpleasant and painful, but it was out and over with very quickly. Unfortunately, I was not spared the tube for long, as I got a bladder infection and he had to put it back in again three days later!

By this time we were firm friends and I really enjoyed the times we could talk together. He seemed to leave himself more time with me so we could catch up on the news together. It was great when he was there and I had a visitor. He got to know Fiona and the kids very well and when they came he greeted them in such a friendly way, always explaining what I had been doing and how I was progressing.

In the first few weeks of my stay, Fiona was not able to drive down to Bonn because of a slipped disc. Friends and family rallied round and chauffeured her to the hospital. She was not able to sit down, so Thomas told her to bring a fold-up bed or sun lounger so she could lie down next to me. This duly happened and Thomas arranged for the bed to be stored in my room and a blanket to be made available. It was such a personal moment for both of us to be lying there in my room holding hands and not actually saying anything. Magical, only made possible by his remarkable understanding. We were both so grateful.

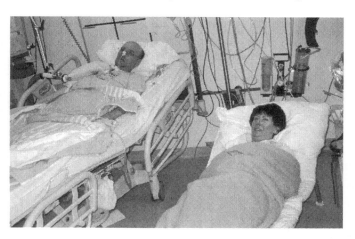

Fiona lying in the fold-up bed to rest her back

There were many other wonderful nursing moments with this remarkable person, but as I progressed, I knew that my time on the ICU ward was coming to a close and I would have to move to a normal ward — on the "other side". This was the main building with access to daily therapy for my further rehabilitation. I came off the life support and the feeding tubes after a total of eight weeks in the hospital, six of which were in Bonn. I was now able to breathe and eat on my own and should have transferred to the "other side". Fortunately, a bed was not available and I was privileged to enjoy another week of constant care. As that final week drew to a close, I knew that I would be moving on Monday and would be really out on my own striving for independence. It was a scary thought and I was really nervous about it. The final Sunday evening, Thomas and I had a really long chat. I would be leaving him the next day and it was a struggle for me. I'd asked Fiona to bring a few bottles of our favourite Rioja wine as a present and we were both choked as I gave it to him. He had brought me back to life and treated me with such dignity and care that I felt humble in his presence. I wished that I could reach the same levels of professionalism and dedication in my life, but I knew it would be impossible. It was an honour for me to have met such a very special human being.

Fiona was with me as I left the ICU the next morning at around 9:00. Thomas pushed me in my wheelchair to my new home on a normal ward, which was so different from the intensive care ward. We said our goodbyes and although I was in the hospital for another seven weeks, whenever I went over to the ICU to meet up with the staff, he was never there. We exchanged Christmas cards that year but had no other contact. This was a shame, but as I moved on in my rehabilitation it only seemed right to distance myself from the intensive care ward and inevitably the staff.

We met again two years later when Fiona and I went back to Bonn to say hello to the staff. I'd called the day before to make sure Thomas would be there and was so excited to hear his voice again when the reception connected me to him. I called from my office and as I put the phone down I burst into tears and couldn't control my emotions. I had to call Fiona and between sobs told her that I'd spoken to Thomas. She was very worried to hear me in this state and naturally thought that I was crying because something had happened to him. In fact, I was crying partly because of the joy of hearing his voice, but mainly because talking to him had transported me back to Bonn and reminded me of my enormous struggle to live.

It was June 2007 and the next day, with my emotions in check, Fiona and I went onto the ward. The staff didn't recognise me at first because I had put on so much weight, but they immediately recognised Fiona. I saw Angelika and Nicole. Thomas was called from nursing a patient to come and see me. It was an awkward moment as we all stood in the corridor and I knew they were busy. I thought about hugging him, but he was in his gowns, waterproof apron, and dressed for nursing action. Somehow it did not seem appropriate. We shook hands and caught up with each other's news. I had moved on tremendously since he had last seen me and he was still there doing the same job with his usual professionalism. After a short time, they needed to get back to work and Fiona and I left. I had closed a circle and seen Thomas again. I did not need to go back and we have not had any further contact since. The ICU ward was a period when I was close to death. My time there taught me a lot about myself and how precarious life can be. I have moved on now.

Jan

I first saw Jan on my first day in Bonn. He was part of the arrival committee with Dr. Mertz, Thomas, and the rest of the team. He immediately stood out because he was absolutely not afraid to speak his mind. He was in his late thirties, had grown up in Poland and spoke good German with a heavy accent. He and his approach to nursing always bemused me. He never seemed to be happy and was always complaining about something. My first real encounter with him was when he and Nicole were round my bed and he told some tasteless joke about showers, gas chambers, and the concentration camps in Poland. Nicole and I were really embarrassed, but it didn't bother him — in fact he would use any opportunity to knock the Germans and his jokes were one of his ways of doing this.

During recovery and rehabilitation, I had to face very unpleasant and usually painful experiences every day. It was always distressing and made even worse if the nurse on duty seemed to be in a really bad mood. And one sure fire way of getting Jan in a bad mood was to have a Pamper full of pooh when it was his turn to clean me up. Courtesy of GBS I had no feeling in and around my bum, so had no idea if I'd filled my pants or not when he was looking after me. He would roll me on my side and I tensed up hoping that I'd not left him a pungent gift. The sticky tape sides of the Pampers were yanked back and I waited with baited breath for the next moment. If it was good, the pants were skilfully whipped away, much like a magician removing a tablecloth with all crockery and utensils left intact. He then grabbed a wet wipe, which was toe-curlingly cold, and wiped me down. He never heard the visible relief and the silent words of thanks to my bowels if they had spared me his onslaught.

When the opposite was true and my Pampers were a delightful mess, he would let out some expletive, in a language I can only assume was Polish. I guessed that the tone and the venom of the delivery would have turned most of his country folk red with embarrassment because he was certainly not a happy camper. On these occasions the Pampers were not ripped off, but instead used as his first line of defence against the faecal feature in front of him. He would grab them and wipe away at my bum with a force that would move me across the bed. All the while, he would switch in and out of German and give a running commentary about "wiping arses" and "shitting in pants". He then grabbed some cloths that seemed to be made of industrial grade sandpaper and proceeded to scrape away at my bum until it was red raw! I was then wrapped up in new Pampers and left in no doubt that it would be a good idea to crap on somebody else's shift tomorrow. Smarting from his mishandling of me, we were both relieved when he left.

Good Friday Jan was my duty nurse on the early shift. He'd been into my room and switched my radio on. A bed bath and clean up were always done on the afternoon shift, so I hoped I had nothing to fear from him that shift. Fiona had told me that two of our neighbours, Lars and Ludger, would be visiting that day whilst she, Gillian, Alexander, and Francesca relaxed at home. Jan had propped me up in bed and I was lying on my left side, with my back to the door. I could hear my visitors walk in and they positioned themselves either side of my bed. I was extremely hot and sweat was running off my forehead. The tubes from the ventilator snaked over my left shoulder and the single tube from the valve was plugged into my neck. Unfortunately, neither Lars nor Ludger was prepared for the shock of seeing me in this state and it robbed us of the opportunity to establish some communication. I was eager to show them that I was not actually hopeless and things were getting better. The day before, I'd seen the very first involuntary movement in my right arm. Looking at Lars I moved my arm upwards from my side towards my head. I could only control the muscles to lift my arm, but once it started moving; I was unable to direct it or stop it. Unfortunately, my hand travelled upwards and hit me in the face, providing quite a comical moment. My hand then flopped down, again uncontrollably to my side. Keen to repeat this, I set my arm and hand moving off again. This time, it hit the valve from the ventilator and knocked the life-giving tube out of my neck! The tube was now free and hissing on the bed, meanwhile I was disconnected from my source of air. I stared at Lars and willed him to do something. I tried in vain to hit the alarm button with my head, but to no avail. It was a helpless situation. I desperately needed the air but could not tell my visitors what to do. I was panicking but it reminded me instantly of one of the most hilarious scenes in the film *Airplane*. A child on a stretcher on the way for a transplant is serenaded by a guitar playing passenger. She swings the guitar around and knocks out the life supporting IV drip from the child. The child rolls her eyes, puckers her lips and tries in desperation to signal that the drip has come out while all the passengers are clapping along with the song and ignoring her!

There was no clapping and singing around my bed, but the hissing of the tube and the fact that it was not connected to my neck was causing me a great deal of anxiety! Lars looked at the tube and asked me if he should connect it back to my neck. I violently nodded my approval. He showed a lot of courage to pick it up and slot it back into place. I immediately felt the rush of air inflating my lungs and was very thankful to him. I looked at Ludger and managed to signal that he should press the alarm button and summon Jan. He did it and in marched Jan who asked my visitors what the problem was. Lars recounted the incident including replacing the tube. Jan scowled and told him very rudely that he shouldn't touch the tubes. He tugged at my cannula, checked it was in place, and left. I was relieved that I had not come to any harm as a result of my stupidity and felt very sorry for Lars because without his action, I could have been in an emergency situation. It was always a roller coaster with Jan.

Apart from the first attempt to switch off my life support machine with Thomas, I experienced the most extreme form of trust in a nurse with Jan. On this occasion he had moved me up from my lying position and held me on the side of the bed. My lifeless legs were dangling down towards the floor and my equally useless arms were hanging limply by my side. Jan was totally in charge of me. He was rarely in a good mood. If anything, he was unconventional but very skilled. He was frustrated with the lack of progress my therapists had made in getting me back on my feet. Consequently, he wanted to show me how much strength I'd recovered in the core muscles of my back and stomach, he felt I needed to push myself harder and place total trust in the nurses and therapists.

He stood in front of me, making sure I was stable. He then moved backwards to be about one metre away from the bed. I had indeed recovered some strength and was able to support my back and not fall. He then told me to fall forward. He reassured me that he would catch me and everything would be okay. I looked at him and looked at the floor. I knew that if I leaned forward, I would fall from the bed. My useless arms would offer no protection to break the fall. I would smash my face into the floor and no doubt severely injure myself. He told me to do it and he once again insisted he would catch me. I moved my upper body forward, further forward and eventually fell face first off the bed. He caught me and lifted me back onto the bed. It was a very real demonstration of the power placing complete trust in a nurse could bring and in doing so I was able to push myself harder and harder. I was very thankful to him for this.

The most memorable session I had with Jan, mercifully, was not punctuated with a full pair of Pampers. I was lying on the bed and he was giving me a bed bath. Jan was not gentle. A bowl of water was placed on a trolley by my side, shower gel, soap, and my deodorant were also lined up. The water was always a touch too cold and the flannel used on the painful side of rough. A wash with Jan was definitely not fun. He talked me through the session as he came to each new area of my body. He looked at me and with flannel in one hand and soap in the other told me, "Okay, now to your genitals." He started washing around my penis and then took hold of it. There was nothing unusual in this, in fact it was normal and all the nurses did it, admittedly with a lot more care and gentler than Jan. He then proceeded to scare the absolute living daylights out of me by announcing that, "We need to pull your foreskin back and clean your penis. I must be careful to put it back to its original position." At this point I started to get really worried and my anxiety levels were rising. He continued in his nonchalant, non-interested way, "Because, if I leave it pulled back, it will dry out and strangle the end of your penis. You will then need an operation to cut your foreskin off!" *What!* I thought and wanted to shout at the top of my voice to him, "Hey, Jan, make bloody sure you've got that foreskin back. I have some pretty serious problems here and I absolutely do not want to have my knob falling off because you have forgotten to pull my foreskin back."

Hell, I couldn't talk or communicate, but I was willing every sinew in my body to move so that I could let him know that I could cope with GBS, but a strangled plonker was one too far. He had no idea how stressed up I was as he merrily rubbed away on my manhood with his gravely flannel, talking away about a fate worse than I could possibly imagine. I dragged myself up onto my elbows and I watched every single minute of the way as he restored my foreskin to its rightful, non-strangling position. I was relieved when he left and vowed never to cross him — lest he let my foreskin dry out.

Ralf, Stefan and Anna — the Physios

From Monday to Friday and occasionally on Saturday morning, I would have physiotherapy. At the beginning of each week, a plan was printed out and delivered to my room showing the type of therapy I would be having, with whom, and at what time. Each session lasted thirty minutes. On the ICU ward, I had speech therapy, occupational therapy, and physiotherapy. When I moved to a normal ward, this was complemented with longer physiotherapy sessions, computer or keyboard skills, sessions in the exercise studio, and on the weights.

In the first few weeks I was not really aware of what was happening to me, but noticed the care and attention that one of the physios, Ralf, was giving me. He was probably in his late twenties; long black hair swept back and he always wore immaculate white Adidas trainers. I have no idea why I felt comfortable with him, but guess it was because he was always professional when working with me. He also never forgot that I was a real person in a useless body and not some object to work on. I appreciated him for that and the dignity he showed me.

The sessions I had with him were probably very boring for his skills because I was paralysed. His job was to provide my legs, arms, and back with some movement to counteract the inactivity associated with long immobile hours in bed. He would sit me up, move my arms around and exercise my legs. As I started to get a little stronger and more with it, he would move me to the edge of the bed and allow my legs to dangle down towards the floor. This was the first exercise on the long road back towards walking, although I never realised it at the time. It was always very strange to have somebody working on my body because they could move my limbs, but I couldn't. I only had limited feeling and in some cases, no feeling, so I had no idea where a limb was unless I could see it! Consequently, I very often felt I was like a rag doll but with a living head where my emotions and thoughts were concentrated. Fellow GBS sufferers told me their horror stories on this subject. They described feeling that their limbs were disconnected from their bodies and lying somewhere over the other side of the room. Josef Berger even had nightmares that he was just a head on the bed without any body at all! It was a really horrible experience that depressed him and threatened to derail his recovery.

The sense of feeling was something that I'd taken for granted. When lying on my back in bed, I could see my legs and knew where they were. When they were covered with a blanket, I imagined that I could move them, that they were perhaps crossed or in a different position. Therefore, if there was no feedback to my brain via sight, or touch, I was unable to say where my limbs were and my mind was given carte blanche to make up virtual effects and movements. As I recovered I found that I craved feedback from my feet and legs, my worst affected limbs. It was a superb feeling when I was allowed into a rehabilitation swimming pool for the first time; the resistance of the water was a significant stimulation to my legs and feet allowing my brain to "feel" it, so understanding where they were in the water.

GBS destroys the nerve linings, but after the worst of the illness has passed, the body remarkably starts to repair them. The extremities closest to the brain have the shortest nerve lengths so they tend to repair fastest. My recovery started with my breathing muscles, my back and stomach, then my arms and finally my legs. The nerves to the face run directly from the brain, those to all other areas via your back. The facial nerves are very short in length, but the repair was very slow, in comparison to my limbs and I am still affected today by paralysis around my mouth. The repair carries on in the body without any noticeable signs, but I would experience uncomfortable pain in my legs, especially at night and also terribly hot feet. Even today, years after contracting GBS, I only have limited feeling in my feet and they throb and pulsate constantly. I have to be careful when I walk barefoot because my big toes hang down and I can easily catch them on a carpet or step and trip up.

After moving to the normal ward, I had a lot of physio sessions with Stefan and Anna. The main difference for me was that I had to go and see them, whereas Ralf had come to see me. The weekly printout was the same, showing my sessions, with whom, and at what time. I was sufficiently mobile to get myself out of bed and into my wheelchair. It was always parked at the side of my bed; I would shuffle on my bottom along the bed — check that the brakes were on and then lean over to grab the arms. My arms were now strong enough to lift my body up and I would flop into the chair and lift my feet onto the foot rests. The first session was at 9:00 each morning. Around 8:40, a whole team of ancillary staff would come to the wards and collect all the patients who could not make it to the treatment areas on their own. I opted for this option once simply because I had no idea where I was supposed to go, but needing a "pick-up" was a further reminder that I was still dependent on others. I was able to accept the dependence in my first few weeks, but once I'd moved to a normal ward, I was desperate to get my independence back as quickly as possible.

The collection service was out of the question for me and I happily toddled off in my wheelchair on my own in the mornings. The route took me out of my room, along the corridor to a lift and down three floors. Out of the lift straight on to the end of a long corridor, a quick left and then a right, taking care to look in the mirrors mounted on the ceiling to check that nobody was approaching in the opposite direction in their chair. I passed the canteen and then had to wait for another lift that transported us down a vertical height of about two metres (probably six or seven steps). There was always a huge wheelchair traffic bottleneck at the rush hour times of just before 9:00, 12:00 for lunch and 1:00 after lunch, so I would dash down the corridor at huge speed, often passing the train of chairs controlled by the ancillary staff in front of me, in order to get a place in the lift before therapy started. Once past this point, I wheeled myself another eighty metres to yet another lift, this time taking me down two floors to the treatment areas. Here, we would all line up in our chairs and wait for the one of fifty, yes fifty, physios to come out and collect us.

It was whilst waiting in this area and at lunch in the canteen that I got to see my fellow patients. For the first seven weeks in Bonn, I was in a single or double room and had zero contact with neighbouring patients, most of whom were so poorly they were unable to communicate. Here though, I was one of many people in a wheelchair. Most were older than me, there appeared to be more men than women, and a lot of them seemed to be in a bad way.

I looked around and knew that I was into my tenth week of recovery and I was getting stronger and improving every day. Many of the folks there were not. Some had serious neurological problems such as ALS, motor neurone, or multiple sclerosis, so they were not improving at all. Many others had had strokes and were paralysed to a greater or lesser extent. I felt as though I was lucky at "only" having GBS because, I knew I was recovering and I had a near normal life to look forward to. Many of my fellow patients did not have the same optimistic future. I felt as though the physios recognised this with me and the two other GBS patients and they enjoyed working with us simply because we could achieve remarkable results in a short space of time. For example, when I started on the normal ward, I could not walk and was not strong enough to stand up on my own. Within four weeks, I was able to take some tentative steps, admittedly with some support from Anna. Not only was this a great motivation for me, but also for the physios because they could see the results of their work. I got on really well with all my physios and not only enjoyed working with them, but enjoyed spending time in their company.

Occupational Therapists

The occupational therapists also came to work on me when I was in the ICU. As a complete amateur, I was not able to distinguish any difference between the therapy they did and that of the physiotherapists. I had a favourite therapist, Monica, who spoke to me in excellent English, as she had worked in the U.S. She was only five feet tall, about my age and always greeted me with a smile and a pat on the shoulder (physical contact always worked wonders).

The first time we met she concentrated on getting me to sit up with my legs dangling over the side of the bed. This seemed like an extremely tedious exercise until I learnt later on that it was designed to strengthen my core muscles, which are essential for walking. Monica made sure I was lying flat on my back; she then activated the controls to raise the head of the bed up. I moved gently upwards and was in a half-lying, half-sitting position when she stopped. The bars on the right hand side of the bed were then pushed down and I was told to roll onto my right hand side. Monica helped me to turn over and held me to prevent me from falling out of the bed — boy was I grateful for that because it reminded me of the masochists in Düsseldorf that had let me fall (or not).

She stood in front of me and placed one hand on my hip, the other then moved to my legs, which were on top of each other. Her right hand went behind my legs and then she put her left hand under my shoulder. With one movement, she swung my legs down and simultaneously pulled my shoulders up so that I was sitting on the side of the bed. I was impressed with her dexterity but was not able to offer any help. As my legs moved down they were bent into a ninety-degree position and an excruciating cramp, similar to a red hot dagger, immediately sliced into both calf muscles. At the same time the movement of my legs had trapped my catheter tube under my body and as I was brought to a sitting position it felt as though somebody was trying to pull my willy off. Her hands were now on both shoulders to support me. I looked at her and opened my mouth in a long silent scream. I shook my head violently and tried with terrified eye movements to let dearest Monica know that she was doing me out of future sexual enjoyment. Through telepathy, ESP, osmosis or some undiscovered communication method she realised that I was in severe pain as my willy was stretching out in front of me like a piece of elastic. She deftly moved my legs back up onto the bed and let my shoulders down. I had tears in my eyes as she realised what had happened, swiftly moving the catheter tube into its normal position. She apologised profusely and I silently noted that this form of penis enlargement must never fall into the hands of a terrorist regime. I would have confessed to anything or any crime at that moment!

The cramp was caused by complete immobility of my legs over hours, days, and weeks. The catheter was caused by stupidity or bad luck. I remember the pain from the catheter more, but the cramp in my legs became a recurring problem whenever I was moved from a lying to a sitting position or worse when I was transferred from my bed to a wheelchair. It never happened when transferring back to my bed, so I was always tense when I was lifted and moved. I knew as soon as my legs were bent that I would get the stabbing pain again. It was another of the daily problems that I had to put up with and one of the minor ones in the grand scheme of things. Once again my mind amazed me on how I approached this. It was counter-intuitive to look forward to being moved, because I knew it would hurt. Yet, I was happy to take on the daily challenges like a punch-drunk boxer walking back into the next onslaught of fists simply because it was survival and I would have endured double the pain and discomfort to reach my goals.

Poor old Monica was responsible for giving me another painful session, causing us both to laugh. A week or so after the catheter incident, she bounced into my room, giving me the customary cheery hello and pat on the shoulder. I was great to see her because she was always happy and she seemed to genuinely enjoy working with me. I was told we were going to practice shuffling along on my bottom and "walking" across the bed by lifting and moving one buttock and then the other. She raised the head of my bed, and with her arms under my neck and legs she swung me round and turned me so that I was on the edge of the bed with legs dangling — yes I got cramp again. I now had sufficient strength in my core stomach muscles to sit up without falling over, but she kept a caring hand on my shoulder and walked around the foot of the bed. She was now positioned behind me. I was told me to lean to my left side, taking weight off my right buttock and then to move my right buttock backwards. Then I had to transfer my weight to the right buttock and move the left one backwards. Repeating this process would result in small "steps" across the bed and represent the first movement under my own control in about seven weeks.

Monica was still standing behind me when she transferred her caring grip from my shoulders to the seat of my tracksuit bottoms. I sat upright, a little unsteady, with my legs dangling. She went through the instructions again and called the directions out. "Move your weight over to your left buttock, now move your right backwards." As I did this she helped me by pulling on the seat of my tracksuit bottoms from behind. We repeated the same with the right buttock and she pulled hard again. I was indeed moving backwards. She called out the instruction again and grabbed more of a handful of my tracksuit. What she did not realise was that as she was grabbing and dragging more and more of my tracksuit she was pulling it so hard backwards that my testicles were somewhere up my lower back by the time she had finished! I was in agony. Monica, her hands still gripped tightly on rolls and rolls of my tracksuit bottom, congratulated me on my efforts as tears rolled down my cheeks. "Martin. Well done! How do you feel?" I turned slowly around to look at her. "Monica," I replied through clenched teeth and with my dead pan expression, "I am okay, but I don't think I will be able to have any more children!" There was silence for a split second as she looked at my face waiting to see if I was going to break into a smile and give away that fact that I had made a joke, *huh, I wish*. Realising that this was beyond me, she looked at her handfuls of tracksuit, released them in an instant and burst into uncontrollable laughter. Her joy was about evenly matched to the relief I felt in my genitals. We were both happy!

Other therapists prepared me with exercises for a return to an independent life. The first targets were simple things such as cleaning my teeth, shaving, and taking control of my own personal hygiene. Further into my recovery, we worked on building up strength, manual dexterity, and ultimately walking. I suppose it would have been better if these targets and my programme of rehabilitation had been explained to me. I might have then understood it — well maybe. My problem was that I didn't know why the therapists were doing all these different exercises. I always enthusiastically carried out what they asked and I looked forward to and enjoyed being with them, simply because it broke up my day. But, I was focused on walking, so anything I considered to be irrelevant to this came well down my list of priorities. I found it difficult with some of the occupational therapists when they gave me tedious exercises to do; like picking up various shapes and placing them in the same shaped holes, *yawn*.

On another occasion, I was placed in front of a desk on which sat a deep tray filled with gravel, the likes of which you would normally find in an aquarium. The therapist showed me six pieces of wooden dowel, approximately twenty-five mm in length and about eight mm in diameter. She buried all of them in the different places in the gravel and then covered it with a tea towel. My hands were then placed under the towel and I had to feel about in the gravel and locate the dowels. It seemed to be another totally useless exercise until I realised that I could not distinguish the difference between the gravel and the dowel. I had recovered some feeling and movement in my fingers, but I was still affected because of poor sensitivity. Imagine your face after the injection for a filling at the dentist — it is there, you can feel it, but somehow it is not completely there. Consequently, I really struggled with the test and could not find all of the six dowels before the end of the session. This was an eye opening exercise and a test that I would use later to improve my keyboard skills. At the time though, I dismissed it as not relevant for walking, so it was not important. If I had known it would be good for learning how to hold a toothbrush or a razor, I would have given it more attention! Hence, whilst it is vital for the medical staff to communicate with patients and explain what they will be doing, it is, in my opinion equally important to say why they are doing it. I know I only have my experience to go on and admittedly I was very guilty of pig-headiness, but I felt as though I missed out on this information, which possibly prevented me from getting the best out of some of my therapy.

Speech therapists

As with so much in my rehabilitation, learning to talk again was not an easy process and whilst the motivation to succeed was high, I have to report that it was associated with mental effort, panic, and discomfort. I was still attached to the life support machine via the cannula. In the diagram below it is possible to see how it is placed via a hole in the neck and down the throat below the vocal cords.

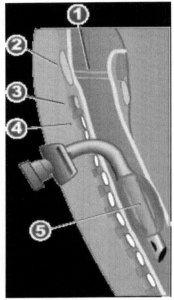

Tracheotomy:

1) Vocal chords
2) Thyroid cartilage
3) Cricoid cartilage
4) Tracheal cartilages
5) Balloon cuff

I never saw this tube before it was inserted in my neck. The first one was placed when I was under anaesthetic. The second one was placed four or five weeks later. It was a very distressing procedure but Angelika, one of my favourite nurses, took charge. She first covered me in a protective sheet. A colleague was then called and two of them readied themselves for action. I was disconnected from the ventilator and Angelika swiftly removed the old tube through the hole in my neck. It was extremely uncomfortable, like being choked and strangled at the same time as she removed it. I then coughed violently and green slime shot out of the raw hole and plastered her gown, just like in *The Exorcist*. Air hissed in through the opening and the second nurse plopped in the new tube. Phew it was over. I never saw the tube, so had no idea that it also contained the balloon cuff (see diagram), which I first came across this during my speech therapy sessions.

Right from the very first day in Bonn, a speech therapist came to see me. I was not able to talk but this is only one area covered by these specialised therapists. With complete facial and throat paralysis, they concentrated first on stimulating the muscles in my face to respond to signals from my brain and then on learning how to swallow. I was seen by a total of three speech therapists, I cannot remember any sessions with the first one because I was too drugged up or too tired. The second was Frau P, slightly younger than me with brown hair. I never really hit it off with her, perhaps because I felt she was too intrusive. Her first sessions were very often at 7:30 a.m. just after I had woken up. It was pleasant to see somebody, but the next thirty minutes were so boring that I must admit I very often fell asleep during the session. She would bring several cubes of ice in a paper cup and position herself close to my left shoulder, ready to work on my face. An ice cube was wrapped in a coarse piece of gauze and held between her thumb and forefinger. She would then lean on my left arm, so we were very close to each other and stroke the now cold and damp gauze in various areas on my face. The problem with this intimacy was that I wasn't comfortable because I had not cleaned my teeth. I couldn't taste or smell if my mouth was rancid or not. But, I had seen the quite disgusting deposits that gathered on my tongue every day —a horrendous orange colour that was scraped off using a tongue cleaner by the nurse, so I was convinced my mouth smelt like a festering bear pit. It would have been really easy for Frau P to say to me, shall we just clean your teeth? Then you will feel better.

Frau P was oblivious to my dignity and set about stimulating ten areas on my face with her ice cubes. Each position, for example the corners of my mouth, were stroked three times with the cloth, first the left side. She would then put the cloth down, lean over me very close to my face (and that festering bear pit) and position her forefingers on the edges of my mouth. Then, on her command, I was supposed to activate the muscles and move the corners of my mouth upwards into a grin. As I tried to do it, she would move my muscles and manually produce the grin. This was repeated three times. We then started again with the ice and went through the same routine another three times finally finishing with another three attempts. She worked on a total of ten positions on my face and each position was moved nine times. So a shockingly boring ninety exercises were induced in my face which was the closest I found in the hospital to a cure for insomnia. It was a complete and utter waste of time and I am nearly falling asleep writing about it. The fact was that I had full facial paralysis resulting in zero movement — otherwise known as looking like a miserable bastard.

No amount of stimulation using ice or rough gauze would induce any reaction whatsoever. In fact, the very first miniscule movement I had was in the right side of my mouth after thirteen weeks in the hospital and this only came about because my body was healing itself.

I was not best pleased with Frau P and we had some tense moments together, usually when she tapped me on my face to wake me up after another ice session! As usual though, I was completely in her hands and I had learned that to progress through my therapy with any of the medical team, I had to trust them implicitly. Therefore, I put full trust in Frau P as she told me that she was going to do a swallow test with jelly and we could also practise speaking as well.

She moved towards my neck and started working on the cannula, causing irritation as she pulled the bandage around my neck tighter. As she worked she told me that she "was now inflating the balloon in the tube". I had no idea what she was talking about, but subsequently have read up on it and it is possible to see from the diagram that the balloon effectively seals the tube inside the trachea. In our throats, there are effectively two tubes, the trachea (windpipe) for breathing which leads to the lungs and the oesophagus for eating, which leads to the stomach. When we are preparing to swallow food, the epiglottis acts as a valve and closes the windpipe, so food only enters our stomach. My problem was that I had no control over the muscles required to swallow and Frau P did not know if the epiglottis function was affected, so she inflated the balloon to prevent the food entering my lungs. As usual, I fully trusted her and was actually looking forward to having a spoonful of jelly, my first "solid" food in six weeks. But, she did not tell me *why she had inflated the balloon and what she was actually looking for*. My position here is that as a patient, it is much easier to get into the zone of discomfort if you are told, or at least have an idea what is being done and why! Personally, the WHY was extremely important to me and she was poor at this. In contrast, I always found the best nurses or therapists were the ones that told me what they were doing and why.

I was fed a tiny spoonful of red jelly. It was nice to have the sensation of food in my mouth again, even if there was no taste. I looked up at her with staring eyes as she encouraged me to try to swallow it. I had to stop and think — how do I swallow. What do I do? I had absolutely no idea of the processes involved, because, like talking and walking, it is an automatic reaction. I had to think fast or it would dribble out, but damn Frau P didn't explain anything. As usual, I panicked. Somehow, I got the stuff to the back of my throat —again not easy as I was lying down — and made an attempt to swallow it. A miniscule amount might have gone down, but I coughed and choked on the rest, presumably as it went down the trachea. It was very unpleasant. Frau P took her stethoscope and checked to see if any had entered my lungs. I presumed it was negative, but she didn't tell me. This was the first and last time we attempted this together and I was glad it was over. Unfortunately, worse was to come when she decided to let me have a go at speaking.

She cleaned me up and told me that I could try talking. This was exciting and I was ready. Yet again though she did not tell me why she was doing something and what I had to do. I was informed that a speech valve would be connected to the cannula, but not what this meant and what I had to do. An attempt to talk could only be carried out when I was disconnected from the life support machine. This was a major issue in itself. For hours, days and weeks, I had lain next to a machine that was keeping me alive. When the machine is switched off it is extremely difficult at first to cope. I felt so vulnerable and isolated. The swallow test had upset me so I was not really in the best frame of mind.

The life support tube was disconnected from the cannula. A speech valve was applied and I breathed in heavily. Frau P told me to talk. Again, I had no idea what to do but suddenly realised that the gulp of air just taken was stuck in my lungs and I was not able to breathe out. I took another huge breath and tried in vain to expel it. I really began to panic and once again gasped more air in further inflating my lungs to what seemed like bursting point. I wanted to scream for help! I couldn't breathe! Oh shit, not again! The problem was not getting the air in; instead it was getting it out. I tried to push it out with my lungs, willing my chest to expel it, but my lungs were so weak. I daren't breathe in any more air and pushed my chest yet harder. To my huge surprise, I pushed so hard that I produced an audible groan. *Wow, I thought, where did that come from?* It was the first vocal sound that I had made in over six weeks and it was from the speech valve, (thanks for telling me what I needed to do Frau P)! The groan was only possible because air was actually expelled from my lungs and through the speech valve. I pushed again, expelling more air and reducing the pressure on my over-inflated lungs. Frau P recognised that I was in trouble and removed the valve. I gulped in air and rejoiced as I could expel it easily. I lay there gasping, sweating, blood pumping through me with my heart banging into my chest. I felt, admittedly rather melodramatically, that I had narrowly avoided dying at the hands of this woman and I was so angry. I tried to let her know the depth of my feeling, but I just couldn't transmit to her how upset I was and how unprofessional she had been. In the space of one thirty-minute session I was so traumatised about swallowing and talking by Frau P that it would be three weeks before I dared to try it again.

I had never realised that we can only talk when we are breathing out. We contract the muscles in our lungs and expel air, which passes the vocal chords so allowing us to speak. Likewise, I had never thought about swallowing something. I now know that movement of the tongue and the muscles in our cheeks work the food into smaller packages and onto the correct position on our tongue. We then use the muscles at the back of the throat and the tongue to swallow it. With a tongue, cheeks, and throat muscles still paralysed or weakened from the GBS, I had no way to get the jelly on to my tongue and then down my throat. If I'd known or been told this, I might have been able to cope with what happened to me. Instead, I was just so angry at this woman. Two months later I could talk and met Frau P whilst sitting in my wheelchair outside the office of another therapist. I told her about my experience and how she had set me back at least two to three weeks in my recovery, but perhaps worse she had really scared me. I think she was genuinely shocked about how upset I was, but appreciative of the fact that I'd told her. ICU nursing and caring is a very difficult and demanding job and in many cases the patients are not aware of what is happening to them and sadly, very few in the ward I was on, ever make it back to normal life. Consequently, there is very little opportunity for feedback to the nursing staff. For just that reason, I thought it was absolutely necessary to recount my experience to her for the sake of others.

Unfortunately, as you can no doubt gather, Frau P was not my favourite therapist and I always found hers and the other speech therapy sessions to be either boring, useless, or both. I am probably being unfair and I have no doubt that most of them were extremely dedicated and as professional as the physios. Unfortunately, my face did not recover as fast as the rest of my body, so I was probably not in the right frame of mind when working with them. Maybe their methods were not suitable for my facial paralysis, or possibly it was because they were used to working on speech therapy with stroke victims. I am not sure, but I was always glad when the sessions were over.

In my eighth week I was off the life support, but still had the nasal feeding tube. An ENT doctor and speech therapist arrived in my room with their equipment and what looked like a small tray of canapés. I recognised the speech therapist, but could not place her. She then explained that she had worked on me during my first three weeks in Bonn and I was very often drifting in and out of consciousness, so it was understandable that I did not remember her. She also politely told me that I was always very hot and had sweated a lot. Thanks mate I remember thinking, but hoped that I'd been polite to her! I then looked at the equipment and implements that she had wheeled into my room. I knew I was in for a swallowing session, but mistakenly thought the tools were for my mouth. Wrong again!

The doctor explained that they were going to test the strength of my throat muscles. I would be given small amounts of liquid on a spoon, then they would progress to yoghurt and finally to small pieces of bread with cream cheese on top. "Fine, bring it on, doc," I told him. The trolley with the equipment was brought close to my wheelchair. I transferred myself into it and looked at the small black and white video screen with a long flexible black tube connected to it. I was tilted back slightly in my chair and the various culinary delights were placed on my tray in front of me. The feeding tube was still in my left nostril and after more than seven weeks in-situ, I was used to it, despite it being the constant irritation in my throat. The doctor then explained that the black tube containing a video camera would be inserted into my right nostril! *Hey no*, I thought, *do they need to use every bloody orifice here!* I was asked to move my head further back, very much like on a dentist's chair and the tube was fed into my nostril. "Swallow. Keep swallowing," the doc said as he fed the tube expertly into my nose. He stopped and told me to look up. I now had a white plastic tube, discoloured to a rusty brown in my left nostril and a thicker black tube in my right nostril. I wanted to laugh. Here I was conversing with two people. I had two tubes stuck up my nose and it must surely have looked bizarre, if not comical but nothing other than seriousness came back from both of them. I looked at the screen, but could only think of the scene with the stammering Michael Palin in the film *A Fish Called Wanda* where he appears with a thick cut chip up each nostril. I wanted to say, "Come on guys laugh. I must look an absolute bugger." I found it difficult to avoid giggling and pulled my attention away from Michael Palin on the big screen to the small black and white one in front of me. I could see what looked like the house of horrors and the doc explained with almost comical seriousness, "It is your throat."

I was given a teaspoonful of water and asked to swallow. The water was placed on my tongue and I suddenly had to go through the thought process of what to do. *Erm, okay, position it on my tongue, move my tongue back and then … well, swallow.* I tried and the water seemed to disappear, whilst the house of horrors convulsed, contracted and then shot back to its original position. A stethoscope was taken to ascertain whether the water had entered my stomach or my lungs. All seemed well and we practised this with more liquid. We then moved onto the yoghurt. It was bliss, the first liquid for eight weeks that I could taste in my mouth because the cannula had been removed the day before and now had my sense of taste and smell back. The yoghurt went down okay, but I struggled at first with the solid food. It was just strange to have something in my mouth and I really had to dig deep in my static memory banks to remember what to do with it. The camera doesn't lie and I was concerned that the two comedians might not pass me as fit to swallow. I was wrong and they told me that I was fine! *Yoh.* The camera was extracted, much to my relief and then the speech therapist proceeded to pull and pull the stomach tube out. It is really a very strange sensation, especially as it moves up the back of your throat and then finally down your nostril, full of green-brown grunge. The feeling of relief when it was removed was superb and I was suddenly tube free! No more breathing or feeding tubes, the catheter had gone the week before and it was two weeks since I'd had a drip. I was now well and truly free of all equipment and living unaided. A very nice feeling!

I was immediately allowed solid food and a lunch tray was wheeled into my room. I was just about capable of holding my knife and fork, but not very skilled, much like a young child. The nursing staff recognised this and cut up the large piece of meat for me. I then hungrily ate my first solid meal in several weeks with a huge virtual smile on my face. I was smarting from the tubes and very happy. I was no longer a nostril virgin, but had no desire to ever have anything stuck up my nose again!

The Doctors

I must unfortunately report that not many doctors caught my attention and made me feel that they were really on top of their game. During my time in Bonn, I only saw the doctors occasionally. During a normal stay in the hospital, the doctor or doctors make their rounds sometime during the day and one has the opportunity to speak with them every day. This was not the case in Bonn. A doctor was present on the ward twenty fours a day and he or she was consulted for any medical decisions, but I would very often go for several days without seeing them. When I did see them, they seemed to be strangely out of their depth or they made the wrong call. One time I was in my wheelchair talking to my visitor, Pia. I was not on my life support and started to cough and then to hyperventilate. Pia could see I was in some distress and she went to call a nurse. The nearest person passing in the corridor was Dr.Mertz. He came in and I was starting to feel weak and struggling for air. He looked at me then at my monitor and seemed frozen by indecision. Pia explained that I'd been talking without any problem and then had rapidly deteriorated. Still seeking answers in the equipment, he did nothing. A nurse then entered and immediately recognised that I was not breathing enough oxygen. I was rapidly transferred to my bed, hooked up to the life support and the panic was very quickly over. The doctor had not reacted, but the nurse knew what to do; this was all too often the case.

Earlier on I wrote about the problems I had with the new nasal feeding tube that irritated my throat. In my opinion, the doctor made the wrong call and prescribed unnecessary anti-nausea drugs to stop me being sick. I wasn't nauseous; it was because the tube in my throat was making me gag.

When on the normal ward in Bonn I came across another problem that had nothing to do with medical skills and everything to do with the ridiculous bureaucracy associated with the medical profession. I'd been in the hospital for more than ten weeks and wanted to make a claim to my insurance company. I asked the duty doctor to write a covering letter to the company and he readily agreed. A week later, after hearing nothing from the company I called them and was told that my doctor had not yet sent the required letter. I challenged him and he told me he had indeed dictated the letter and passed it to the typing pool. He told me apologetically, "Unfortunately, it has not come back yet from the typing pool." What other kind of profession today works on these lines where the doctor is waiting for somebody to type up his report more than a week later?

However much the nurses were in control of the day-to-day medical decisions, they of course had to refer to the doctors for the extra shot of drugs, for the amount of medication that was required, and for any vital changes in my treatment. I have to be honest though and say that I very often struggled to connect with the doctors. However, one doctor I did connect with was Dr. Meyer. A Registrar neurologist, probably in his early forties and looked to be very fit. He had a quiet, practised manner and talked me through the tests I had with him. He seemed to understand and empathise with me and I was impressed with his experience of GBS. I suppose that because it is such a seldom seen illness, only very few doctors have some detailed experience of it. He was one of them, so I was pleased to talk to him when we met in his office in my eleventh week in the hospital. I was able to propel myself there in my wheelchair and could converse verbally without any problems. However, I was not able to move any facial muscles and had not yet taken any steps. His office was on the third floor and a welcome escape from the noise and constant poor health so evident in the rehabilitation area on the ground and lower ground floors. I knocked on his door and went in. We shook hands and exchanged pleasantries. I sat in my chair and he moved closer to my height by sitting in front of me. This was always a good sign. When somebody stands and you are in a wheelchair, you feel intimated, almost childlike. An experienced and sensitive medical professional will always take themselves down to the height of their patient. This is the correct way to talk to a person in a wheelchair — eye contact should be at the same level. It is a simple but very effective form of respect. Incidentally, the next time you fly with an Asian airline, observe the cabin staff if they are called to a passenger. If they are engaged in a conversation that appears to be more than a request for a drink, they will crouch down and talk to the person at eye level.

He confirmed that I had a very serious form of GBS and that I should not expect any quick or significant improvements in my condition. He then told me he would be doing an EMG (electro-myograph) test on my arms, legs and face. The test involved sticking two needles in the same part of my anatomy (face, arms, and legs). With the needles in place, he would induce a signal through one of them via his expensive looking equipment and measure the time it took to reach the sensor attached to the other needle. Essentially this involved passing a mild electric current to the first needle which then travelled along the nerves in my body and out through the second. The equipment could calculate the speed of the signal transfer provided the distance between the two needles was known. Bizarrely the distance was measured with a simple tape measure, which seemed very incongruous next to the hyper expensive kit in his room. It sounds complicated, but in fact was a very simple experiment. When the results were compared to a healthy person, it would give an accurate indication of the amount of the nerve or nerves that were working. I'd understood the physics, so told him to get on with it.

Two extremely thin needles, similar to acupuncture ones were removed from their sterilised packets. One was placed at a shallow angle into my forehead — *ouch!* The second was placed at a similar shallow angle into my top lip. *For fuck sake that one hurt.* Looking like a piercing victim, the signal electrode was connected to the needle in my forehead and the sensor to the one on my lip. A current was applied and my forehead twitched. There was no reaction on the sensor. The current was turned up and my forehead twitched more violently. Again there was no reaction. It was then yanked up further and I was wincing with pain, but still nothing. He then started twisting and moving the sensor needle in my top lip. *Youuch!* It hurt and was devastatingly uncomfortable. No reaction whatsoever. The conclusion was that my facial nerves were severely affected and that no signals were reaching the muscles. Consequently, the prognosis for a recovery of nerve activity was very poor. The same tests were carried out in my arms and legs. My arms revealed that the nerve signals were travelling at about half the normal rate, which indicated I had progressed significantly over the preceding weeks. In contrast, my legs only registered about a ten percent speed, which meant that I had a lot more recovering to do if I was to walk again.

I left him and we kept in touch whenever we met up during my final five weeks in the hospital. He was one of the very few doctors that impressed me with his skill and patient manner. The essential difference he showed was the dignity and respect he afforded me. This is not a medical, but a social skill that seems to be sadly lacking in doctors, as they tended all too often to disappear up their own self-important backside.

Chapter 12 — Family and Friends

The week before I entered the hospital, Fiona was really struggling with a very bad case of the flu. We were both ill in bed over the weekend but I was able to drag myself to work on the Monday. On Tuesday, Fiona woke up and told me she was in desperate pain from her back. She tried to move but screamed. I helped her up, but she clutched her lower back and told me in no uncertain terms that we needed to get to the doctor as soon as possible. I had no idea what the problem was, but it was not the time to argue. She needed help.

The doctors' surgery was a five-minute drive away. The car journey was excruciating for Fiona as she tried to find a position of comfort in the seat. We presented ourselves at the reception and Fiona begged me in English to get some pain relief for her. She was now crying uncontrollably. The receptionist ignored her and completed the usual formalities, finally telling us to take a seat in the waiting room. Fiona exploded, refused to talk to the receptionist and told me that she could not sit down, she needed to lie down and she needed help NOW! Unfazed, the receptionist carried on and I had to negotiate with her to get a bed to lay Fiona down on. After recognising the seriousness of her condition, our wish was granted and I led Fiona into an examination room. Once again I pleaded with the nursing staff to get the doctor to a background chorus of sobs from the bed behind me. Eventually Doctor Wagner came and after a series of questions and his examination he diagnosed a possible slipped disc. He administered a pain killing injection in her back and prescribed some very strong pain killers. An x-ray was arranged and she was told to rest and take it easy. The immediate problem was over and we both returned home. Fiona went back to bed and I carried onto work where the Ibuprofen helped me get through another day, despite feeling lousy.

Four days later I was in a coma and fighting for my life. The shock of being woken up at 1:50 in the morning by a doctor telling her that I'd stopped breathing would have been too much for most people to cope with. But Fiona is made from extremely strong stuff and is much tougher than I am. She contacted our friends Pia and Jörg and organised the kids to go to friends and made plans to spend time with me in the hospital. When I was in the coma, she put her own health problems aside and was at my bedside for hours every day. Her own life was now effectively on hold. She directed all her efforts towards me, hoping that I would pull through, because in those first few days, this was most definitely not a certainty.

It was bad for me, but my family had to cope with daily life as well as the stress of separation and not knowing how my condition would develop. Three weeks into my illness, it went from bad to worse for Fiona, and it hit Alexander and Francesca hard. She was diagnosed with a slipped disc and was told to go immediately into hospital for an operation on her back! She had to make arrangements for the kids. Pia and Jörg and Andrea and Stefan were wonderful and took in Alexander and Francesca. Clothes were washed and prepared, bags packed, timetables and routines sorted out. School was informed and Fiona even found time to go in and explain our situation to the head and the classroom teachers.

Ever resourceful, Fiona checked into her hospital in Düsseldorf and then somehow found time to get down to Bonn to see me before she went under the knife. I only vaguely remember her arriving and telling me. Frankly though, I was not with it and do not have any recollection of the ten days that I did not see Fiona or the kids.

Our lives as a family were now on hold. I was on life support in intensive care. Fiona was having serious back surgery, which necessitated a ten-day stay in the hospital plus a six-week convalescence, during which she could not drive (a trip to Bonn was impossible unless somebody drove her). Alexander and Francesca were staying with dear friends but had no parents on hand to comfort them. To cap it all, I was self-employed and had recently started a business. I was the sole breadwinner and the livelihood of the family was directly related to my health. It was a desperate situation, but as life kept on throwing more and more grief towards us, family and friends would compensate with yet more practical support and help, filling Fiona and I with huge amounts of gratitude. It was human nature at its very best.

I was unfortunately not there to help and support Fiona through her surgery. Whilst nobody wants to stay in a hospital, her ten-day stay was some relief from the stress of having to worry about me. She'd been constantly organising her days around visiting me, or asking others so as to give her some time off. The phone at home had not stopped ringing as family and friends called to ask for an update or offering to help. My business was also a huge worry for her. I was the sole signatory for all official documents, so legally nothing could be signed. Fiona was then thrust into my business life, having to answer questions from the two staff in my office, trying to reassure them that they would have a job in the future (she hoped) and all this whilst running a family and not knowing if I would survive or be permanently handicapped. Consequently, in comparison to all this, hospital was a bit of light relief. Quite frankly she was a tower of strength and she prevailed where many would have gone under with the stress. It made my recovery a lot easier.

Alexander and Francesca struggled with my illness. It is probably no surprise to report that they both failed their school years and had to repeat them. Instead of school showing an understanding of their plight, they showed such a cruel, cold indifference that was borne most probably out of stupid ignorance more than animosity. Sadly, it is a damningly poor trait of human nature that when someone is faced with adversity, many people are unable to actually address that person or to offer any positive action. It is the "crossing the road" syndrome — easier to avoid the situation and pretend it is not there than to confront it and offer help or support. I am not sure why people react like this, but I suppose it is that they feel uncomfortable. A very clever person once told me several years ago that when we are faced with this situation and we do not really know what to say — the best thing is to say, "I don't know what to say." Try it, it works every time. This usually promotes conversation and the initial difficulty is overcome and generally a conversation ensues. Unfortunately, one of the (allegedly) best academic schools in Düsseldorf and worse one that is controlled by the Church "crossed the road" and left my kids to struggle and sink. I will never forgive them for this.

With no support from school and both parents in the hospital, my kids were really on their own in a very uncertain world. Alexander was fourteen, Francesca only twelve. They both faced it in different ways. Alexander was that little bit older and saw the situation with a great deal of angst and worry. He took it upon himself to assume the alpha male role in the family and focused his attention on making sure Fiona was okay and doing practical things like cutting the grass and helping with the shopping. He was very fortunate in that he'd recently joined a youth group in Düsseldorf which was run by a very caring leader Stu and his wife. The group is church supported but non-denominational and its aim is to provide a safe environment for third-culture kids. A third culture kid is generally from an internationally mobile family. The parents could be from one or two different countries. The child may have been born in another country and he or she could be living in a third country. This mobility can outwardly seem like an enormous opportunity for the Facebook generation of today, but in reality it often leads to a huge feeling of insecurity and a challenge to oneself of "who am I". The youth group recognised this and set up in Düsseldorf, allowing kids of vastly different national and religious backgrounds to meet, share, and support each other, all under the superb leadership of Stu. The time Alexander spent at the group meetings were a stress release valve from the dreadful situation at home and allowed him, however briefly, to forget the troubles that he and the family were having. Stu also counselled Alexander, offering a shoulder to cry on and an adult friend to "offload" to. He did a superb job and navigated him through the minefield of our illnesses and hospital stays. When I was able to talk to him two months after entering hospital, he'd matured by two years into a confident, caring, and thoughtful lad.

Francesca was much younger at only twelve. The group did not appeal to her and so she didn't have the luxury of a Stu to talk or escape to, preferring instead to tackle it on her own. On the first day of my illness in the Clinic she walked into my room and the sight of her father lying there shook her to the core. Her beautifully large eyes were usually so full of expression and warmth. On that day the warmth was replaced with fright and never in my life have I seen such an expression of fear. I wanted to lean over and comfort her. I wanted to tell her that it would be okay, but GBS did not allow me this wish before it strangled me.

I cannot imagine how traumatic the whole episode must have been for Alexander and Francesca. You want to be there to protect your kids, to provide for and look after them. Suddenly, they had to go from youngsters and turn into young carers for Fiona and me. They had to see me on life support in the hospital, help Fiona at home after her back operation and perhaps the ultimate indignity, take me to the toilet. Both of them had no idea if I would recover and if we would have any money in the future. This was far too much for any young kid to handle. They both tried in different ways to cope with the situation, with Alexander turning to practical help and Francesca showing that she loved us by producing wonderful presents for Easter. Without any prompting, she put together three photos in a frame with a picture of me, one of Fiona and her sister Gillian, and a family shot of the four of us on holiday in 2003. She'd captured her entire family in that frame and presented it to me as a present. She must have been so scared and obviously didn't want to lose us. The photo still hangs in my office at home and I have looked at it many times with a great deal of pride while writing this story.

Sometimes we hesitate about asking for help in order to avoid appearing weak, stupid, or helpless. In our case, Fiona had absolutely no other choice but to ask for help. She first activated the support on Sunday 13th February after being told I'd stopped breathing. *How on earth do you cope with that?* But, my wife is so strong, so practical, and a rock in turbulent times. I don't think if you asked her she would describe herself like this, but I've witnessed her in times of utmost adversity and she copes with it all! After calling Pia and Jörg then Bernie and Dennis in Brussels, a massive operation then swung into place. Pia helped Fiona with emotional and practical support. Jörg helped with my business and all the myriad of details that need to be organised in Germany when it is not clear if a patient may die or indeed may be incapacitated for the rest of their life.

My business was only fifteen months old. I had two staff, plus a partner with several staff in Taiwan, many customers, and a turnover of around €1mio to deal with. Fiona and I had deliberately agreed when I'd set up the business that we would not (could not) work together. This suited us both, but in this time of crisis, my staff turned to

Fiona for help and advice. It was far too much for her to cope with, so Jörg stepped in to steady the ship. It was a stupendously unselfish act for a friend in need and one that I will be eternally grateful for. He went to the office talked to the staff, organised meetings with my partner, and generally saw that the company was still on course. A very significant problem was that nobody else in the company had the authority to sign any legal documents such as invoices. A meeting was then organised with a Notary, whereby Fiona had to give consent to transfer the power of attorney for the company's legal signature to Jörg. This was just one of the many problems that he sorted out and that Fiona was faced with whilst I was oblivious in my hospital bed.

For the seven weeks I was in the intensive care in Bonn, somebody visited me every single day. It was a huge logistical exercise coordinated by Fiona and one that I greatly appreciated. She could not come every day as she was unable to drive, so family and friends rallied round to organise a lift for her, or to shop for the family, provide cooked meals, take the kids to their activities and to just be generally on hand to offer help. When Fiona came out of the hospital, her sister Gillian travelled over from New Zealand to help and to be with her. A great act of generosity as Gillian herself was suffering from cancer (she unfortunately passed away in November 2008) and was not a well person. She stayed for two weeks and came to see me several times. Sometimes alone, sometimes with the family and it was always a joy to see her, as she seemed to be unaffected by the gravity of my situation. She was totally at ease and happy to just talk to me, which was in stark contrast to many visitors who often froze when they saw how bad I was. I guess this was because she herself was ill and she knew she just had to get on with it. I would like to believe that having been seriously ill myself, I would also be more relaxed when visiting a sick person, but I suspect that Gillian was much better than I will ever be. As a special treat she massaged my feet, which was absolute bliss. Normally, I am so ticklish and I can't bear anybody touching my feet, but GBS had robbed me of most of the feeling so a massage was a wonderful treat, especially when carried out with menthol moisturising cream to combat my dry skin.

When Gillian eventually had to leave to go back to New Zealand, it was emotional for all of us. Our friend Fiona then came from the UK to stay for a further week. She drove Fiona, cooked for the family and even had her husband Iwan mowing the lawn! He's probably not picked up a lawnmower since! Bernie and Dennis came many times from Brussels; they visited me, looked after the kids and provided great emotional comfort for Fiona. Pia and Jörg did so much and took in Francesca. Andrea and Stephan were constant visitors to Bonn and looked after Alexander whilst Fiona was in hospital. My business partner David in Taiwan visited me three times and made sure that Fiona was okay. Christian and Andrea, our neighbours, did a lot and drove me back to the hospital after my visits home. Noah visited from the UK twice. Hans came many times to Bonn and I enjoyed our long chats. Lars and Ludger, two neighbours came to see me. Mark made the journey over from the UK. My sister Lesley came over from Manchester with her husband,

Brian, and looked after me for a weekend in Bonn whilst the family took a well-earned break in Spain. Nick drove over in his new Aston Martin, visited me for two hours and then drove back! Mick and Máire lent me a portable DVD player and brought Fiona several times to Bonn. The British Women's Club ladies and friends of Fiona, Ros, Caroline, Angela, and many others provided meals and shopped for the family. I was overwhelmed with cards and get well messages which was incredibly comforting. Last but not least, my customers supported me by continuing to order products, keeping the ever resourceful Renate in my office extremely busy and ensuring that I had a livelihood. To all the others that I have forgotten to mention, I apologise, but I would just like to say that when every one of you visited me, it was magical and every time it helped me get through the long motionless days.

Chapter 13 — Roommates

I had several roommates in Bonn, two on the intensive care ward and four on the normal one. I started off with somebody whose name disappeared into the morphine-induced haze of my first week. I can only remember that he coughed an awful lot. A deep rasping cough that was loud enough to annoy me and drown out the noise from the array of machines that were keeping us both alive.

I guess I was about five days into my stay in Bonn when Thomas came in and told me that I was to be moved to a room on my own. My fellow patient had contracted some highly contagious bug — I guessed it was MRSA, and he was put in isolation, together with another poor sod that had the same problem. The last thing I needed was yet more problems, so I was happy as my life support equipment, tubes and bed were moved to the sanctuary of a single room. The discovery of the bug was always a trial for staff and patient alike. I'd seen how the medical staff had to gown up and literally scrub everything clean. Any person entering the room had to take precautions and wear gowns, which cannot have been easy for people visiting their loved ones.

I very quickly got used to being on my own. It was better for my visitors, as they could stay as long as they wanted without disturbing anybody. That room was my home for more than four weeks and saw me through the darkness of the worst excesses of GBS and into the first light of recovery. To all intents and purposes, I'd started a new life there. The forty-seven years before GBS were history. I had to get used to living the rest of my life in a different body and those initial weeks were spent coming to terms with it. I was then told I had to move out and share with somebody else. It threw me off my stride because I'd become institutionalised and very averse to change. As with all aspects of my treatment, I had to take it on the chin and get on with it. Each day was a struggle and so hard, therefore a change of room was really only a very minor hiccup on the long road to my goal. Nevertheless, it was a wrench as my pictures and belongings were unceremoniously removed from the walls and window ledges, all piled onto my bed and I was pushed down the corridor and into a larger room with a fellow patient.

My roommate was on the right and I was given the "berth" on the left side of the room. I only used my ventilator now at night so it was wheeled in behind me and it took up residence on my right side. My panzer wheelchair followed and my belongings were distributed around the table, also to my right. In fact, I had very few possessions with me. I wore my own T-shirts during the day, which were always loose enough so they could easily be taken off over my head with the nursing staff disconnecting me from my tubes and drips and then plugging me in once again. I also had a nice line in older T-shirts, each with a cut down the back from the collar to the bottom. I placed my arms in the sleeves and the shirt was then tucked in behind me as I lay in bed. No need then to negotiate and disconnect all the tubes into my neck and nose etc, although not very elegant.

When my bed was positioned I could look over to my roommate for the first time. He was in his seventies and half propped up in bed. His eyes watched me, but there was an empty look about them that seemed to convey only minimal understanding of the world around him. I am a little ashamed to say that I found his staring eyes quite creepy. I was pretty sure he could not understand me as I greeted him with a hello after we were left on our own together. I always said, "good morning" to him and, "hello" whenever I returned after treatment or an excursion in my wheelchair. There was never any recognition or acknowledgment, but his eyes did seem to follow me if I moved across the room in my chair. The contrast for my visitors from the single to the shared room was huge and whenever I received visitors, they spoke in a lower voice and stayed for a shorter time so as not to disturb him.

I never knew his name, but I felt so sorry for this chap who was in the twilight of his life. He had been out for a late evening walk with his dog and was hit by a car driven by a young driver while crossing the road. His head smashed onto the bonnet of the offending car, suffering severe injuries. His dog carried on home and alerted his wife who came dashing to the scene, her worst nightmare unfolding in front of her. When I first saw him in his hospital bed, he appeared to be conscious, breathing on his own and not in any obvious discomfort. His arms and legs were in traction and covered in huge bandages that must have masked severe wounds because they were dressed at least twice each day.

His wife visited him regularly. I was able to speak to her and she explained in a very matter of fact manner and in front of him, that he had most likely suffered brain damage. She was scared for their future and did not know what would happen to him. She was a lovely older lady and fate had really dealt her a cruel blow. One day when the neurologist came, I asked what would happen to him. He told me their job was to stabilise him and try and put him back on the road to physical recovery. Once that was done, he would be transferred to a normal ward for further rehabilitation. If there were no signs of neurological activity, he would be confined to permanent care in a vegetative state. A frightening thought.

I was now in my eighth week of recovery and in my sixth week in Bonn. I was able to talk during the day as I was not connected to the ventilator. Food was still administered via the tube in my nose, so I still had no sense of smell or taste. I was able to sit myself up and shuffle on my bottom to the end of my bed and transfer myself to the wheelchair. I was not able to move my legs and had to lift my feet on and off the foot-rests in the chair. *Hell, life was looking up and compared to the other nine people on the ward, including my roommate, I was extremely well.* Consequently, I did not want to be reminded of the utter seriousness and in some cases hopelessness of my fellow patients around me. I was on the up, but here in my room was somebody that was definitely on the way down. So I often asked for the screens that we had in our room to be placed in front of him as he was being tended to, or just when I lay awake in the room. It was simply a way for me to get away from the staring lifeless eyes that reminded me of the dark days that I'd emerged from.

At the beginning of my tenth week, I was moved from the all-consuming care of intensive care ward to a normal ward. Luckily, I was put into a room of my own. There was space for two beds, but I was alone. It was much larger and less personal. The staff only came in when it was necessary and the nursing care was much less hands on. I was now starting to develop a more independent existence within the confines of the institution, which did seem daunting at first. I had to work with schedules and appointments and get myself to them on time. It was a big step and one that left me feeling bewildered and confused. I kicked myself into action and just got on with it. I was determined to get into a normal routine as quickly as possible, but still had to rely on the nursing staff to help me shower in the morning.

Week 10 in my room on the normal ward. *I was alone for a few days. Note the extreme weight loss and the huge plaster on my neck covering the tracheotomy hole. Whenever I sneezed, air would expel through the hole in my neck — most disconcerting.*

My solitary peace was disturbed when Damien was wheeled into my room and his bed filled the berth closest to the bathroom. He was a twenty-year-old lad that had been involved in a traffic accident, hitting his head on the windscreen and being thrown out of the car. Remarkably, he had few external injuries but appeared to me to have brain damage. He was not really able to talk and had difficulty controlling his limbs. Once again I was confronted with a desperately sad situation, Damien was so young and a tragic accident had cost him the quality of life that we all take for granted. It was quite heart-breaking to see his friends visiting and he struggled to recognise them. His mother was at her wits' end and she would often turn to me and ask my opinion on how he'd been earlier in the day or the previous night. We talked frequently and on more than one occasion she cried the desperate tears of a mother who'd seen the life ripped out of her son. She saw that I was on the mend and I believe she tried to seek answers in my illness, desperately hoping that Damien would also improve. It was difficult, but I had to put her straight about my condition and how it was not a result of an accident. Strangely, I never got emotionally upset about any of my roommates' plights. I guess most of my energy was taken up in focusing selfishly on my own recovery. I didn't seem to have room in my heart to take on the emotional troubles of others.

On our 3rd day together, Damien had a very restless night and was in obvious discomfort. He ripped out his catheter during the night and was moaning in pain. The nurses came, got him sorted out and he was eventually sedated. Exhausted, we both then got some sleep. In the morning he seemed worse and the stench coming from him was quite repulsive. I got myself dressed, transferred myself to my wheelchair and went to call the nurses. On my return, I watched him as he continued to writhe about on his bed and he seemed to be terribly distressed. The nurses came and pulled back his covers. His bed was soiled and he'd once again pulled out the catheter. A doctor was called and eventually an x-ray and blood tests were ordered. Within two hours everybody was back, including Damien's mother. The poor lad had a burst appendix and he was rushed off to theatre for an emergency operation. I was alone again.

Unfortunately, it only lasted one night. The very next day Mr. Z was wheeled into my room. He was a pleasant looking chap of sixty with rosy red cheeks and what appeared to be a very healthy complexion. The two nurses fixed everything and introduced him to me. For the third time, across two different wards, I could see that my new roommate was not really aware of what was going on around him. He was groaning and staring into space and he reminded me so much of the seriously mentally handicapped people that I'd seen as an eight year old when I'd visited my grandfather in a horrible mental hospital in North Manchester. Mr Z had suffered a heart attack and had stopped breathing for several minutes. He'd been revived and appeared to be in reasonable physical condition, but the lack of oxygen had resulted in brain damage.

I was able to cope with these patients, but the sight, sounds, and smells of very ill people gets you down after a while, especially when they rob you of sleep. Mr. Z did that all the time as he groaned his way through the night. He also managed to pull his catheter out three times! The next day, he was taken to his rehabilitation classes and I did mine. I'd finished first and was in the room catching up on some work at my desk. He was wheeled in and two nurses lifted him onto the bed. They then did something that surprised the hell out of me. Four belt type straps with huge buckles were produced and attached to each wrist and ankle. He was then literally strapped to his bed. He was able to move each arm and leg to some degree but not enough to get at his catheter or to fall out of bed. It was 6:15 in the evening! The nurses left him and I could not help but think of straightjackets and Victorian mental asylums. Yet, here I was in 2005 watching a brain damaged and very bewildered man tugging at his straps and to my ears, groaning his disapproval. I wasn't happy and couldn't help but think that the staff had only done it to make their lives easier.

I kept shaking my head and looking at this poor man. I'd been a prisoner in my own body but I was now able to rediscover the joys of moving again as nerves reconnected. Here was a man that was already a prisoner in his own body and had now been made a prisoner to his bed by the staff who were supposed to be helping him. It seriously bothered me and I'd made up my mind to ask the night shift for a knock out sleeping pill so that I could get some sleep despite the moaning and groaning beside me. Just after 9:00 p.m. two lovely nurses at the beginning of their shift came into the room. Without any questions and the least amount of fuss, they told me that I was moving to another room where the patient was not as ill as Mr. Z and I would be able to rest more. It was a relief and I was very thankful as my belongings were piled onto my bed and wheeled down the corridor to the end room.

My new roommate was a young Turkish lad of twenty-eight called Mehmet. He'd had a tumour on his spine that was successfully removed; it was a serious operation that could have left him totally paralysed. Fortunately it went well and he was able to walk and move around; only bending down was difficult. He was the first roommate I could talk with and we exchanged pleasantries as I made myself at home in my new room. I relaxed as I realised I was finally rooming with somebody who was physically in much better shape than me. I got my sleeping tablet from the nurses and I soon drifted off.

The first problem I noticed was the earth-shattering snoring erupting from Mehmet's bed. It was quite unbelievably loud and one I was certain would wake him up. Unfortunately, it didn't and I searched around in the bed-side drawer for my earplugs — essential equipment for rooming with the three previous roommates. The earplugs worked and I made it back to sleep again but my peace was only short-lived. At 4:30a.m. Mehmet was up and out of bed, standing on his towel facing towards me and chanting! I searched for my glasses to see what he was doing, desperately hoping he wasn't chanting at me or wanting anything from me. He had his reading lamp on, his eyes were closed and he was praying to Mecca — at 4:30 in the naffin' morning. *Yikes, if it wasn't ruddy groaning it was chanting.* With absolutely no consideration for me, he just carried on in an almost trance-like state. What could I do? Once again in my recovery it was either get on with it or let it get you down. The latter was negative and I am not wired that way. So, I popped my ear plugs back in, they were always falling out and I forced myself back to sleep.

I got to know Mehmet quite well. He seemed a decent enough lad who had worked in a warehouse. Due to his tumour he was invalided off and no longer employable.

Curiously, this didn't seem to be a problem for him and when he proudly told me that he got €980 per month unemployment money and his apartment was paid for I begun to understand why. He had a wife and young son. His wife was chosen for him, by her family in Germany. They had met a couple of times, prior to their marriage in Turkey, got married and then he came to Germany. He had no qualifications and little opportunity of getting a job. However, €980 per month and an apartment was a lot better than he could expect in his home country.

I've had very little contact with Muslims but have observed from afar that it is very much a male domain. I have no idea if this is better or worse than my domain, but I knew with my struggles in the hospital, I would have never been able to come through them without the constant love, support, and attention of Fiona. Mehmet had come into hospital not knowing if his tumour was malignant or benign. He was also told that without the operation he would be paralysed from the waist down. It was a complex procedure and there was a fifty-fifty chance he could be paralysed afterwards. It must have been a stressful time and one that I would have found difficult to cope with on my own. However, in the three weeks I was with him, I never saw his wife. I just thought it was really very sad.

We managed to get on during our time together. His snoring disturbed me, as did his chanting five times a day, but hell I'd had worse problems to deal with, so I never mentioned anything, preferring instead to keep the peace. I didn't have an awful lot to do in the evenings after my treatment sessions and was able to observe Mehmet more closely. I began to notice his personal hygiene and it became a constant source of fascination. He always washed his feet before praying, but I never once saw him change his clothes. Admittedly, he may have had five different identical pairs of grey sweat pants and five white T-shirt vests, but there was no evidence of this. My sense of smell was back, but I never detected any body odour. Bizarrely, he sprayed his under arm deodorant on every day, but always onto his T-shirt — arms raised, but never onto his skin! He then set about beating himself with his towel, slapping his back and chest and readying himself for his prayer sessions. I am not sure if all this had any roots in his religion or he was just a bit strange. I tend to think the latter was true.

We got into conversations about the Koran and I was genuinely interested in his devotion, but to be honest, not when his praying kept waking me up. He told me he read the Koran every day but it was the abridged version. He offered to get me an English copy, which I politely declined.

Mehmet was not in any rush to go home. He'd been in for five weeks and was trying to convince the doctors that he should stay for another week. I was angry about this because it was at the same time as I was being told by my health insurance company that I had to go home. They simply refused to pay for anymore treatment! I was unable to walk and had severe difficulty living a normal life. To my eyes, Mehmet looked perfectly healthy and there was no need for him to stay. He tried his best with the doctor but common sense prevailed and he was sent home. Once again there was no sign of his wife. I felt sad at this, but he was perfectly happy.

My last and final roommate was Nick from Romania. He was sixty-three years old and a local restaurant owner. He got around in a wheelchair since a stroke had left him paralysed down his left side. We got on well and watched the Champions League Cup Final together when Liverpool went down 3-0 to AC-Milan and then won the game on penalties. It was a great game that we both really enjoyed. He was shocked by the severity of his disability after the stroke, but the physios were working wonders and he was on the mend. We spent just over two weeks together and in that time developed a bond with each other. We were never going to be best friends, but my final roommate was a joy to be with and he didn't keep me awake at night by groaning, snoring, or chanting! Finally, a result!

Chapter 14 — Personal Hygiene

Lack of dignity is one of the most challenging issues when you are seriously ill in hospital. For me this was best illustrated by my total lack of independence in personal hygiene issues. For those who know me well, I could best be described as someone who feels the heat. Or to put it bluntly, I sweat a lot. Put this together with a well-heated room, huge amounts of medication, masses of blankets to prevent me rolling onto my back, and it was a recipe for mass perspiration. The sweat would roll off my forehead and down my face. I was bathed in it, making me feel more anxious, causing me to perspire more, especially when visitors arrived! Logic told me that I must absolutely stink, but I had no sense of smell. The only way I could actually tell was to watch my visitors and hope they would not recoil in horror or collapse on the floor clutching their noses as they came close to me!

That first shower Thomas gave me was a huge sense of relief and afterwards I was pleased to present myself to my visitors in a fresh state. Yet I was still dependent on the nurses. The same went for shaving, cleaning my teeth and washing the little amount of hair I have. Personal hygiene is not exactly of great importance in the grand scheme of things — when you are totally paralysed and being kept alive by machines. However, it was unbelievably important to me and I would wager a large sum of money that the vast majority of people in my position would have felt the same. I knew I was ill, but that was no excuse to smell like a rugby player's jock strap or to look like a down and out. No, I wanted to present myself with the same pride and dignity that I always do. The problem was that I had no control of how I was presented or how I looked after myself, always relying on the nurses to do it for me. I was, therefore, excited to try to shave myself, or to clean my own teeth, and as the dexterity and strength came back into my fingers and arms I was able to do so on a regular basis.

After the catheter was removed, I started to regain some control over my personal hygiene. I could move around in bed, even assist the nurses when getting into and out of my wheelchair. Crucially, I could talk and was off the life support machine during the day, meaning that I was much stronger and had more bodily control. To my huge relief, all of this meant that the Pampers came off and I was rid of them. I would like to spare you the less savoury details but I cannot recall any problems associated with my solid waste. I guess that since I was fed on liquids, the resultant output was also only ever liquid or semi-solid, which was easy to expel whilst lying down, certainly I never felt it. Once I had started on small amounts of solid food, my insides reacted by solidifying the waste and I was in agony. I spoke to Nicole, my duty nurse about it and she brought me a bedpan. I'd heard the expression bedpan before, but had fortunately never had any reason to have seen or use one. I was amazed to see her bring what looked like a large deep stainless steel frying pan, complete with lid, into my room. She lifted the covers and asked me to lift up my bum. She moved my gown aside and slipped the pan, without the lid, under me. I lowered myself onto the cold metal — wincing as I touched it and tried to adjust myself into a comfortable position whilst Nicole replaced the covers. I looked at her with enormous incredulity and wanted to say, *How, on earth, am I supposed to pooh in this thing?* She read my face and told me, "Just push and try to use it. If you have any problems, call me."

She left me to it and I was lying prone in bed with a large pan under my bum. I was in agony from the contents in my stomach and I needed to rid myself of them. I pushed and writhed on that damn pan, but nothing, absolutely nothing moved. I tried and tried for at least half an hour, shifting positions, thinking about other things to try to trick my body into forgetting the pain and then using all my energy to push as hard as I could. I felt my face go beetroot red and my eyes nearly pop out of their sockets as I pushed, but to no avail. I had to stop. Breathing deeply and feeling exhausted, I pressed the alarm button for Nicole to come. I told her that I'd not been successful and it was removed.

As usual, my mate Thomas came to my rescue. It must have been the next day and I told him that I was really struggling and needed to have the bedpan again. "Martin, don't worry. It is not a problem. I will take you to the toilet." These words were like the sweetest pudding dripping with hot chocolate, honey, and coated in sugar. So welcome. Thomas readied me for the transfer to my wheelchair and he then wheeled me into the bathroom and placed me in front of the toilet. I stared at the grab rails on either side of it and at the welcome sight of a seat and not a ruddy bedpan. It was to be the first time I'd used a disabled toilet and as with so many other things in my illness and recovery, I had no idea what to do.

Thomas positioned me at about forty-five degrees to the toilet and applied the brakes on my chair. These simple implements are your safety belt on a wheelchair and you learn very quickly to apply them at all times. "I'll leave you. There is an emergency button. Call me if you need me." Once again, Thomas demonstrated an amazing amount of nursing experience and skill. He instinctively knew that I was ready to work at sorting myself out in the toilet. He knew that it was best to leave me on my own and in doing so he gave me back my dignity.

I was normally dressed in very loose tracksuit bottoms — horrible shell suit type ones from Adidas that were at least a size too big. In hospital, it is always easier to have things that are too big and very baggy, essentially for comfort reasons, but also because you are constantly taking them on and off for various examinations. I had not thought about removing them in the toilet, but suddenly I was left alone and had to negotiate several actions at once. With the brakes on, I dropped down the side of the wheelchair closest to the toilet, bent down, and lifted my feet off the foot rests and placed each one squarely on the floor. My ankles were very weak and would give way if I tried to stand up, so it was arm strength that was the key to this exercise. I leant forward in my chair and grabbed the nearest u-shaped rail. It was the first time I'd lifted myself out of my chair unaided and I was a little apprehensive. I was scared of falling because I knew I would not be able to pick myself up. Heart in mouth, I summoned up the strength in my arms and lifted myself up onto my feet, paying attention never to put all my weight on my legs. I was now up but facing towards the toilet, not the ideal position when your stomach is boiling with anger and desperate to get rid of its contents. I leant onto my left arm and transferred my right hand to the grab rail on the other side. I steadied myself on my feet and then turned slowly round but always keeping one hand gripped tightly to the bars. Once facing away from the toilet with it behind me and supporting myself on the rails, I released one hand and pulled my tracksuit bottoms down. I was finally able to sit down.

What followed was relief of orgasmic proportions. It was not only a huge load off my mind, sorry for the pun, I was also immensely proud that I had taken on the significant challenge of the toilet and won. The main achievement was that I had got some of my dignity back. The relief in my bottom lasted a few moments. That of having back my independence remains with me today and like so many issues in my recovery; it was a small step that motivated me even more to take on the next challenge.

Thomas was extremely pleased with me and congratulated me on my achievements. Having done this once, I was able to take myself to the toilet whenever I needed to go. I would shuffle across my bed, transfer into my wheelchair and wheel myself to the communal toilet area. The first time I did this, I didn't tell my duty nurse, Nicole. She came into my room to find an empty bed, missing wheelchair and no sign of yours truly. She castigated me when she eventually found me in the toilet, having banged on the door to check if I was there. In my stupidity, I'd locked the door! I'd taken dignity too far and put myself in danger. Suitably chastised, I was not to do that again and was happy to stay within the rules.

Thomas and I laughed about this the next day when we met. He knew that I'd been silly, but he was also very sympathetic and understood perfectly that I was learning to live again. He helped me with my next step, too — having a shower. Unfortunately, this was still not possible on my own. He was the only nurse to offer me a shower, I guess because it was actually a lot of work for them. I was wheeled into a large walk-in shower room which had a shower head, a fold down seat and grab bars. A drain in the floor, a lone radiator and a frosted window completed the sparse room. He always turned up the radiator when we went in, so that I would not get cold. Possibly because I had shivered like a freshly poured jelly when he'd first washed me.

To have a shower I had to get out of the wheelchair by grabbing the bars and then turn round and sit on the chair. Meanwhile, Thomas changed into waterproof clogs and put on a plastic apron. My clothes were taken off and the water turned on. The shower-head was on a hose and not fixed to the wall, so Thomas had to spray me with water. I was now able to move, so could hold the bar with one hand and use the shower gel squeezed into my hand to wash myself with the other. Thomas would soap and wash my back and then help to dry me. It was bliss.

The final step towards full independence came after my first week on the normal ward. The nurses came to wake us around 7:00 when breakfast was delivered. I was able to get myself into the bathroom in my wheelchair. At the sink I could wash my face, shave and clean my teeth. The toilet was no problem but I did not have the confidence to shower myself. I would call for a nurse who would supervise me, much as Thomas had done, and wash my back. We only did this three times because I started to resent having to ask the nurses to help me. It was a chore for them and I wanted to do it on my own. On the final of the three days, I told my nurse that I was confident enough to do it on my own now and my journey back to personal hygiene independence was complete. I wasn't mobile, I had very little strength in my legs, I was confined to a wheelchair but I could take myself off to the toilet, I could wash, shower and shave myself. Life was looking up and I was beating GBS. *Who cares about money, possessions, and supposed status? Being able to go to the toilet and wipe your own bum is Dignity with a capital D.* It is a very precious gift that when we are healthy we take far too much for granted.

Chapter 15 — Wheelchair

I had a very bi-polar relationship with my wheelchair. Actually, I had two wheelchairs. The first was a tank-like contraption that was extremely heavy and had support for my neck, back, sides, and feet. It was built to support the occupant and not for speed. Then, when I was strong enough, I was given a racier model that was much lighter, which I could handle on my own. I hated the first one. I hated getting into it and out of it, I hated the pain I suffered when I was in it and I hated that it showed me how useless my body was. My racier model became my first taste of mobile independence, it was my surrogate feet and I used it to scoot around all over the place, occasionally with very dangerous turns of speed. It was as important to me as my legs.

I was only allowed into the first wheelchair when I was recovering and stronger. I knew I had to get into one but was not prepared for the trauma it gave me when I was wheeled in front of a mirror during the first outing in one. I saw myself in that chair, looking so desperately disabled and it is so deeply etched on my memory that it continues to haunt me today. My gaunt face, open mouth and dark sad eyes are all associations I have with that chair. Add to this list: pain, terror and exhaustion and you begin to understand why I had such a dark relationship with it.

My first chair, the tank, was moved into my room close to Easter. I'd started with my first trials of separation from the life support machine and I was surviving. The physiotherapists, Ralf and Monica, had worked with me on getting up and sitting on the edge of the bed. I was stronger in my core muscles so I could hold myself upright unaided. The chair was moved to the side of the bed, the brakes applied and side dropped down. I was soon to learn that the nurses had very different methods and techniques to lift me from the bed and into the chair. Some did it alone, some did it in twos. The two best ones were slight female nurses, who always transferred me on their own with the minimum of fuss and the maximum amount of skill. The worst was a nurse who very nearly dropped me, closely followed by Thomas, he always seemed to get me caught up and twisted, struggling to get a better grip and then just dumping me into the chair.

The transfer started with the nurse manoeuvring me into a seated position on the side of the bed. My useless arms hung down by my side, my legs dangled down towards the floor with feet hanging. The nurse would stand in front, facing me, one hand on my shoulder to steady me, the other checking the position of the chair. My arms were taken and placed over their shoulder as they leaned forward and bent their knees. I was told to lean forward and had to put my head on their shoulder. The nurse put their arms around me in a bear hug, straightened their legs and lifted me off the bed. A half turn was made to their right and I was then placed (or dropped) into the chair. So much for the theory, the reality was often very different. Sometimes, their grip slipped or I was in the wrong position, my catheter was caught on more than one occasion and I would get cramp in my legs as soon as my weight was lifted off the bed.

Honestly, I hated the transfer, every single time. It wasn't that I was scared or apprehensive about the pain it was simply that I was so graphically reminded how useless my body was every time it was carried out. Lying in bed with my tracksuit bottoms and running shoes on, I was not able to see my legs. With all the time I had to think between treatments and visitors, I would retreat into my head. In the virtual life I lived there, I was never paralysed. I could walk around the room, reach the cards and presents on the tables and take myself off down the corridor. My legs and arms worked perfectly and there was no reason to contest this figment of my imagination, until I was readied for a transfer. The first problem was the nurse having to place my arms on his or her shoulders. I desperately wanted to help, but was not able to do anything. Secondly and most devastatingly, as I was lifted off the bed and airborne, my legs flopped down like a rag doll with useless lifeless limbs. It was a horrifying reminder of the devastation GBS had had on my body. As I hung there in mid-air between bed and chair, I despised the bloody chair for reminding me of my predicament.

I had to endure at least a two-hour session in my chair every day. This first time was wrought with anxiety and I was preoccupied with mastering shaving and cleaning teeth, so the two hours passed without too much trouble. The second time I was transferred to the chair and simply left in the room with full view of the clock. After fifteen minutes of sitting in the same position on my backside, numbed by the hours and hours of lying in bed, I was screaming with discomfort. I tried to shift my weight but was not able to relieve the pain. I pressed my alarm button and wanted to get back into bed. It was Peter who came in and told me no. I had to sit there for two hours. In an attempt to relieve the pain, he reclined the chair so my weight was transferred through my back to the chair and at least I was able to use the new position to shift around a bit. The clock dragged and I had no stimulation other than the metronomic ticking of the hands. It was a very hard two hours that taught me a very valuable lesson about severely disabled people — if a person is not able to move, sitting in a wheelchair is very close to torture. I felt ashamed with myself because I'd never given any thought to this and had wrongly assumed that it must be a welcome relief from lying in bed. How wrong I was and how I feel for people I now see in that position.

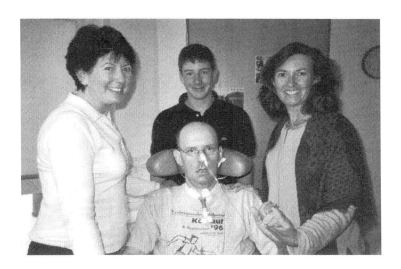

In my tank-like wheelchair with Fiona, Alexander and Gillian on the 25th of March 2005. My expressionless face hid my huge levels of anxiety. Francesca took the picture.

March 25th, Easter Saturday, was a very big date for me with my wheelchair. Spring had arrived. I was expecting Fiona, her sister Gillian, Alexander, and Francesca. Peter was caring for me, we had built up a rapport and he was pushing me to do new things. When the family arrived I was excited to hear him ask if I would like them to take me outside in my chair! *Wow,* I thought, *Yeah, let's try it,* but as usual not thinking about the organisation and the difficulties involved.

The usual horrible transfer was carried out and I was positioned in the chair. I was still connected to my feed tube and catheter, so they were hung discreetly on the side frame. The tube from the life support was removed and I was left with a short stubby tube in my neck. A small gas bottle containing oxygen was connected to the white T-valve at the end. Oxygen did not flow directly into the T-valve, but around it, so I could breathe in some pure oxygen as well as air. I was then connected to a portable blood/oxygen saturation meter. With weak lung muscles I was in constant danger of not being able to breathe in enough air, which of course contains life-giving oxygen. Hence, it was necessary for the meter. Peter dictated strict instructions to my visitors that the meter should normally read between 95 and 98 percent. If it reduced to below 85 percent, they were to bring me back immediately.

I could hear and understand all the instructions and the meter was in full view, so I could watch the display dance about as I dragged air into my lungs. In the comfort of my room the meter was at 95 to 98 percent as Peter had predicted. He patted my shoulder and told me to enjoy myself with my family. Alexander took charge of the chair and pushed me towards the door. Francesca held my hand and I had such a warm and immensely proud feeling that they were looking after me. Suddenly, I became very nervous about leaving the safety and sanctuary of my room. We were now at the door, I was two metres away from the life support machine. It was the furthest I'd been away from it since I entered hospital on 12th of February and I was scared. Fiona held my other hand as we passed through the door and turned right towards the lift. I stared at the meter as it beeped away, registering my heartbeat as well as the blood oxygen levels. We moved slowly down the corridor, passing the nurses room. A couple of staff on duty shouted out messages of encouragement as we rolled past.

Nobody could see how horribly anxious I was. The family and staff were all full of smiles and obvious joy that I had progressed so far in my recovery that I could now contemplate a journey in my chair down the corridor and outside. My thoughts were dominated instead by the distance I was away from my room and the life support machine. The meter beeped away and my heart rate went up over 100. The saturation level started to come down and it hit 92 percent. My palms started sweating and I could feel the sweat forming into beads on my forehead as we reached the lift. On my right was a massive floor to ceiling mirror and as Alexander turned me towards the lift controls I caught sight of myself in the mirror. I saw that horrible, badly paralysed Terri Schiavo image and it scared me rigid again. I hated how I looked — just so damn ill!

As Gillian pushed the lift button to take us from the third floor down to the ground floor my saturation level hit 90 percent. I noticed myself starting to breathe harder so I tried to avoid hyperventilating. The lift doors slid open and I was pushed in. Although I was surrounded by my loving family in a large modern lift it felt very claustrophobic. As the doors closed the air seemed to be so stale and it felt a lot warmer than on the corridor.

The lift jerked into life and began its slow descent to the ground floor. My saturation levels dropped to 86 percent and I tried to breathe harder. I flashed glances and clicked my tongue to try and signal to the family that we should go back — I wanted right then to crawl into the safety of my bed. Despite my desperate signalling I was not able to communicate in any intelligible way, so my pleas were ignored. We jerked to a halt and the doors opened. With that came some fresh air and the saturation went up to 88 percent. I'd passed the critical level. We moved down the corridor and I could look outside into the world I'd used to live in. The idea of entering this world had felt absolutely wonderful in my room but as I approached it, I was consumed with anxiety about what might go wrong. I felt terribly vulnerable and although the warmth of the spring sun was a very welcome relief from the stale air in my room, I wanted more than anything in the world to get back to the safety and security of my bed and my life support machine.

Alexander gently pushed me over the aluminium frame of the door and out into a small garden courtyard. The path was made up of small stones laid in a crazy paving way. My panzer chair was equipped with large wheels, but no suspension, so I felt every bump and all the unevenness. Each jolt worried me disproportionately, so much so that was not able to enjoy the journey round the garden. We stopped in the sun and Fiona could see I was obviously in distress. She asked me, "Do you want to go back?" I nodded and was wheeled ever so gently back to the lift and up to the ward. As we arrived, I was facing the lift doors and when they opened I was confronted with my reflection in the huge mirror on the opposite wall. For a split second we waited and then Alexander pushed me out and away from my image that made me shudder with horror once again.

As we went passed the nurses' office, Peter came out. My whole excursion had lasted ten minutes. He had spent forty minutes preparing me and was understandably not best pleased that I was back so soon. Fiona told him that I was very distressed and wanted to go back to bed as soon as possible. Peter looked at me with total and understandable exasperation telling me, "You are not getting back into bed now. You need to spend at least two hours in the chair." I then had the family wheel me back into my room and I struggled through the remaining hour and fifty minutes. My only consolation was that I was surrounded by my family who distracted me from the discomfort I was suffering. Eventually, I was allowed back into bed and hooked up to my life support machine. I was so relieved and I finally felt safe. It had been a hard but eventful day.

Outings in the chair eventually became less stressful, but always as painful. I became reasonably comfortable away from the ventilator, so did not need to take the oxygen with me anymore. Once in the chair, after the dreaded transfer, I was usually wheeled out onto the corridor where I could see some human activity and maybe one of the nurses would stop to talk to me. I rarely saw any other patients, other than through a hastily opened door as the staff busied themselves with their nursing activities. What I did see was not pleasant and provided a constant reminder that there were some very seriously ill people around me. I was one of the extremely lucky ones, I could look forward to a tediously slow improvement but I would eventually get better. The other nine patients on the ward would be stabilised and eventually moved to another ward, their prospects of recovery were close to zero. It was heart breaking to see. I knew I was in a bad way, but I was lucky, things would not always be like this. I was on my way back.

It was vaguely more interesting to sit on the corridor rather than in my room, but the tortuous pain of two hours in the chair had to be endured with the minimum of stimulation. It was Peter who introduced me to the leg exercise bike. He asked if I wanted to have a go on the bike, I thought, *Mmmmhh, how on earth am I going to get on a bike?* I had little to worry about. This contraption had two pedals with a motor to drive them. It was low and on wheels and placed in front of my wheelchair. My legs were moved from the foot supports of the chair and secured in the pedals on the exercise bike. The speed and time were then programmed-in and my legs started turning as the motor kicked into life. Obviously the essential difference to a normal exercise bike was the motor that turned the pedals, so moving my legs. I sat and watched as my legs circled very slowly and the counter reduced from the programmed ten minutes to zero. A very simple movement and exercise, yet it was wholly welcome. I was a frustrated amateur sportsman who could not move, never mind exercise, so this was superb. My ten minutes were up and I decided to carry on and see if I could move the pedals with my own strength. To my amazement, I was able to turn them very slowly. *Heh! I had some strength.* It was exhausting but ultimately successful.

Peter came past and noticed that I was pushing the pedals myself. He bent down by my chair (classic pose to show the patient respect) and said, "Martin, brilliant. Don't do too much. Just take it easy. I know you are determined, but take it slowly." He had seen my determination and I had recognised I'd found an exercise here that I could relate to. I wanted to walk; to do that I knew my legs needed to be stronger. I was a keen cyclist and this exercise suited me perfectly. I now had a distraction from my daily torture in the chair and I would spend as long on the exercise bike as the nurses would allow me. It was usually kept in the corridor, but after a while it was relocated to my room so that I could pedal away on my own and I could let my mind drift. One day I drifted towards sport and exercise. I was still angry that my fitness had not kept GBS at bay. Yet here I was positively enjoying the challenge of exercise and I rapidly got back into the mindset of a sportsman in training. I could see the number of revolutions that I had pushed and the time taken to do it. I made a mental note of them and pushed myself to increase it the next day. I was back in training! I knew from the years of running and triathlons that I needed discipline, I needed time and I needed strength. I was hugely elated and looked at my therapy differently. A two-hour session in the wheelchair was like a run on a cold, wet and windy night — horrible, but essential and something that needed to be done so that I could reach my target. The bike helped me and the staff could see it, especially Peter.

A few days later, probably in a reflective state, I returned to my anger with sport whilst sitting in my wheelchair outside the hospital. I looked back on the hours and hours of training, the hurt and the injuries. The joy of finishing was forgotten, but the discipline required for early morning starts and six sessions per week training made me shudder with disbelief. I decided there and then that I would never run another marathon. Despite the buzz I'd got thinking about using the exercise bike, I decided that cycling and swimming for triathlons would never again enter my life and that I would hang my sports kit up for good. I was finished with sport and told Fiona so when she came to see me that day. I said, "I never want to do another marathon or triathlon again!" I expected her to say something like, "Well, finally you have realised that you are no longer a teenager and you cannot do these things." Instead, she surprised me as she so often does and replied, "Scattie, I don't mind if you want to do a marathon again. I just want you to get better." I thought about her reply again and again over the weeks and months that followed. I did not realise it as we were talking, but I was of course in a fragile mental state at that time. My struggle to survive had pushed me to my mental limits and I looked at sport as a scapegoat; it had not saved me, despite all the official advice to live an active life, so why waste my time doing it. Writing this, I realise now that I was unable to mentally cope with anything other than my recovery. The thought of training for a marathon when I got out of hospital was too much for me to cope with. The perverse point here, and an indication of the fragility of my mental state, was that I attacked the bike and subsequent exercises like a sports training session, which I'd decided never to do again!

I continued to improve my leg strength through the exercise bike and also in my core muscles allowing me to sit without any side or neck support in my chair. It was unfortunately too heavy for me to move on my own so I was extremely happy when during my final week in intensive care I was told I would get a racier one. I was taken over to the physios' workshop on the lower ground floor and presented with my more manoeuvrable chair. It was about half the weight of the panzer version and with no head support. I was shown how to operate it and told to ensure the brake was on whenever stationary and avoid getting my hands caught in the wheels as I propelled myself along. Apart from that, I was free to try it and it was now mine. I transferred myself from one to the other and was amazed how I could turn and move it with great ease. The overriding difference was that I was now able to operate the chair on my own. I now finally had some freedom and pushed myself back to my room, learning how to steer with my new "wheels" as I went. It was a further move towards full independence.

I used the chair for four weeks and developed a new relationship with it. After moving to the normal ward, I had to, but also wanted to be independent and my chair was literally my vehicle for this journey. I could now take myself off to the toilet, wheel myself to my therapy sessions and when I had some free time, go to the library, or to the computer room to work on the keyboard. There was also a café where we could get coffee, drinks, and wonderful cakes in the afternoon.

During my first week on the normal ward, I would scoot back to my room in the chair after the morning therapy sessions for my hot lunchtime meal. I would eat it in solitary silence, struggling to cut up the meat or eat it in time before the start of therapy again at 1:00. I was eventually told about eating in the canteen by the ward nurses, who explained it was a lot more sociable than being alone in my room. I tried it out at the end of my first week and all the staff there was marvellous. The main dishes of the day were shown on the menu by the entrance, those of us in wheelchairs then went to a table and one of the army of servers would ask what we wanted, collect it, and bring it to us. Wheeling a chair and holding a tray was not impossible, but it was very difficult. It was a nice touch and indeed very sociable. I now had more time for lunch as the canteen was near the therapy rooms and it was possible to meet up and talk to fellow patients away from the stress of our medical care.

Eating was a slow affair, mainly because I had trouble holding and controlling a knife and fork. I would often ask the staff to help me cut particularly thick pieces of meat and it was invariably cold by the time I'd eaten it all. My facial paralysis was very severe, it not only made me look like a miserable bugger who could not smile, but it also seriously restricted my eating. Chewing was difficult because my cheek muscles, which are used to push food back into the centre of your tongue to allow you to swallow, had ceased to function weeks before. I developed my own strange technique of eating. I would use a fork to place some food in my mouth then use my hand to massage an immobile cheek pushing the food onto my tongue. The other hand covered my mouth to prevent food from falling out, as my lips were not strong enough to close them tightly. Despite my best efforts, food and especially liquids would fall or dribble out, producing an unsightly set of stains down my chin and on my T-shirt. Unfortunately, as soon as I started chewing, my left nostril would start running and my left eye would well up with tears, which eventually cascaded down my face. The facial nerves from the brain run down the left hand side of our face and fan out to the eyes, nose and mouth. The reaction of my eye and nose to chewing was because the nerves were no longer isolated from each other and had short-circuited together. My brain told my mouth to chew, but the same signal also went to my eye, which responded with tears and to my nostril, which started running. When surrounded by fellow patients who had suffered severe neurological difficulties, it was not such a problem to juggle hands, knead my face, and wipe away the excess of food, tears and water with tissues. Visitors were different; when they came to see me I could not help but feel embarrassed about my lack of control during eating or drinking. I continue to suffer from residual problems of facial paralysis today, more than five years after the start of GBS. My left eye and nostril still run, but thankfully, I have sufficient control of my lips to be allowed to eat in public.

I particularly enjoyed the next few weeks of sessions with my occupational therapists. Their rooms were on the same floor as the canteen and so after a hearty lunch I would line up in my chair, side by side with the other patients outside their treatment rooms. The therapists would come out and collect us and I would roll off with one of them into a particular corner or section of a room dedicated to the exercises we would do that day. I consider myself to have been lucky to have worked with two great therapists who both seemed to take a real interest in my development. They focused very heavily on building up my stomach muscles so that I could first learn to stand up, the essential precursor to walking. It was tiring and exhausting work. In parallel, I did strength exercises every day alone in the fitness studio. I was one of only a handful of patients in the room and I would wheel myself between fitness equipment which I used still sitting in my chair. I also did leg presses but had to clamber onto the equipment to do them. All in all, thirty minutes of exhausting circuits, but they were essential to build up my leg and stomach strength.

At the end of my eleventh week in the hospital and the fourth on the normal ward, one of the occupational therapists told me to ask my doctor if I could go home for the weekend. It was a lovely suggestion. I asked and to my great delight received the required approval. As usual for anything associated with my recovery, it meant a huge logistical exercise for everybody looking after me. The therapists gave Fiona two portable aluminium ramps to be used for getting my chair up our front door step. Fiona organised a bed for me in the lounge, as I didn't have the strength to get up the stairs to our bedroom. The nurses prepared my cocktail of drugs for the weekend and provided the essential wee bottle. Fiona, Alexander, and Francesca made the journey to Bonn on the Friday afternoon to pick me up and take me home.

Fiona and me outside the hospital ready for my first weekend at home after eleven weeks in the hospital. Although I look like a miserable bugger, I was smiling and glowing inside.

Fiona and the kids helped me to pack my bags and collected the ramps for the chair. The nurses and therapists wished us a great weekend and we set off to the car. Fiona was able to park by the main entrance and I was wheeled to the front passenger seat. Suddenly, I was confronted with the reality that the outside world is not wheelchair or handicapped-friendly. I had no idea how I was going to get from my chair and into the car. Alexander and I had a conversation and decided the best thing to do would be for me to pull myself up on the passenger door using the handle on the underside of the roof and he would move the chair away. I could then lower myself into the seat, avoiding bashing my head if possible and swing my legs into the front well. It worked, but it was exhausting. It was also a complete role reversal with my fourteen-year-old son looking after me. He had to move the chair, store it in the back of the car, buckle my seat belt, close my door and carry out the reverse when we arrived in Düsseldorf.

Safely strapped into the car, Fiona started the engine and moved slowly off towards the main road. I felt terribly vulnerable and very scared as we drove away from my institution. We stopped to let a car pass and Fiona drove down the hill. Everything was happening too quickly. We were moving, cars were coming towards us, and the kids were chatting away in the back. I grabbed my seat belt out of fear and was convinced we were going to crash. The outside world was big and dangerous. I longed for the slowness of my hospital life and the comfort of the inside, not the rush, rush, rush of the outside. As we approached the first traffic lights, I pushed my foot down on an imaginary brake pedal and hoped Fiona would slow down in time. It was a very nervy journey!

Alexander and I in front of the house with my "Welcome Home Dad" banner.

Arriving home, Francesca collected the bags and Alexander moved my chair to side of the car for me. I was able to haul myself out and flopped into the chair. I was pushed to the door and the kids had made a fantastic "Welcome Home Dad" banner and I had my photo taken by it. Still the same miserable bugger look on my face, but I was so proud of my family. Alexander and Francesca were marvellous and looked after me like doting parents. The ramps were collected from the car and placed on the front step. Alexander turned me around and wheeled me backwards up them and into the house. Home at last. I could start relaxing. We all just sat around talking. I moved from my chair to the makeshift bed in the lounge and I was really happy to be out of hospital.

Unfortunately, there was a difficult moment when I needed the toilet. I had to ask the kids for help. I positioned my chair outside our downstairs loo and asked them to make sure I did not fall when pulling myself up on the doorframe. They opened the door and helped me into the bathroom and towards the toilet. Fortunately, I was able to take care of myself from there, but asked them to stay outside in case of any difficulty, as we did not have any grab bars at home. It was hard for Alexander and Francesca to see their dad like this.

Eleven weeks is a very long time, I'd left home in winter and arrived back in late spring. Life went on in the outside world but mine had stood still and gone into reverse. Eleven weeks prior everything was good, yet in the interim I'd nearly lost that life. I'd been nursed back and had to relearn how to breathe, talk, eat, and move myself about. It was necessarily a very selfish existence. I was not able to think about others or my business; I had to use all my energy to focus on getting myself back into life so I could re-enter the outside world. Sitting in the lounge at home I was now faced with that world and I had to learn to not only consider myself, but also others. Fiona was exhausted with the stress of having a sick husband and looking after two emotional and hormonal teenagers. Alexander and Francesca were suffering at school because their dad was extremely ill and there were a hundred other problems to be addressed. To her superb credit, Fiona kept most, if not all, of these problems from me and we could both use the hospital as a smokescreen. At home, we just talked and talked about the issues that I'd missed and needed to catch up on.

I was struck by Alexander's maturity and I immediately noticed that he'd grown up so much. He cut the grass, he did the jobs and he looked after Fiona. It was a real pleasure to see. On the Saturday, we had our friends Barbara, Jochen, Pia and Jörg over for a meal. It was a long-standing arrangement as we met regularly for an evening meal, taking it in turns at each other's house. Barbara and Jochen used to live locally in Kalkum and their son Nick and Alexander were friends at primary school. They'd recently moved to Hamburg and used the occasion to bring Nick along so that he and Alexander could spend some time together. As we sat down to eat, the two boys went out to Kaiserswerth around 7:00 p.m. We told them to be back at 10:00 and were a little concerned when they'd not arrived by 10:15 so Fiona called Alexander on his phone. Strangely Nick answered, telling Fiona that Alexander was in the toilet and they would be home soon. Around fifteen minutes later, we heard a commotion at the front door and Fiona went to investigate. Alexander was slumped on the front step in a drunken stupor! The stress of the past weeks and months had got to him and he'd had to endure far more than any normal teenager of his age. The sight of his dad at home, albeit in a wheelchair, was no doubt a huge relief for him. The combination of his stress and relief, together with the visit of one of his oldest mates created a potent mixture for Alexander's first boozy night. I secretly laughed as Fiona shouted at him as he staggered about downstairs in the guest room. *This was real life. Yes, of course he shouldn't have got drunk but it was really nice to be back in the world of problems and not to just have my therapy to stimulate me.*

I spent a further five weeks in Bonn. I came home for another weekend two weeks later. That time, I felt confident enough to travel without my wheelchair as my legs were stronger and I had a Zimmer frame to support me. I was to only use the chair for another week or so and I was glad to leave that phase of rehabilitation behind; I appreciated it for the freedom and opportunities it gave to enhance my quality of life. I had very little opportunity to use the chair in the outside world, so was really only moving about in the unreal world of hospital. However, the experiences that I did have confirmed to me how far we have to go to have a wheelchair and disabled friendly society.

Chapter 16 — Walking

As soon as Dr. Mertz told me, "If you want to walk out of here…" it became my target to do so. My motivation to reach the goal was enough to push me through the mental and physical pain barriers on many occasions. Consequently, I am now almost evangelical in the advice I offer to any poor bugger that will listen, telling them that if they set a goal and really want to do it, they will achieve it — no matter what gets in their way. I started towards my goal during week three in Bonn and it was the end of week sixteen when I walked out, unaided. Of course the main issue was physical, but without my brain in gear with the good side pushing and pushing — just like the four-hour marathon target in Hamburg — the body would probably not have followed. As with breathing, talking and eating, GBS had robbed me of these abilities and I had to relearn them. Walking was the hardest but most satisfying of these skills to regain.

One day at about week nine, I was having one of my regular occupational therapy sessions with a chunky therapist named Nick. His colleagues and the physios had worked hard during the previous weeks at practising to get me into a sitting position on the edge of the bed. I appeared to be strong enough so Nick asked if I would like to try to take some steps. "You bet," I replied enthusiastically. My trainers were placed on my feet and Nick summoned the help of a fellow therapist. I was eased off the bed with the two therapists either side of me. My feet touched the ground and my arms were placed around their shoulders.

"Okay Martin. You are now on your feet. Try and walk."
I stood there marvelling at my achievement to be upright
and I wanted to walk, but had no idea what to do. How do
you walk when you have forgotten what to do or you do
not have the strength to do it? I strained to lift my right leg
upwards. As it came up, my foot hung down limply. Nick
tried to move me slightly forward. I brought my foot down,
but due to lack of muscle control, the side of my foot hit
the floor first. I was moving forward and transferred my
weight onto the leg, which caused my ankle to give way
and turn over. Nick stopped me from falling and moved
me forward onto my left leg. To our dismay, the same
thing happened with that leg, my feet fluttering about in a
random way. *Mmmmh. Not really a good start.* After such
a long period of lying in bed, the inactivity had rendered
my ankle muscles totally useless. I had a pronounced
"drop foot" problem despite the best efforts of the nurses
to prevent it.

The attempt was abandoned and I was returned to bed
for some ankle support. Two large bandages were
produced and wound tightly around each ankle, under and
over my trainers — a very strange sight. I was now ready
for a second attempt. I stood again on my now heavily
bandaged feet, once again supported by the two therapists.
I was willing my legs and feet to move as I looked down
and stared at them. "Martin, look up, not down — eyes
forward," bellowed Nick. I lifted my right leg; I felt it
move slowly upwards as though being dragged through
porridge. My foot still hung down, but with the bandage
support I was able to keep it in a relatively good position
in relation to my leg. Nick moved me forward and I

transferred my weight back onto my foot. The same procedure was repeated on the left leg. With some enormous support from the two therapists, I was able to move forward about ten metres and then a further ten metres back to my bed. Both ankles collapsed and I turned over painfully on them during this attempt so I was happy to stop. It was not a very successful exercise, but I had managed twenty metres. It was the last attempt I would make for another four weeks. My legs and ankles were simply not strong enough.

Those of us who are fortunate to be healthy and have no trouble walking do not give this complex action any thought. I was now subjected to learning the whole process from start to finish. Before walking, the first action is to stand up straight on your feet. Assuming we are sitting down, we need to use our stomach muscles to move our torso forward. Once our centre of gravity is over or beyond our knees, we have to use our stomach and back muscles to balance ourselves. We push up with our leg muscles and use our feet and toes to keep us in balance, possibly also with our arms out wide to provide extra stability. Once on our feet, the muscles in our lower legs and feet are working hard to make sure we stay upright and do not sway off balance. I had to relearn all this. I was now working very intensively with the physios and the occupational therapists and was in the fitness studio every day to build up strength in my legs, preparing my body to do nothing more than simply get to my feet. We trained and practised this laborious action for three weeks. I did sit ups, bum raises, leg presses, arm raises, back exercises and balancing exercises and didn't take a single step in anger.

Walking is in fact controlled falling. The core muscles in our backs and stomachs are used to move our weight forward. Once our centre of gravity is beyond our knees we will fall forward. As we do this, we roll one foot forward, shift weight to that leg and lift the other leg up. As we fall further, the airborne leg is brought down to the ground. As it nears the ground, we automatically lift our ankle upwards so that the heel of the foot hits the ground first. We then transfer our weight to this leg and start to roll forward on our foot. When the middle of the foot hits the ground, our toes then start to move upwards and when we have the full weight on the foot, the toes move down again. To be honest, it was an absolute revelation to me to see how our feet and toes react when we are walking (go on try it — walk slowly in bare feet and watch how your foot moves upward when you walk, allowing the heel to strike first and then the toes also curl upwards). The muscles to lift my ankles were extremely weak. I had to compensate for this by flipping my feet upwards, as though trying to flick some mud from the end of my shoe during each step. The muscles in my toes and especially my big toes were also non-functional, so I had to be extremely careful when walking bare foot and make sure that I did not catch my hanging big toes and break them as I put my weight down. In addition to the ankle and toe weakness, I had to add general leg weakness.

I knew I was in a bad way and that to rush my first steps would be a mistake. However, after more than three weeks of exhausting exercise and no attempt at walking, I was getting frustrated. I talked to Anna and told her how I was feeling. She understood, but assured me that I had to build up my strength first, quite a blow, as I was in a hurry. Then something happened to focus the minds of my therapists. I was in my thirteenth week and received a letter from my delightful health insurance company advising me that I would have to leave the hospital that week. I was told, somewhat discourteously, that they would no longer pay for my rehabilitation! Just like that! I consulted with my doctor on the ward. He could see that I was not able to walk unaided and whilst I could use the wheelchair and Zimmer frames in the hospital, I did not have my own that I could use at home. He told me not to worry and assured me that I would not be thrown out. I just needed to get on with the selfish business of looking after myself.

As one of life's worriers, it was not easy for me to get this out of my mind as I imagined the insurance company coming to turf me out of hospital. It did however serve as a catalyst for Anna and the others to accelerate my treatment. They could see that I now only had a finite time left in their care and I needed to start walking. Anna allowed me to start with my first tentative steps in week thirteen. Bandages were again used to beef up the support in my ankles and I was given a Zimmer frame on wheels to support me when walking. My delightful frame had bicycle style handles with a brake for safety, a lovely seat that I could use when tired and a metal basket on the front to carry my notes or shopping! I had hoped that I would have made it into my seventies before the need for a frame, but here I was in my forties and extremely happy about it.

My first excursion with Anna was from the therapy rooms back to my ward — a journey I could do in five minutes in my chair, it took fifteen, but I was moving under my own steam. It was great to have my legs pumping again and whilst it was a laboured movement, I was forcing my muscles to work, so they would get stronger. I was anxious and fearful of a fall but help was with me. It was simply a matter of confidence because I was out of my comfort zone. When I arrived on the ward, the nurses were in their room and I proudly announced my arrival by pointing to my legs and showing them that I was walking on my own two feet. The three of them came up to me and I actually said, "I am really proud of myself!" They shook my arms, slapped me on my back, and told me that I had every right to be proud. I was encouraged to carry on with the excellent progress.

I was chuffed. I'd had to push Anna and the team to let me progress from the tedious exercising of my legs and muscles and then on to standing up and finally walking. I'd focused on these movements and getting back to walking during all the pain and heartache of my rehabilitation. At first it seemed impossible because my initial thoughts at the start of my treatment were whether I was going to survive. As recovery progressed, I gained in strength and could imagine walking, but was still physically unable to do it. Instead, I focused on learning how to breathe without the life support and then how to talk again. These two skills brought an enormous improvement in my quality of life. I was able to communicate and was independent of the machines keeping me alive, but both new skills required extremely high levels of survival instinct. Learning them required me to challenge and face fears of death through oxygen starvation. They involved horrible pain and huge moments of anxiety. In contrast, learning to walk was associated with exercising and building up strength. It did not require me to confront fears of my own mortality or involve pain. I was mobile because of my wheelchair, so my first walking steps with the Zimmer frame I could argue, perhaps controversially, that they did not even bring any improvements in my quality of life. This was a shock to me. I had focused on walking for so long whilst lying motionless, that I'd imagined it to be a utopian moment when it arrived. It wasn't, but I was mightily relieved when I was able to do it.

I was allowed home again at the end of the thirteenth week and this time I left the wheelchair behind and only took the Zimmer frame. Fiona and Alexander picked me up and I was able to walk with their help into the house, pushing my frame triumphantly into the kitchen to sit down. It was fantastic to be at home away from hospital. Fiona and I just talked and never seemed to tire of things to chat about. She updated me about the kids and what was happening at school. It was nice to hear about non-medical issues and brilliant to be surrounded by healthy people. It is very easy in the hospital to become focused on just yourself and your ailments. Here at home, I had three other people to think about.

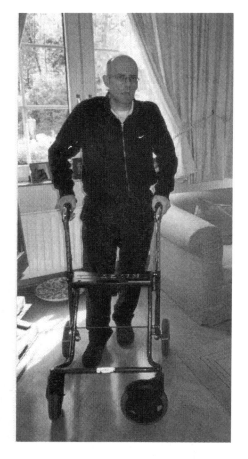

With my wheeled Zimmer frame at home at the end of week thirteen. I was to go back to hospital on Sunday, but did not know who would be paying for my treatment.

Fiona made me a cup of tea and asked if I would like to see some photographs taken earlier in my rehabilitation, where I was in bed, paralysed, and hooked up to the life support (they are all shown in previous pages). I took them off her and looked at the first one. I immediately burst into uncontrollable tears and sobbed as I looked at my pathetic body in the prison of my intensive care bed. All the pain, the stress of my immobility and my daily struggle came rushing back. I was suddenly very aware about how much I'd gone through to survive. How I had suppressed and kicked all negative thoughts out of my head so that I was never unhappy and had never broken down. Tears dripped from my face onto the photos as I looked through misty eyes at Fiona and said to her, "It was hard, so fucking hard! You have no idea how hard it was. It was so, so fucking hard!"

Shaking with emotion, I wiped away the tears and looked at the rest of the photographs. They were a traumatic reminder that ripped my emotions wide open; exposing a rawness that was so deep it frightened me. Somehow, I'd managed to work my brain into being positive, I'd ignored all the possible negatives and focused only on getting better. My reaction made me realise that I'd expended nearly all of my energy on surviving. I was aware that I'd been dangerously close to the edge, but I knew that I had never ever once looked over. I'd whipped it and survived, it had damn nearly taken me down with it, but I had survived.

Fiona held my hand and we cried together. There was nothing she could say to me that was of comfort, her being there was more reassuring then any number of words. I told her of the one major fear that I still had. I'd faced all the other life threatening issues and overcome them, but there was one point that I knew I would never be able to beat. It was my fear of getting GBS again. It was probably an irrational fear, especially only thirteen weeks after getting it for the first time — yet it continues to be a very real fear of mine. Around two percent of GBS patients contract this awful illness for a second time, a truly horrible thought and not without precedent even in Düsseldorf! Some kind soul had given me an article in the hospital from the Rheinische Post, our local newspaper, describing the case of a young woman contracting it twice within three years!

Fiona told me not to worry and tried to assure me that it wouldn't or couldn't happen again. I knew it remained a very slim, but nevertheless real possibility and this fear gnawed away at me as I progressed further in my rehabilitation. At that moment in my kitchen as I saw my pathetic self in an emaciated body, I knew that my survival reserves were empty and there was almost nothing of my fighting spirit left. A second dose at that time would have killed me — I have absolutely no doubt about that. Writing this we are in the middle of a possible Swine Flu pandemic and as more than fifty percent of patients' contract GBS after a bout of flu, there is a very real threat that more and more people will succumb to it. As I have shown a susceptibility to the illness, I remain at risk.

Fiona distracted me and we returned to the normal humdrum world of family life. Only two weeks had passed since I'd been allowed to come home for the first time, but the improvements in my condition during that time were dramatic. I was now confident to move around with my Zimmer frame. Home was not exactly disabled-friendly, but the doorways were wide enough for the frame and I was able to hold onto furniture and walls, as well as my frame, to prevent me from falling over. A huge relief for us all was that I no longer needed the kids to wheel me to the toilet in my chair.

During the previous week in hospital, Anna and I had practised climbing and descending stairs. For our first sessions I perhaps naturally, focused on going up. I was worried that I didn't have enough strength in my legs, but was surprised that I could take one step at a time, whilst simultaneously pulling and steadying myself on the banister. I was chuffed with my leg strength when I got to the top of the first flight of stairs, it being a nice reward for the hours spent in the gym working on the leg press and other exercises. What I was not prepared for was the walk down! I'd assumed this would be the easy part, but as I turned and stood at the top of an imposing flight of stairs I was suddenly very concerned for my safety. My leg strength was okay, but my ankle strength was poor. When practising walking with my frame, I had learned to push some of my weight down through my arms to prevent me from painfully turning my ankle. At the top of the stairs a frame is useless, a safety blanket was only provided by the banister which I gripped very tightly with both hands. I took the first tentative step down with one foot and moved the second one down to it. I paused, caught my breath looked down and moved down a further step. Anna was now behind me ready to hold me should I collapse, all the time passing on lots of encouragement. Twice my ankles gave way and I was saved from tumbling down by my iron grip on the hand rail. Anna told me that it is actually easier to walk down backwards, so we practised this as well, which reminded me of the horrible muscle ache that you have after running a marathon that makes descending stairs a nightmare. The solution is to go down backwards! Therefore, if you ever see any fit-looking person descending stairs in this way, they don't have a screw loose, they have just run a marathon!

Armed with the skills and confidence that I learned in the hospital, I tried at home and got upstairs. My bed was still in the lounge but I wanted to sleep upstairs with Fiona. I had sufficient furniture and door frames to hold on to so that I could get into the bedroom and bathroom without any problems. The shower was a different matter because there were no grab rails. Fiona had thoughtfully bought a small collapsible stool which she had put in the middle of the shower tray. To get in, I needed somebody, usually Alexander, to help me up through the doors with a steadying hand. I faced forward and he held me as I sat down onto the stool. Alexander closed the doors and I was then able to pick up the shower head as in the hospital and wash myself.

Getting out or down from the shower was more difficult than getting in. Our shower tray is 30 cm off the floor and it was too high for me to step down without any support. Once again, as with the stairs, I reverted to reversing out, backing down and steadying myself on the side of the cubicle. All in all, a challenging process and made me realise how a house is not set up for a disabled person and in some cases, it could have been quite dangerous.

Having mastered the stairs and the bathroom, I was able to enjoy the weekend and I felt part of the family again. I could sleep upstairs and as an added bonus, we had a visitor from the UK — Rachel. The three of us went out for brunch at a local café on the Sunday. My frame was packed into the car and Rachel helped me into the restaurant. We sat and chatted over a simple but deliciously appetizing brunch. I drifted away in my head and was a million miles away from the problems of my rehabilitation, the hospital and being surrounded by ill or distressed people. Those hours and the weekend at home were so important to me and I am sure they accelerated my recovery, giving me further strength the face another week of tortuous exercises and the sterility of the hospital.

The two hours we spent in the café were brilliant and we could have stayed longer, yet I had to break the party up because I was not sure if I could get down and up the very steep spiral staircase to the toilets. It was a cruel reminder of the precariousness of my condition. I was recovering rapidly now, but I was not able to cope outside on my own and I had to choose the places or at least the amount of time I spent in a place by the accessibility of the toilets. This is a daily problem for a person in a wheelchair and one that restricts your life. Surely it cannot be a big problem to equip all places with wheelchair or disabled access?

The weekend was a great success and I was pleased when Christian, my neighbour and great friend, offered to take me back to Bonn on Sunday evening. It relieved the stress on Fiona and we had the chance to have a chat about life and my recovery on the journey back. Christian brought two bottles of alcohol-free beer and offered me one. I opened it and tried to drink, but the taste was just horrible. It was a problem I was to face with all types of alcohol or even alcohol free beer for several months. Perhaps it was the medication or perhaps I was just not ready for it, but I was off booze for about nine months in total.

We arrived back at the hospital around 7:30 p.m. of a lovely evening. Several of my fellow patients were sitting outside drinking coffee, chatting, and enjoying the warm sunshine. Christian helped get my frame from the car and he carried my bag up to the room whilst I walked, pushing it in front of me. The enjoyment of the weekend started to seep out of me as we entered the institution again and I was once again surrounded by sick people. We took the lift to the third floor and I shuffled slowly to my room, desperately trying to hide the fact that I was not happy to be back at all. We reached the end of the corridor and pushed open the door to the room I was now sharing with Mehmet, the young Turkish guy. Unfortunately, as we entered we were confronted with several men involved in a prayer session!

Christian and I made a swift departure and retired to the corridor. The prayer meeting broke up a few minutes later and at last I felt comfortable enough to move back into my own room. I placed my bag on my bed and as it had been an exhausting weekend I sat myself down in my wheelchair and accompanied Christian to the lift and to his car to say goodbye as he made his way back to Düsseldorf. It was always really hard when my visitors left and especially after such a great weekend — where I was really close to normal life again. I pushed my chair back to the lift and noticed for the first time how small I was in the chair compared to walking with the frame. I'd not used my chair for three days and I was much taller without it. Now, sitting in it, I suddenly felt more vulnerable and isolated. I pushed myself back to my room, applied the brakes and climbed out onto my bed. I didn't use the chair again. It had helped me make the transition from immobility to mobility as my strength returned but it was no longer needed. I had passed through that phase and was ready to only work with my frame. It was a smooth transition but not, if you pardon the pun, a huge step in my recovery. Consequently, for the first time I felt slightly deflated with my progress. My expectation of the sense of achievement when I could progress from wheelchair to Zimmer frame was so high, but the reality, although very pleasing, was easier than I thought, tempering my satisfaction somewhat.

I was now installed back in my room and had to get back into the swing of being a patient again. I longed to be back with the family and not in a room with a stranger. My thoughts turned to the insurance company. I noticed my weekly plan detailing the therapies that I had every day was lying on my bed. It clearly showed that I was to have a session every day, so as the doc had said, I needn't have worried.

I was more confident and more mobile yet I still needed further help and support in hospital. The doctor on my ward had done a great job and had managed to secure a further three weeks of funding for my continued rehabilitation from the German pension authorities. It was a relief and I concentrated hard on getting the best out of my remaining treatment as possible. I had finished with my wheelchair and moved it away from the bed and placed it by the table. It became an ornament. I was on the home straight now.

The following three weeks were made up of yet more exercises to strengthen the muscles and develop more coordination in my feet and hands. I was measured up for my very own Zimmer frame and more importantly, leg braces. The braces were made from fibreglass and were used to provide support to my ankles, so avoiding my legs giving way as I walked. The weather was now much warmer and although the braces would be uncomfortable to wear in the heat, they were designed to give me confidence to walk without my frame. Until they arrived though, I had to make do with bandages wrapped around my ankles — not a very endearing sight.

The worst of the illness was over and like the weather, I too had come out of a very dark winter and summer was dawning. I was able to move around and meet two other fellow GBS sufferers on the same ward: Francois, an artist from South Africa who had lived in Germany for many years, was a year or two younger than me, and Agnes, a feisty woman from Aachen. Francois and I got on really well and we could chat away to each other in English, which was hugely comforting. We'd both been on life support and had seriously paralysed facial muscles. Fortunately for Francois, he came out of his paralysis faster than I had and he was able to walk without the aid of a frame. We would meet up for lunch after the morning's treatment and then agree to have a mug of hot chocolate after the afternoon session had finished. We both had enormous difficulty keeping food and liquid in our mouths because of facial paralysis, so eating and drinking was always accompanied by hands over our mouths and a tissue to mop up the food or chocolate that dribbled down our chins. It was a comical sight and one that made us both laugh — it also reminded me of the two grumpy old men in the Muppets. Neither of us could smile and we both struggled like two old men, but in fact we had a great time chewing the fat together. When the weather was good, we sat outside with our hot chocolate and just chatted. It was very comforting to have a fellow GBS sufferer there that I could discuss with and I know Francois thought the same. It was also great to be able to speak in English as we could both express what we really wanted to say or ask the other something without worrying if we had chosen the right words. I am still in touch with Francois. We talk intermittently on the phone and update each other about how we are doing. His facial paralysis only improved slowly, whereas mine is now better than before. I had and continue to have problems with my legs, but Francois still suffers from chronic tiredness, unfortunately an all too common problem for GBS patients.

In my fourteenth week, Thursday was a bank holiday. More than six months prior, we had booked a long weekend away in Spain with our friends Fiona and Iwan. I was not well enough to go away with them, so Fiona and I had decided around five weeks beforehand that she and the kids should go anyway. They all needed it, it was very stressful having an absent husband and father. I would be on my own on the bank holiday Thursday, but my sister Lesley and her husband Brian came to see me on the Friday and Saturday. It was a real treat to see them. The weather was superb and we took a trip out in the car to a local village on the Rhine. Saturday was spent downtown in Bonn and I was learning to move around in crowds with my frame. The worst part though was always the stress of having to find a toilet that I could access. Unfortunately, this always seemed to be degrading, as I had to rely on my visitors to help me with physical support in walking to the toilet if access with my frame was not possible.

I had another two weeks left of hard exercising. A further weekend at home and then I was into my final week — my sixteenth in hospital. I was now confident enough to walk from my bed to the bathroom without my frame. I first stood at the end of my bed and steadied myself. I then looked at where I wanted to go, not down at my feet and pushed myself off forwards, towards the bathroom via the end of my roommate's bed. I had to concentrate hard on lifting my feet up and then placing them flat down at the end of my stride. It was three steps to the end of the next bed and I grabbed hold of the frame to steady myself. It was another two to the wall and then a further two, using the wall for support to the bathroom. Once I had my hand on the door, I could swing it open, using the handle for support and move inside to the grab rails and safety. These first unaided steps were a challenge and I was told on more than one occasion by the nurses to be careful. However, I knew that I would be leaving on the Friday and I'd promised myself that I would walk out unaided.

I received my leg braces on Thursday. They were L-shaped, made from fibreglass with a sole designed to fit into my shoes. I stood on the sole in my socks and tightened the two wide straps; one around my ankle the other my calf. I took my training shoes and loosened the laces as much as possible so that I could slip my foot, plus the braces into them. I stood up and supported myself on my chair. The support for my ankles was impressive. The braces kept my feet at right angles to my legs and allowed me to concentrate on the movement of walking without worrying about my feet hanging down and tripping over them. I pushed my frame to the side and started to try and walk unaided. Unfortunately, it was not a natural movement and I had to swing my legs forward, rotating my upper body via my waist. I stretched my arms out wide to provide balance and I moved one step at a time. I found myself leaning forward to aid the swinging of my legs and consequently my bum would stick out. Suddenly I thought of Kenneth Moore in one of my all-time favourite films *Reach for the Sky*, where he played Douglas Bader, the World War II RAF pilot that lost both legs in a plane crash. My exaggerated leg movements were so similar to those shown by the actor depicting this great man. It gave me a further boost and I walked a few more steps away from the comfort of my frame. It worked and I was nearly ready to walk out of hospital after sixteen long hard weeks.

It was my final evening in Bonn. I had been to hell and back and I was now on the mend. I was able to move around on my own but with the frame for safety and support. It was a warm Thursday evening, 3rd of June 2005. I'd arrived on 25th of February, heavily sedated and on a life support machine. Life could not have got any worse. Fourteen weeks later, I was able to talk to my fellow patients and the medical team. I could move around and I was almost ready to go home. I'd come a long way and I wanted to see Thomas one last time to show him how much I had progressed before I left the next day. I decided to set off to walk on my own to the intensive care ward, with my braces on and my frame for support. This was by far the furthest I had managed to walk and it would take me at least twenty-five minutes to accomplish.

I could have taken the quickest route out of the main door of the hospital, but would then have to cross the road running between the two blocks of buildings. Instead, I took the longer, but safer subterranean route under the road and arrived at the lift to take me up to the intensive care ward quite exhausted. I pressed the buttons in the lift and whilst looking around noticed how everything seemed so different. I'd not been there for seven weeks and previously had only seen everything from a bed or a wheelchair. Now as I was standing upright, my whole perspective was different. The doors opened and I pushed my frame forward and moved out. I looked around and all was quiet. All the doors to the patients' rooms were closed and there was nobody on the corridor. I edged forward to the nurses' room, taking in all the sights on the ward where I'd experienced the worst seven weeks of my life. I passed one room and the clinical smell of a severely ill patient wafted towards me, reminding me that my sensory experiences on this ward had fortunately not included smelling anything. As I got to the nurses' room, Peter came out and beamed a huge smile at me. "Martin. You are walking!" He moved to shake my hand and I thanked him for all his help in getting me back on my feet again. At this moment the boss nurse came out as well as Katharina, one of my favourite nurses. They were extremely pleased to see me and asked how I had managed to get there. I recounted my journey, which drew further praise from these wonderful professionals. I thanked them for their help but each one told me that it was all down to me. They praised me for my dedication to getting better, which made me feel warm inside, but uncomfortable because I knew they had been the catalyst for my motivation. Peter leaned towards me and said, "I knew you would do it. You really worked hard." He made me feel good!

I looked around and asked after Thomas. Unfortunately, he had been on the early shift and I was not able to say goodbye to him. I asked the others to pass on my regards and after a few more minutes of chatting I knew that my time was up and I was ready to leave this very special place for the last time as a patient. I moved off waving goodbye with a whole bunch of emotions sweeping and swirling round me. It was on that ward that I experienced the worst that a sick body can endure. I'd been trapped for seven weeks in my useless body here. I'd choked, I'd shivered, I'd thrown up, I'd sunk to the lowest depths of my physical and mental limits. I'd also experienced extreme levels of professionalism and felt privileged to have known and been cared for by these people. It was as though I'd gone through a whole lifetime from birth to middle age in the space of seven weeks and it was such an emotional time that I did not know whether to cry tears of sadness or joy at my departure. I walked to the lift, pressed the button to go down and entered. I turned round and as the doors closed, I stood and looked at the polished aluminium sides of the lift and my initial sadness was replaced by happiness. I'd whipped it, was almost on my way home and on my own two feet! I felt the onset of ever such a slight smile. I was chuffed with myself.

The next day, the formalities were completed and I was given my very own Zimmer frame to take away with me. I said my goodbyes to the nurses, physios and waited for Fiona, Alexander, and Francesca to arrive to pick me up. My bags were taken downstairs and I pushed my frame in front of me, my legs protected by the braces. The car was parked near the main entrance and Alexander, as helpful as ever, ferried my bags and belongings to the car. Without any fuss or any comment, I left my frame in the entrance hall and I walked for the first time totally unaided to the car. Nobody noticed and I did not mention it, but I had fulfilled my target and my promise to myself to walk out of that bloody hospital on my own!

I sat in the car and Alexander closed my door. Fiona started the engine, manoeuvred away from the hospital doors and down onto the road. Sixteen long weeks had come to an end. I was no longer a patient in a hospital and was free of all the connotations that brings with it. I could say goodbye to the institutionalised and rigid system and I was now on my own and free to decide what I wanted to do. Eight weeks prior I would not have been able to contemplate going home because of the poor physical state I was in. I was now physically able to move around, albeit with a great deal of care and support from my Zimmer frame, and I was mentally very ready to break out of the stifling existence of hospital. I was uncertain of what treatment I would now undergo. I'd received notice that I could go as an outpatient to a local day clinic in Düsseldorf, but that was three weeks off. Right at that moment as I looked out of the window at the trees lining the street to the clinic, I didn't care. I could now be with my family and I was bursting with excitement at the prospect of living a normal life again. The most traumatic period of my life was now at an end. I was on my way home!

I'd done it and I am convinced it was only possible because my head was in the right place. Sixteen weeks previously if I'd not had the strength of mind to recognise my situation and told myself to get on with it, I wouldn't have made it. If that single target of walking out of the hospital had not been set, I might have got lost in the maze of pain, discomfort and terrifying treatment. The positive side in my head was switched on despite the most mentally and physically demanding of circumstances and I refused all attempts to switch it off. That very simple act of walking out showed to me in a living and extremely vivid form how the power of the mind can drag the body through almost anything and make it survive. It will remain as one of, if not the greatest achievement of my life.

Part 3 — Starting Life Again

Chapter 17 — An Outpatient and Further Rehabilitation

It was a sunny early summers' day when I got home. Friday 4th of June 2005. It was magical to be finally away from the rigidity and inevitable boredom that a prolonged stay in hospital thrusts upon you. I was able to walk into the house on my own. I had my own brand-new walking frame and my leg braces. I walked into the lounge and looked out into the garden. Fiona and I went outside and sat at the table and I just soaked up the warmth, the sounds and the beauty of the open space. It was freedom. I was alive and I was, quite simply very happy.

I only cried once in hospital. I was into my ninth week and able to talk and move around in my wheelchair. Christian was with me and in contrast to his previous visits I was now able to talk. I'm sure this was much easier with a two-way conversation possible — no need for the dreaded alphabet board. He could finally ask me how I was really feeling and we eventually got onto what I was really missing. I looked at him and explained that I missed my family and friends and was really looking forward to having them round to the house and sitting outside in the garden drinking a nice cold glass of white wine. As I explained this, I suddenly got very upset. The dreamy vision of my garden, sunshine and loved ones just seemed so far away from the sterile and immobile world I was then living in. The tears rolled down my face and I longed to be away from my hospital bed. Wind on eight weeks and I was now finally able to live that vision. I was outside with Fiona and just so happy. The wind on my face, the warmth of the sun, the fresh air and all of the sounds associated with home, it was so far away from the institution that had reluctantly become my home. I felt alive and very grateful.

I was in reasonable physical shape. The hole from the tracheotomy in my neck had healed over and I no longer wore a bandage on it. (It didn't look very pleasant then and I still think now that the scar looks like somebody has taken a wooden stake and driven it into my neck). In the first few days I used the Zimmer frame to move around the house downstairs, but soon relegated it to a corner using doorframes and walls as support instead. Climbing stairs was no longer a problem as long as there was a banister for additional support. Upstairs the major challenge continued to be the bathroom and I very quickly realised that we were not set up for disabilities. I longed to have a bath, but this was out of the question as I would not have been able to lift myself up once I'd sat down. A shower was my only option. In the hospital I'd always sat down on the fold out chair and steadied myself on the grab rails. It was unfortunately very necessary to do this because as soon as I closed my eyes I lost balance. Standing on one leg was impossible, so support was needed when drying myself or putting my trousers on. Showering was always done sitting down on the fold away stool and I had to exit backwards out of the cubicle so as to avoid tripping or falling over.

The weather was glorious for the first weekend at home. On Sunday the four of us went out in the car to Baldeney See near Essen. It is a beautiful area where the river Ruhr flows gently past and is perfect for a Sunday outing. We parked the car and Alexander retrieved my

Zimmer frame from the boot. We decided to walk along the water's edge and targeted a restaurant a short distance away for a lunch stop. I suddenly felt very vulnerable and my initial confidence for tackling and taking on the outside world had a swift reality check. The first problem was the unevenness of the surface in the car park. Whilst I was able to walk, all the practice I'd had was on flat and very even surfaces in the hospital. Now I was presented with gravel, holes and puddles and I had to negotiate cars and other people. In the hospital, fellow patients with various disabilities, plus staff and visitors, are willing to assist you or at least allow you space or time to complete your movements. Out in the real world, that awareness, in most cases, is non-existent. The Sunday afternoon strollers had no idea what I had been through or that I was gripping the handles on my frame so very tightly because I was very concerned about falling. I had help, in the form of Fiona, Alexander, and Francesca with me, so my fears were unfounded, but a fall on my own would have resulted in an almighty fight to get back on my feet. Sure I would have been able to ask for help, but falling is counter-intuitive. Nobody wants to fall and I found people, through no fault of their own, would get far too close to me or allow their dogs to approach to me. It now seems petty and irrational but out in the real world, on our first Sunday stroll in five months, these concerns were very real to me.

We reached the water's edge and could hear a cacophony of sound coming from a canoe water polo tournament further down the bank. Sleek sail boats glided through the water and a passenger boat chugged its way to the jetty close to where we stood. I edged forward very slowly and marvelled at the multitude of activities that danced away in front and to the sides of me. People were happy, smiling and laughing. They were out in the fresh air, moving in, on and around the water. I could not help feel for all the patients that I'd left behind in the hospital for whom this beautiful Sunday was just another day in their two dimensional world. Many of the patients I'd seen, and some that I'd spoken to, were terribly unfortunate and would never again experience what I was now enjoying. Some were getting worse by the day and some would die soon. I know it sounds perverse to put it like this but GBS, whilst there is no doubt it is a terrible illness, is the only neurological condition that shuts the body down and then reverses the effect. I knew after a few weeks that I was going to get better and I would regain some or all of my strength and mobility. I reflected on this and the strange fact that I'd reached the grand old age of forty-seven but was shuffling along in the warmth of the sun like an eighty-year-old. Nevertheless, I felt so very fortunate.

Joggers of all shapes and sizes passed us on our walk to the restaurant. I maintained my studied and concentrated movement forwards and marvelled at how a couple or a group of runners could talk and seemingly be oblivious to the skill they needed to remain upright. I'd not re-learned that skill yet and I knew that the last time I'd trodden this very same path was during training for the Hamburg marathon, just over a year earlier. Christian, Stefan, and I had run the length of the lake twice, completing 28 km on a Saturday afternoon. We'd sprinted back to the car park and were all in great shape for the run in April 2004. I was the strongest that day and was very happy with my training. Here, just over a year later I was unable to walk without the aid of my frame. Jogging would be impossible for another year. Toddlers and pensioners alike were much faster on that path than I, but nobody was as proud of their fitness as I was. My hospital stay had been my marathon and I'd reached the end in well under the magical time.

Monday brought me back down to earth with a bump. Family life had to move on again and the kids needed to go off to school. I stayed in bed whilst Fiona got them ready. They only had a couple more weeks before the summer holiday, but my illness had already taken its toll on them. It was blindingly obvious for any sane person that Alexander and Francesca were both going to struggle whilst my life hung in the balance and further, when Fiona and I were both in hospital. Instead of compassion and support, the school provided the continued expectation of thoughtful work and the achievement of the minimum grades; unrealistic expectations from such vulnerable twelve and fourteen-year-old children. I was furious with the school, with the head and the teachers because of their miserable and absolute failure to be proactive in helping them. I lost an enormous amount of respect for both the school and the German teaching profession in particular. Rarely have I experienced such unjustified arrogance and aloofness from any professional group, not even the doctors I'd dealt with over the previous weeks, and it ultimately lead to us taking the kids out of that damn school. At the end of that term, they both flunked the year and were made to repeat it again. It was a hugely demotivating act that they both had to endure through no fault of their own and within twelve months we'd enrolled them both at the International School in Düsseldorf. The contrast was enormous and is a decision we have never regretted, despite the financial cost. Ultimately a happy end to the sad saga of my kids' education at a very prestigious German school, but one that could easily have been so very different if a little care and compassion had been scattered around.

As thoughts turned to my on-going care Fiona took me to register at a local neurological out-patient clinic, which was only 1.5 km away from home. It was attached to a rehabilitation centre and sheltered old age accommodation. The clinic was able to provide medical care with an on-site neurologist, physiotherapists, occupational therapists, speech therapists, masseurs and medical fitness trainers. In short, I could expect the same daily care as in the hospital, with a midday meal and door to door pick up and drop off thrown in. I registered and was initially granted a three-week stay by the German State Pension fund that would foot the bill. The only problem being I could not start for another three weeks.

It was actually a relief to have some time off from treatment and to just enjoy being at home. My condition dictated that I couldn't move fast but I discovered that slowing down was actually very rewarding; with hours spent doing nothing, reading or watching television. It was all new and I really enjoyed it. My life before GBS was so hectic, I'd started up and was running my business before I fell ill. I usually worked between twelve and fifteen hours per day at least five days a week. I travelled a lot and was in Asia every six weeks. I flew out on a Monday afternoon and arrived Tuesday morning after a twelve-hour flight. I worked from Tuesday until late Thursday evening and returned home overnight, going straight into the office after a quick shower on Friday morning. Besides work, I'd trained for and run the marathon in Hamburg in April 2004 and I'd spent that summer and most of the winter months doing triathlon training four to six times per week. I had no time in the evenings, so the triathlon training either swimming, running or cycling, had to be done in the morning before work or at the weekend. Here at home, I was now just sitting down and doing nothing. It had seemed alien to me before because I considered it a waste of time. Ultimately, my lifestyle most probably contributed in some way to a lower immune system so that when I went down with the flu, I was susceptible to GBS. Thomas warned me in the hospital that I needed to avoid stress and, to be honest, in those first few days and weeks over the summer of 2005 it was very easy to do. I tired very quickly so I would have a sleep in the afternoon. I enjoyed just sitting and relaxing and I didn't consider it a waste of time. Fiona and I also took time getting to know each other again spending a lot of time sitting in cafes and talking — I didn't even object to walking around town and visiting the shops as long as we were together.

My face had regained some limited movement and I was able to raise a very tiny smile. Unfortunately, the other muscles in my cheeks, my tongue and my lips were all still severely affected. Eating would remain a problem for several months. First I had to make sure that everything was cut into small pieces. I was only able to have a small amount in my mouth at any one time and would spend a long time chewing it. I always ate with my hand in front of my mouth (and sometimes still do) because my lips were too weak and food would fall out. Once I'd finished chewing, I had to stroke my cheeks with my fingers to massage the food out from between the inside of my mouth and my gums and finally to swallow it. Eating was a very slow affair. Drinking out of a glass with a thin rim was okay, but the lip of a cup or worse, a mug, were too wide for me and the liquid always dribbled down my chin. To avoid making a fool of myself, I held the cup in one hand and a serviette in the other to catch the drips. I'd not touched any alcohol for more than six months and although I'd dreamt of a cold glass of white wine, I had absolutely no desire to touch any. I guessed this was because I was still on medication and it would be another two months before I had my first beer. The lack of facial movement still affected my speech and I talked with a very pronounced lisp —with "copy" sounding like "coffee" — which became worse when I got tired as the fatigue affected my lips. To make myself understood, I often used my thumb and forefinger to push my lips away from my teeth so I could speak more clearly. Not a sight that one would call attractive.

I started as a day patient in Düsseldorf at the end of June 2005. I planned to be there for three weeks, but spent a total of five weeks, finishing my treatment time there the day before our summer holiday to Turkey. I received a lot of physical therapy, which was the same or very similar to that received in Bonn. The main difference was the help from the occupational therapist who worked hard to put my business or professional life back in order. We worked on typing skills, relaxation and most importantly the removal of stress from my daily routine. Previously after a ten or eleven-hour day I would have carried on working at home after my evening meal. Consequently, I wouldn't get all my jobs done in the office and I found myself working on quotations and checking invoices late into the evening. I knew then that it was stupid, but it is all too necessary when you are in a business start-up situation. Pauline, my therapist, worked with me to structure my day in a different way so that I wouldn't leave my e-mail and to-do actions until the evenings, finishing them during the day instead. She told me to take regular breaks, to avoid sitting at my desk eating a sandwich for lunch and instead to walk to the local bakers or restaurant, leaving my phone behind. I'd known that I was working too hard. The business, the risks, the money and the travelling all contributed to my enormous stress levels. To counteract this I spent hours each week exercising and convincing myself, with some justification, that it was my stress release valve. It all worked well for a while and I never ever believed that anything would happen to me, but to be honest, who does? I suppose I got some warning sign when I became ill with the flu and I took myself off to bed for two days. Stupidly, I then dosed myself up with ibuprofen and went back to work, succumbing five days later to GBS. Admittedly, I have no idea if the stress or the return to work contributed in any way to my illness; the only certain thing is they didn't help. So, here I was nearly six months later and I not only had to slow down, I also wanted to slow down, and to my amazement I really enjoyed it. I took all of the advice from Pauline on board and still follow it today.

After five weeks in the clinic I was ready to finish. Twenty-one weeks of treatment spread over twenty-four weeks was enough. I wanted to do the rest myself and I was ready to. I was happy to leave and relieved to be looking forward to two weeks in the sun in Turkey. It was a great holiday with our friends Bernie and Dennis and their son, Tom. We returned home tanned and relaxed. It was time to get back into my business and to pick up my baby that I'd started with such pride at the end of 2003.

Chapter 18 — Running My Business

I had been self-employed from late 2001 when the company I worked for went into liquidation. Having always wanted to run my own business, I set about getting the legal issues sorted out, but actually had no idea what I wanted to do. In the end, after trying my hand as an interim manager and working as an agent selling technical items, I stumbled into a business area selling electronic RFID components, working in much the same way as I had over the previous fifteen years, except this time it was for me.

2003 was a transition year for the economy and for my business life. Business picked up and I was forecasting sales of $200k in RFID. I had stock in Germany, which I kept in my garage. I found customers who placed an order to my manufacturing partner. I shipped the parts writing invoices, delivery notes, calling UPS and packing the boxes in my cellar. All orders were payment in advance. As soon as the money was in my account, I would ship the goods. I was surprised how much time non-productive work such as invoicing and organising shipments took of my day. Inevitably, I found myself doing this work in the evenings and spent the days trying to find customers. Little did I know, but this routine was probably the start of my high stress levels.

One warm Sunday evening in September 2003 my neighbour, Christian, asked me if I would like to go for a quick blast on the mountain bikes before our evening meals. We were on the home stretch of a fast 15 km circuit, on a bike path just a kilometre away from home. It was glorious weather and we really pushed it hard on the final section reaching a speed of 37 km an hour. I was riding very close to Christian's back wheel. Unbeknown to me, there was a cyclist on the path coming in the opposite direction. Christian had him in his sights and judged that he would pass him just before we reached a part of the path where a bush protruded out into it. His calculation was correct and they crossed at high speed. Christian then shimmied around the bush. Unfortunately, I'd not seen it and my handle bar struck the foliage. It jerked the front wheel violently round to the right and I was catapulted over the handlebars into a long flight. As I was in mid-air I remember thinking I was glad I had my helmet on because this was going to hurt. I landed on my left shoulder then my head and felt my collarbone disintegrate on impact. I knew it was broken and when I came to a halt lying on my back on the grass verge, I felt strangely content with the world. I knew I was injured, but I was not in pain, no doubt due to shock. I could move my hands and feet, so I knew my neck and back were okay. I tried to get up, but as I moved my shoulder the pain shot into me like a red-hot poker. I decided to just lie there.

I was eventually taken to hospital and after the x-rays was told that my collarbone was broken in four places. I was admitted and told the surgeon would talk to me in the morning. During his rounds the next day, I was informed that I could have surgery to screw a 10 cm plate onto the bone. I would then be able to regain almost total movement in my shoulder within a few days — the only downside being that it was an operation. A second and less invasive option was to wear a butterfly sling for four to six weeks to allow the bone to heal itself, but this would mean very limited movement (including typing) for maybe the whole four to six weeks. It was a no-brainer and I had to go for the operation because I needed to return to work and very quickly!

Lying in bed that Monday after the surgeon had left, I realised for the first time the perilous position you are in when you are self-employed and completely on your own. I was about a year into my own business, it had started to show signs of going well, I was very busy and some, but not enough money was coming in. I was then thrown off my bike and my business stopped in the same length of time as it took to smash my collarbone. I got Fiona to bring my PC to the hospital and I wrote several mails to inform my customers. I'd set out on my journey of self-employment with the intention of being independent, working at home with the lowest possible risk and no staff. This accident told me that I really needed support and it was a pivotal moment because I decided there and then that I needed to employ staff to share the load in the business. At the same time I made up my mind that I would need to incorporate the company into a GmbH and to start trading. A relatively simple accident had transformed my thinking and the new direction was one that would ultimately save my business when GBS struck eighteen months later.

I registered the limited company in December 2003 and took on two staff in 2004. Sales hit €1.5mio at the end of 2004 and things were looking good. On the way from the doctors to the hospital on Friday 11th February 2005 the day that GBS finally got the better of me, I called the office to say that I wouldn't be coming in. As for my business, for the second time in eighteen months, I was removed from it without any warning. But this time, I had a manufacturing partner and staff to keep things going.

Our friend Jörg was in the office with Fiona at 7.30am on 14th February 2005. It was the Monday following my admission into hospital. I was in a coma in ICU. My business had to carry on. My staff of two in Germany, several people in Taiwan, Fiona, Alexander, and Francesca all needed money to live, money that the company had to earn. Everybody was naturally very shocked and nobody knew what would happen so Jörg set about reassuring people and putting actions in place to allow the business to continue. I meanwhile had no idea what was going on and once I had woken up from the coma, I cannot remember my thoughts ever turning to business.

The effect of GBS on my business was kept to a minimum by the skill, dedication, and determination of many people, most especially by Jörg, my manufacturing partner in Taiwan and the staff in Düsseldorf. Jörg provided some stability in Germany and a focus for any business questions. My partner took it upon himself to visit and inform some strategic customers. He was in Europe three times during my illness and organised help for the company from Taiwan with one of his staff coming to stay for two weeks. The office staff worked tirelessly to keep everything running and customers happy. My customers were also brilliant and they did everything they could to keep my company going by placing orders and working around the obvious deficits we had. I will always be grateful to them and can happily report that I did not lose a single one, despite the fact that I was out of circulation for six months!

I eventually returned to my business in a full time capacity after six months out. It was a struggle and I tired easily but I was great to be back and work definitely helped with my recovery. I avoided stress and still try to do so today. I make sure that I am always in time for meetings or a flight or the train and I no longer do everything at the last minute or take on too much. When I am travelling, I avoid driving too far to meetings and I always try to get a good night's sleep. When in the office, I take breaks and if I am under the weather, I go home. My business survived because of the hard work and dedication of my staff and the willingness of my customers to keep purchasing from me. It was yet another humbling experience of kindness. I was so proud when I opened my business and I never once thought what fate would have in store for me. I'd thought about failure, about money and cash flow, but never about a serious illness and six months in the hospital. Once again I was lucky.

Chapter 19 — Sport

Sport has been a part of my life for as long as I can remember. I turned on it during my recovery because I'd truly believed that sport would somehow protect me from any illness. I was still angry with "sport" in my ninth week of recovery when I told Fiona that I never wanted to do a marathon or triathlon again. My mind-set, at that time, was reminiscent of the minutes and hours after finishing the Düsseldorf and Hamburg marathons. I was extremely uncomfortable and couldn't get any relief or respite from the dreadful tiredness by standing, sitting, or lying down. In those moments after almost collapsing over the line, my overriding thought was, *Never again. Never.* Yet, when the pain had subsided, the legs had recovered and the brain had turned the mind-numbing tortuous 42 km into an "experience that I really enjoyed", rose-coloured thoughts replaced the negative ones and the mind looks towards training for the next event. Think of Sir Steve Redgrave at the end of his race in the 1996 Atlanta Olympics when he won his fourth gold medal. He said that he never wanted to see a boat again, but four years later he was there in Sydney winning his fifth. It is a long stretch comparing me to Steve Redgrave, but when I was sitting in the hospital garden with Fiona telling her I didn't want to train again, I'd just endured a very stressful eight weeks of immobility, had not heard the sound of my own voice or had the ability to think clearly or express my thoughts. After the struggle, I was able to start to enjoy life but the pain of my experience was very raw and sport was at the heart of my grievances. Hence my rather brash comment. Needless to say, my thoughts turned to sport eventually, but it was a much longer rehabilitation than I thought.

After two months at home, I was able to dispense with the Zimmer frame and walk around unaided. It was now eight months after I'd contracted GBS. I had very little feeling and movement in my feet, so I always had to be very careful on uneven ground or when walking close to others. For example, I couldn't feel if I stood on somebody's foot! Month by month I started to gain strength and a little feeling in my legs and toes, so by October 2005, I felt confident enough to go for short walks on my own, using Nordic walking sticks for support.

My first attempt at jogging was in April 2006. I was now walking without any sticks and I'd recovered sufficient movement and strength in my legs. I was actually going for a fast walk and had my training shoes on. Ten minutes into my exercise I was in the middle of the fields close to home with not a soul in sight. I suddenly thought about jogging and decided to give it a try. Unfortunately, as with walking I had to re-learn it and I'd honestly forgotten what I needed to do. I referred back to my exercises in the hospital and leant forward. I lifted one foot exaggeratedly up from the floor and staggered onto my other foot. I repeated the exercise and moved forward, each time lifting my feet up high and then down as gently as possible. It was not pretty and very awkward, but I managed to avoid falling over. After 50 metres I was exhausted and had to stop. I repeated the 50-metre stagger two more times in a walk of 2.5 km. I didn't feel good and as I'd promised myself that I would now live my life by listening to my body, I decided that it was too early to start jogging.

I tried again in June and by September was able to manage 2 km. In January 2007 I was up to 8 km and getting stronger all the time. I'd also tackled swimming and cycling in 2006 and was able to complete modest amounts of exercise. Swimming breaststroke was very difficult because of the lack of movement and dexterity in my feet (a problem that still persists today) but freestyle was okay. Once I was confident with my balance, cycling was also possible. One of my proudest moments was trying skiing again in February 2007. Again it was a little ugly, I was slow at reacting or turning and I tired very quickly, but hell I could do it. Unfortunately, all the sporting activities came to a halt in late February 2007 when I was diagnosed with a huge kidney stone.

After strenuous exercise I always had blood in my urine. Fearing the worst, I went for a series of tests, which proved inconclusive. A CT scan eventually showed up the stone, about the size of a golf ball as the cause, so I required another series of hospital stays. Three times I was admitted for treatment to smash the stone using external ultrasound. I was in for between seven and ten days at a time. When stone free, I started jogging again and completed in the Düsseldorf 10 km race in September 2007. I finished in a respectable time of 53 minutes, 40 seconds. My previous attempt in 2004 was 47 minutes, 40 seconds. I was surprised and pleased to see that I was less than fifteen percent slower! Unfortunately, I picked up an injury in that race and I was unable to train again for several months.

Five years on, I exercise four to five times per week to keep my head clear and my body in shape. I cannot move as fast or for as long, indeed, I injure very quickly especially when jogging. My arms are probably at ninety percent of my previous strength, but my legs and feet are still only at seventy-five to eighty percent. The large muscles in my legs are working and allow me to exercise to a reasonable level, but the myriad of small muscles are not functioning one hundred percent because the nerves are still not completely connected. Consequently, I can run, but cannot sprint — so squash, one of my favourite sports, is very difficult. I can jog, but when on uneven ground I am very unsteady and have fallen, because the small muscles that keep my feet level and my body in balance do not work. I must emphasise that whatever my limitations are I am happy and extremely pleased with what I can do.

Chapter 20 — Counselling and Going Mental

Recovery was brilliant. I was enormously proud of any improvement in my physical condition when I was in the hospital. The first time I could move my arms I moved them up and down to show Katharina, one of the nurses. She instantly understood and congratulated me on my improvement. It felt good. The same encouragement was there throughout my time in Bonn and also as an outpatient, possibly because I was one of the lucky ones that was at the bottom but was now on the way up. In the first weeks of intensive care all my visitors offered the same support and willed me to get better. Before everybody's eyes an amazing transformation took place as I progressed from a paralysed wreck kept alive by machines to self-sufficiency within the space of a few weeks.

When I moved from the ICU to the normal ward in Bonn, I was physically able to look after myself, although a long way from normal. It was now a matter of time until I would be able to re-enter society and it was obvious that I was not going to die or to be permanently disabled. I had mental stimulus and was fully able to cope with my world. We were all relieved. Consequently, and very understandably, the number of visitors dropped dramatically from at least one every day to a visit two or three times per week. As I improved further, returning home, attending a day clinic and finally full time work, my physical appearance returned to almost normal. The only physical signs that betrayed my previous condition were my limited smile and the exaggerated walk as I flapped my feet around. If you hadn't met me previously, nothing would have indicated the struggle of the previous months. Consequently, I was treated as normal; the encouragement had gone because there was no obvious physical recovery to encourage. I was asked time and time again, "Oh, you are okay now. Is everything back to normal?" Slowly, stealthily and unconsciously this started to get me down, gnawing away at my confidence. I would reply, "I am physically at about seventy-five percent" and would then go on to describe what I could not do. *What I could not do!* The glass was not half full it was always half empty. The poison of mental problems had started to seep into my confidence and I had no idea it was happening.

I had used my mental strength in hospital to channel all of my energies into my physical recovery and to avoid the minefield that was depression. I was sufficiently mentally sharp enough to use this ever present danger as a tool to keep my mind focused. I instinctively knew that if I was not positive I would fail. Once I had overcome that danger and I knew I would be okay, albeit possibly in a very limited way, the sharpness of focus shifted ever so slightly. I now had more to concentrate on than just surviving. When I was totally paralysed, my only goal was not to die. Once that survival was a certainty, I could concentrate on many issues including learning how to talk, to eat, walk, and to live independently. Yet paradoxically, these successes brought physical triumphs, but also mental torture as I began to examine how much my life had hung really by a very, very tiny thread. That thread could really be traced back to the experienced Registrar in the local hospital who had thankfully seen GBS twice in twenty years and then to the consultant surgeon and his team in the Düsseldorf Clinic who intubated me when I'd stopped breathing. When I heard from Fiona what the surgeon had done in the ICU it was a sledgehammer blow that aggressively exposed my own vulnerability, shocking me to the core and playing on a sensitive mind. That mind had guided me so positively through hell on earth, but when a return to normality was in sight it started to turn on me, bringing doubt and negativity.

The more I progressed and the more I improved, the more time I had to think about what could go wrong again and what I could not do. The source of my worry was twofold: 1) my almost primeval fear of contracting GBS again and; 2) my own vulnerability as I had almost departed this world. *Was it rational to think that I may get GBS again?* It was possible and this was my worry. I was convinced that I would suffer the same fate again and I tried so hard to banish those thoughts, but they hung around me like a bad smell and intensified whenever I was reminded of my illness, plunging me further into negativity. My fear continues today to be very real. I am almost one-hundred percent sure, even now, that I used up all my survival points fighting off GBS. It was a monumental, at times titanic struggle. It was worse, more painful, more uncomfortable and more tortuous than anything you can possibly imagine and quite literally the only thing worse would have been death — but even that seemed like blessed relief. With the painful memories so fresh in those first weeks after leaving hospital and the day clinic, I was constantly worried that GBS would come again and I was absolutely sure that I would not have the strength or the will power to fight it.

I became irritable, worried, and increasingly nervous because of my fears. I knew from my stay in hospital and long chats with Thomas that I had to avoid stress at all cost. Stress had not caused GBS, but it had possibly been a contributory factor. Here was a paradox, I was stressed up worrying about something that might happen and I needed to avoid that to stop it happening again. My stress levels became very real and I would feel it in my stomach, almost like butterflies before I was due to make an important speech, only worse. My head was heavy and I could only think negatively. On a few occasions, it was even worse and I saw an imaginary dark room with a door invitingly open ready for me to enter. I felt drawn to the door propelled by negativity and although I was trying to resist, I moved relentlessly forward. I could see darkness beyond the opening and I was sufficiently aware to know that should I enter I would suffer a total and utter break down. I had to stop moving towards that damn door, which seemed so seductively inviting and totally frightening. I had to kick myself out of my negativity.

When I saw that door for the first time, I was strong enough to recognise that it was a crisis situation. I did not think I was ill, but knew that stress was possibly the cause and I had to avoid it. It was my first active decision to get away from a potentially destructive situation. Without any reference experience, I did what I would have done if I'd been physically ill. I switched off my computer, left the office, drove home and took myself off to bed. The warmth and the familiarity of my surroundings induced a more positive frame of mind and I was able to walk away from that door. The dark room entered my life on two more occasions and I was only able to move away from it with my old mate mental strength. I forced myself to think positively and shut off or move away from the situation or circumstances that had triggered these mind games. I was entering a critical period in my recovery and one that was unseen by all those friends and loved ones that had been so supportive in my first few weeks in the hospital. Frankly, I needed them just as much, possibly even more now, but as usual it was my incredibly patient and long-suffering wife Fiona that kicked me out of it.

I was not aware that I was actually changing or that I had a problem. Fiona kept on telling me I was going mental, but I just laughed it off. I honestly thought that she and everybody else had the problem and that I was perfectly okay. I arrogantly thought that neither she nor anybody had or ever would have any idea of the struggle that I'd been through, so how could she judge if there was something wrong with me. I was only shaken out of this stupendously selfish state of mind when confronted by a spectacularly stupid incident that occurred in front of the house. It was mid-October. Fiona and the kids had been to England for a few days. I'd stayed at home on my own and was looking forward to welcoming them all back around 7:00 p.m. on the Saturday evening. I heard the car arrive and went outside to see Fiona reversing it into the path between our house and next door. It is narrow and tricky, especially as you need to negotiate the car parked opposite, which prevents an early line-up into the path. As usual after a trip to England, the car was packed to bursting with plastic bags from Sainsbury's, preventing Fiona from seeing out of the rear window. Relying on the rear view mirrors she moved the car close to the path, but I could see she was not lined up correctly and was heading for one of the three lights standing guard and illuminating the edges.

I shouted "stop", but Fiona didn't hear me and carried on oblivious, directly into the light, crushing the cheap aluminium frame and glass top with crunching ease. She realised that something was wrong and opened her door. I shouted at her, "Didn't you hear me? Look what you've done!" It was cruelly delivered, aggressive, and wholly over the top. Fiona rightly reacted with disbelief. Through tearful sobs, she said, "Oh I was so looking forward to seeing you. I've really missed you this week but you have definitely changed. There is something wrong with you." Her words hung in the air. I looked at the tangled mess below me with a value of 10 euros, then at Fiona and the kids who were priceless to me. I realised for the first time that perhaps there was something wrong in my head and that I should go and seek some help. It was very painful but it took the hurt inflicted on my loved ones to get me to realise that I needed to act.

Fiona and I talked. She told me that I'd changed so much and that I was really different. She was also pretty direct in describing the fact that maybe I was going mental and that I needed to go and see somebody. I wanted to believe her but I was unable to realise or define what was wrong with me. I knew I had a problem because my loved ones were telling me so, but I reasoned that I could only sort out a problem if I knew what was wrong. Together we agreed the solution I needed was to go to counselling. I was happy to do this as I'd promised Fiona I would do it, but I had no idea where to start. I checked the internet and yellow pages but found it difficult to come up with the German equivalent of counselling, so I decided on a visit to our GP, to ask his advice.

I made an appointment and honestly had to think what I was going to say. I couldn't say I was doing it for the sake of my family and ultimately for my sanity, so I told him what was in my mind, but not actually what I thought was wrong with me. I explained that I was preoccupied by my vulnerability (near death experience) and the fear of contracting GBS again. These two issues were in fact the source of my problems that fed the well of negativity that polluted my mind. Ever sympathetic, Dr. Thoms immediately understood and referred me to a psychotherapist. He explained to me that I had undergone a trauma and it was normal to have issues of coping with it after the event. It was the first time that I'd heard my experiences referred to as a trauma.

I was given a prescription for sixteen sessions with a therapist. I looked for somebody locally because I couldn't drive and would need to get there by public transport. I rang two but they had no free appointments and could only offer me something in the New Year. I needed to be seen sooner so I looked further afield, eventually finding a practice close to Dr. Thoms's office. I made an appointment with a great deal of trepidation but full of determination to get this, whatever this was, sorted out.

Getting to the practice was quite a struggle. I had to get a bus, two trams and then walk 500 metres. It was not the first time I'd travelled alone after coming out of hospital, but it was the first time I'd travelled that route. I still had some difficulty negotiating steps. Walking was slow and I had to be ever vigilant that I didn't fall, as getting off the floor unaided would have been a challenge. Finally, I had to allow plenty of time for my connections because I was unable to move quickly should an oncoming tram dictate it. Indeed as I left the bus after completing the first leg of the journey for my initial consultation, I saw a tram approaching. What could I do? In my previous life before GBS, I would have run at high speed and hoped that I could have reached it in time. Now, it was impossible. With a tranquil calmness that really surprised me, I maintained my measured pace and watched with joy as the tram moved away, very safe in the knowledge that: a) there was absolutely nothing I could do about it and; b) another tram would be along in ten minutes. Please allow me to be a little self-indulgent or over the top and to describe this as a life-changing moment. I'd always rushed about hurrying here, there and everywhere beforehand; now here I was actually deriving pleasure from watching a situation unfold that would have previously sent my stress levels into the stratosphere. It was what my occupational therapist had called the "discovery of slowness", taking pleasure from being well in time, instead of seeing it as a waste of time. *I had changed after all* and it was a change in my attitude that I derived a great deal of pleasure from. I was hoping that my therapist could work on the other changes in my attitude that Fiona was definitely not finding pleasurable.

It is always awkward working with any type of therapist. This was my first attempt with somebody who would be looking inside my head. I was nervous because I could not put my finger on what was wrong with me, if anything. My therapist was Frau Schmitz, a rather bohemian "green" trendy type woman a few years younger than me. I knew instantly that she would be okay, but never a great soul mate of mine. She sat me down on a chair in a sparsely decorated room. As is normal with counsellors, the chairs never seem to be comfortable and you never face the person. I sat at an angle to her. A pad in hand we started with pleasant introductions and the formalities of insurance cards and contact details. I duly obliged and all was noted. She then asked me how she could help. I actually didn't know, but recounted my story and focused on the two issues that were in fact my problems. Several questions followed and she continued to write furiously, more questions, more explanations and more writing. I had the usual thought that I guess most first timers have in this situation, *where is the therapy and what are the answers to my problems?*

Eventually, close to the end of our first chat, she told me that I was suffering from post-traumatic stress syndrome. I'd heard this used in terms of soldiers returning from violent conflicts, but had never considered that I might have a similar problem. *Was this why I was being such a nasty bastard at home?* She went on to explain that the definition of trauma is the "loss of control". In life we are controlling and deciding all our actions. Suddenly when we are confronted with a violent incident or a car crash or in my case the extremely close brush with death, we are not in control. The memories of the incident are then stored in our "trauma memory". This memory is characterised by instant flashbacks that transport us to the site of the trauma, so we relive it again and again. The triggers for the flashback can be anything associated with the problem such as a record that was playing at the time, a picture, sound or voice. I was fascinated with what she told me. She was describing exactly what I was going through at an alarmingly frequent rate. She went on to explain that as time goes by or with work on our minds, we slowly move some or parts of the trauma to normal memory, so reducing or neutralising the problems associated with it. Gob smacked, I wrote down in my notebook — trauma, the loss of control. It rang so true to me and I was hooked. I wanted to hear more and I felt as though a huge weight had been lifted off my shoulders.

She then took a few words to talk about my fear of contracting GBS again. She asked how old I was. I replied, "Forty–seven." She then enquired, "And how many other times have you been seriously ill in forty-seven years?"

"Well, never," was my rather curious answer as I was not aware of where she was trying to go with this line of questioning.

"Do you think it is rational to think that you were ill once in forty-seven years and now a few months later you will be ill again?" Her words hung in the air and I was unable to answer as I was thinking hard about her comment. She continued, "You are an engineer and can look at it statistically that you had one illness in nearly half a century and consequently you are now worried that it will occur again within a few months. Applying statistics, you could argue that you will not get another serious illness for another forty-seven years!"

It was a comment that really cut me open and I suddenly felt really exposed. Here was a stranger who I'd known for less than an hour telling me that my primeval fear of contracting a life-threatening illness was not rational. It was hard to take, but I instinctively knew she was right. It was irrational. One in 100,000 people get GBS. Only thirty percent of those people contract the very severe form, which requires life support — meaning one in 330,000 people. Of the people with GBS, around two percent of those contract it again. This puts the odds of suffering a recurrence of the horrors of ventilators and total paralysis at around one in sixteen million people. Statistically, I would have to be enormously unlucky to get it again and the chances are negligibly small. Being an engineer, I could appreciate her comment and it allowed me to look at my irrationality in a cold and non-emotional way. I wrote in my notebook, "No illness in forty-seven years, so chances of another are slim." It helped me enormously.

Finally, in that first session, she turned to her notes for the first time and recounted some of the comments that I had made about my condition. I'd told her that I couldn't smile as my face was still paralysed, how walking was difficult, how I couldn't drive and I'd come to see her on public transport which was really the first time that I'd managed such a long journey on my own. She pointed out to me that I was always discussing things in a negative way. I focused on what I could not do and not on what I could do. She asked me, "You talked about your journey here on public transport and how much of a challenge it was for you. I would like to ask you a simple question — could you have done that journey a month ago?"

I had to reply, "No — I wasn't physically capable and I would not have had the confidence to do it." "Exactly," she replied. "You must look at what you have achieved and what you can do. Do not concentrate on what you cannot do, take great pride in the fact that you can walk, whereas six months ago you couldn't!"

Wow, really simple but very heavy stuff for me. I once again took my notebook and wrote, "Concentrate on what you can do!" It was life-changing advice.

I thanked her and after making a series of appointments for the coming weeks, I left with a spring in my step and a totally new mind set. I took the tram for the journey home and looked at the notes I'd made. They were so simple: 1) Trauma — loss of control; 2) Forty-seven years; no illness; 3) concentrate on what you can do. They opened the door to the problems in my mind that allowed me to understand them. I had really been very sceptical and nervous about going to see Frau Schmitz. With a great deal of professionalism and some incisive comments she had really cut through the fog of my mind. Within an hour she had allowed me to see that I had problems and what they were.

I now knew what I had to do. I had a recognised problem because of my trauma. I wanted to work through it with her; the same would go for my fear of re-contracting GBS. It was the concentration on looking at what I could do and revelling in the achievement of this reflection that brought about the greatest amount of self-healing. In fact, the shift to positive thinking was a repositioning of my mind to the same state I had used in the hospital. There I'd always been positive and refused to think about any negative points. Somewhere between those first critical days in the hospital and my eventual physical recovery the negative or bad side of my brain had taken over my thoughts and infected my character. In running or exercise terms, if I'd been in the marathon and close to the finish and my target time, I would have given up because my legs hurt. This wasn't me. I didn't function like this. I was always positive and I assumed I always would be like that, but something in my chemistry had changed. I was determined to not let it happen again.

I set about rejoicing how much I had achieved, which brought about an almost instantaneous improvement in my head. I had further sessions with Frau Schmitz and we worked through the trauma and fears with detailed chats and conversation. My now positive frame of mind allowed me to see my fears with more rationale. My positivity meant that I was enjoying life, focusing on what I could do and not on what might happen. It was a new lease of life for me.

I only went to see her for a total of six appointments, of the prescribed sixteen. My head was in a totally different position and I felt that I no longer needed her help. Our sessions were not bringing about any further results because I no longer had problems that I felt I could not cope with. The mind and the brain are very powerful when in positive mode. Unfortunately, when in negative mode, the power is worryingly destructive and I was saved from further problems because the person I loved most had had enough. Fiona had saved me yet again.

Chapter 21 — Five Years On

Five years on, I continue to live with GBS every day. If you met me, you wouldn't know I'd had a serious illness. But, I know I did; I am reminded of it by the tracheotomy scar, which I see when shaving every morning, by the constant tingling and limited movement in my feet, by restless legs in bed every night and by my Gumby smile. I can't watch medical or hospital programmes on the television. When I see a life support machine or a tracheotomy tube on somebody I am shaken by the image. Last summer, four years after leaving hospital, I saw a young man in a wheelchair with a tube into his neck. I was amazed to find my legs buckling and I felt physically sick as I rushed to turn away. The worry and my trauma float around me ready to pounce at any visual or audible reminder of the struggle I had. Happily, though I can report the frequency of those reminders are decreasing and I have a greater and improved capacity to cope with them.

I am often asked if I live my life differently now. I do, but I must say that some of the promises I made to myself to never to do this and never do that have faded with some of the horrors I endured. What I can happily report is that I am extremely content in my life and the happiest I have ever been. I am pretty healthy, have a great family (we drive each other mad at times) and am fulfilled professionally with my business. I have a vibrant circle of friends and I am able to enjoy sport. Life is dripping with riches that GBS all so nearly stole from me. I try at all costs to listen to my body. If I feel ill, I pack work in and go to bed. If I am feeling stressed up, I do something to get rid of it. I avoid rushing anywhere. I treasure magical moments with my family and my friends above all else. They make me feel a rich man.

Epilogue

I have enjoyed writing this story and to use a cliché, it has been a journey for me. All the details have come straight from my head and as far as I am aware, are one-hundred percent accurate. I made a few notes in the hospital, but then got fed up and stopped. I did put together a basic chapter outline, but as the writing progressed I chopped and changed it allowing the structure and flow to move as I told the story.

Bizarrely, as I've read over what I've written I found three Martin Scattergood's were involved. The first is the person who lived the experience, the second is the person who wrote about them, and the third is the person reading about them. Of course, they are all one person — me, but when I read back some of the passages I'd written, I'd forgotten about them and what I had been through. I am not a psychoanalyst, but I guess from my experience with Frau Schmitz that my writing helped to move the experiences from my trauma memory to my normal memory. Consequently, the memories were no longer so raw, upsetting or traumatic. My take on this is that writing the story has certainly helped the healing and recovery process in my head. I can therefore only encourage anybody else who finds him or herself in a post-traumatic stress situation to try writing things down. It has certainly helped me.

What you have just read was my first attempt at any form of detailed writing. I tried to avoid any stylised attempt to describe my experiences because I would have failed miserably. Instead, I told it how it was. Sometimes raw, sometimes upsetting, occasionally damn funny but in the end it is just my personal account of fear, struggle and survival. If there is only one point out of the whole story that I would emphasise to everybody it is; never, ever underestimate the power of the mind. A positive mind can force an unresponsive body to struggle against all the odds. A negative mind will fail. Being positive, deciding you are going to do something with a fixed target will bring you extraordinary results. It does not need to be a fight for your life, but banish negativity and you will have the best chances of reaching that target.

Cheers for reading it.

Appendix 1- My top tips when meeting or visiting severely ill or disabled people

1) Talk softly in a normal tone at normal speed. I was not stupid or deaf just because I couldn't move.

2) Talk at the same eye level. If the person is in a wheelchair, bend or crouch down beside him. If they are in bed, pull up a seat. It is horrible being looked down on all the time.

3) If the patient is paralysed and unable to speak or move — try to establish contact. Ask if he can hear you and to reply by nodding, squeezing your hand, or closing his eyes. Taking time to do this will make the person you are visiting feel ever so special and they will love you for it.

4) Get close. I longed for people to take my hand and to have physical contact with me. Please always ask the patient first though and I am sure the answer will always be positive.

5) Make the person more comfortable. Fluff up the pillows or raise the head of the bed so he can see you more easily. Any little gesture like this that makes the person feel special will go down really well — again, please ask first.

6) Help with the patient's physical appearance. This maybe combing his hair (not needed for me), shaving, doing his nails — anything. Even when I was in a really bad way and more dead than alive I was totally preoccupied by looking the best I could.

7) Avoid bringing presents that exaggerate the patient's condition. If the person cannot read, as I couldn't, obviously avoid bringing any magazines or books. On the other hand, I was always very happy to receive cards and flowers. My best presents though were happy photographs from family and friends and a "Zen" type graphic that I stared at every day on my room wall.

8) Give the person a massage. On one occasion I had four people massaging my hands and feet. It was truly magical, connecting me with them and making me feel very special.

9) If the patient's physical condition will allow it, take the person out of their room and if possible outside. I absolutely loved to be away from my room, one on one with my visitor. It was an escape.

10) If the person cannot eat or drink, avoid doing either or even talking about it in his presence. This happened to me on more than one occasion and it incensed me!

11) If talking is impossible, being there is every bit as good. Always visit.

12) I always appreciated humour. Take it easy though and check how the person is responding.

13) Try and see through and past the physical condition and treat the person as you normally would have done. If you always gave the patient a kiss beforehand, make sure you do it when he is ill.

14) Finally, be positive! The patient does not want you to feel sorry for him or to hear your problems.

Appendix 2 - Overview of my weekly progress.

Treatment week	Hospital	Physical condition
1	Local Hospital	Started with tingling in my feet and hands. Severe back ache. Difficulty speaking. Rapid onset of paralysis
	Specialist Clinic Düsseldorf	Complete paralysis. Stopped breathing. Intubated. In coma for five days. Tracheotomy. Life support with ventilator and nasal feeding tube.
2	Specialist Clinic Düsseldorf	Intensive care. Complete paralysis. Full life support
3	ICU ward Bonn	Double room. Complete paralysis. Full life support
4	ICU ward Bonn	Single room. Complete paralysis. Full life support
5	ICU ward Bonn	Single room. Complete paralysis. Full life support. First uncontrolled movement of arms. Began exercises

		off the ventilator. Attempted speech.
6	ICU ward Bonn	Single room. Full life support. Very limited movement in arms, back and waist. Continued exercises off the ventilator. Sat in a wheelchair. First shower. Saw myself in the mirror for first time. Major mental issues because of the Pope and Terry Schiavo
7	ICU ward Bonn	Single room. Life support at night. Speaking with speech valve. Limited movement in thighs and hips. Found out for the first time that I'd stopped breathing.
8	ICU ward Bonn	Double room. Ventilator no longer required. Catheter removed. First use of the toilet on my own.
9	ICU ward Bonn	Double room. Feeding tube removed. First solid food. Managed 20 metre walk. Able to move from

		bed to wheelchair alone. No movement in feet or ankles. Got new wheelchair that I could propel myself.
10	Neurological ward Bonn	First shower on my own. Now self-sufficient. No movement in feet or face. Able to cut food and eat with knife and fork. In wheelchair
11	Neurological ward Bonn	Wheelchair. Managed first weekend at home
12	Neurological ward Bonn	Wheelchair. First steps with Zimmer frame
13	Neurological ward Bonn	Wheelchair. First movement of facial muscle. Took Zimmer frame home
14	Neurological ward Bonn	Zimmer frame
15	Neurological ward Bonn	Zimmer frame.
16	Neurological ward Bonn	Zimmer frame. Leg braces. First steps in room without frame. Walked out of hospital unaided.
17	Home	Using leg braces and Zimmer frame

18	Home	Leg braces and occasionally Zimmer frame
19	Home	Walking without any support —very slowly
20	Out-patient clinic Düsseldorf	Full treatment —steady improvement in condition
21	Out-patient clinic Düsseldorf	Full treatment —steady improvement in condition
22	Out-patient clinic Düsseldorf	Full treatment —steady improvement in condition
23	Out-patient clinic Düsseldorf	Full treatment —steady improvement in condition
24	Out-patient clinic Düsseldorf	Full treatment —steady improvement in condition

Appendix 3 - Return to Triathlon

On 3rd July 2011 I successfully completed an Olympic distance triathlon in 3hrs and 5 mins. I returned in 2012 and reduced my time to 2hrs and 58mins and in 2013 to 2hrs 44mins. The better times are due to more intensive training but also due to a continuing improvement in nerve and muscle activity in my legs several years after contracting GBS. I continue to train five to six times per week for triathlons and feel in great shape.

In 2017, I entered a sprint triathlon in Düsseldorf, for the first time in the 60+ age group. With limited training, I was very surprised and extremely pleased to come in third in my age group! The result meant I had achieved the qualifying standard to represent Germany in international age group triathlon events.

On 13th September 2018, I was extremely pleased and proud to compete in the 60-64 age group World Sprint triathlon championships on the wonderful Gold Coast in Australia. I completed the 750m swim, 20km bike ride and 5km run in a time of 1hr 24minutes and was placed 58th from 68 competitors. The race start time was 13years and 7months almost exactly to the minute since I'd stopped breathing in 2005 in the Düsseldorf clinic.

Follow your dreams. I did and I am now an international age group triathlete that also beat GBS.

Enjoying an energy drink and proudly showing my finishers medal.

Finally, I am happy to report that nerve activity in my face is also improving and a limited lop-sided smile is returning.